I0631016

A GLITTERING GLANCE AT HOW THE OTHER HALF DIES

The mansion was large and luxurious, overflowing with priceless antiques and the pleasures a great deal of money can buy. Beautiful, honey-tanned people frolicked on the white sandy beaches, living the sweet life with a flair. This was a scene out of everybody's dreams.

And then they found the first mangled body . . .

About the author

Leslie Ford has become one of the most widely read mystery writers in America. Her first novel was published in 1928 and since then she has written over fifty others. Miss Ford lives in Annapolis, Maryland.

Among her books are FALSE TO ANY MAN, OLD LOVER'S GHOST, THE TOWN CRIED MURDER, THE WOMAN IN BLACK, TRIAL BY AMBUSH, ILL MET BY MOONLIGHT, THE SIMPLE WAY OF POISON, THE CLUE OF THE JUDAS TREE, THREE BRIGHT PEBBLES, WASHINGTON WHISPERS MURDER, THE BAHAMAS MURDER CASE, THE PHILADELPHIA MURDER STORY, MURDER IS THE PAY-OFF, BY THE WATCHMAN'S CLOCK, MURDER IN MARYLAND, and RENO RENDEZ-VOUS, all published in Popular Library editions.

Leslie Ford
INVITATION
To MURDER

WILDSIDE PRESS

Invitation to Murder

Copyright © 1954, renewed 1982, by Zenith Brown.
All rights reserved.

Published by Wildside Press LLC
www.wildsidepress.com

Dedication: For: Frieda Lubelle

CHAPTER : 1

Fish (James Fisher) Finlay counted eleven.

Thirty-four minutes by the crystal clock on the crystal mantel he'd been cooling his heels in the terrace window in Malvern Towers, waiting for the Countess de Gradoff (nee Dodo Maloney).

"—Ten-thirty absolutely sharp, then, Fish, darling—if it's really important and not too horribly grim," was what the countess had said.

His leg was getting tired, standing. He could sit, but he was also tired of looking at James Fisher Finlay reflected *ad nauseam* in the crystal mirrored walls on three sides of the room. The places to sit were an equal hazard. He glanced from the shell-pink love seat next to a shower of yellow mimosa over to the silver-blue satin job of the same insubstantial elegance with white lilacs beside it. Then he glanced at Finlay, the weather-beaten hide around his hazel eyes wrinkling with sardonic amusement. Six feet two, shaggy-browed, thatched with rusty red iron filings it took a magnetized currycomb to straighten, he was an outsize ox in either shell-pink or silver-blue.

He gave his short clipped thatch a swipe with the heel of his palm, buttoned his gray flannel suit jacket, and gave up. The patina of the well-groomed New Yorker was not for him. No amount of spit and polish lasted long enough for the next layer to build on. It was hard to see why Caxson Reeves, Vice-President and Trust Officer of the Merchants and Mechanics Bank and Deposit Company, officer in charge of the James V. Maloney Trust, had hired him, when he limped back from three months in Korea, half a leg gone, after a year in the Big War without a scratch . . . with no patina and no connections. And harder to see why he'd sent him up here to the present beneficiary of the James V. Maloney Trust on a job that, if it wasn't horribly grim, was certainly damned unpleasant. .

Which was probably why Caxson Reeves had waited until Fish Finlay was leaving the office to spring it on him. His rugged face sobered as he sat cautiously down next to the white lilacs, seeing Reeves behind his desk, dry, inscrutable, a sheet of note paper in his hand, hooded lids raised over the rims of his half-spectacles, waiting while Fish limped back to him.

"A job for you in the morning. Make the appointment before you leave."

He handed Fish the sheet of paper.

"Dear Mr. Reeves," it said. "I wonder if you will please tell my mother I'm not coming to Newport this summer. I'm going to secretarial school as soon as I graduate this June, so I can work this fall. If my mother doesn't want to send my allowance, Anne Linton says she can manage to lend me the money. I will stay with her at Dawn Hill Farm and go in to town every morning. It will save a lot of trouble if you can make my mother understand before they go abroad again next week. I tried to do it myself but she doesn't listen to me, and I really mean it. Sincerely, Jennifer Linton."

"Well, well," Fish Finlay said. He read it again, the lovely peach-blow face and violet-blue eyes of Jennifer Linton's mother, Dodo Maloney, Countess de Gradoff, coming between him and her daughter's letter.

"Did you say a job for me?"

Reeves nodded his grizzled head once. He wasted nothing, money, words or motion.

"How do I do it?" Assistant Trust Officer Finlay asked.

"I've no idea." Reeves took the letter back. "How does anyone tell a very lovely, very spoiled woman her eighteen-year-old daughter prefers potluck with her widowed stepmother on a run-down farm in Virginia to luxury with her mother and her mother's fourth husband in Newport? I don't know. My methods have failed for years. Jennifer adores Anne Linton. Under the terms of the Trust she has no money until she gets it all, when she's twenty-two. But she's your problem, Finlay. That's what you're being trained for. You'll be the buffer state between the two of them for a long time. You might as well start . . . it'll be experience."

"—Experience I'd rather skip," Fish Finlay thought, coming back to the crystal room and looking at the clock again. The more he learned about the Maloney Trust and its beneficiaries the more he admired Caxson Reeves's controlled and apparently inexhaustible patience. He settled back and looked out the terrace windows. They were opened at oblique angles to let in the unexpected warmth of the early April sunshine, and he was aware suddenly of an image of another room in one of them. It looked like a mirage room at first, until he realized it was an image, refracted in the angled window glass, of a sunlit dining-room along the terrace. When he moved his head it disappeared. He moved it back, and it returned. He closed one eye, and the other, playing a game he became so engrossed in he did not hear the door open behind him.

"Oh, Fish, darling, I do hope I didn't keep you waiting!"

The Countess de Gradoff was there, her husband with her.

Fish Finlay 'scrambled to his feet, his awkward leg giving the fragile love seat a jolt that lurched the white lilacs.

"Oh, don't get up, darling!" Dodo de Gradoff's lovely eyes were filled with understanding and sympathy. "It's so stupid to have pots of things sitting around, anyway."

She smiled at him, enclosing him in the warm and pearly aura she diffused about her, as fragrant as a sun-washed rose. Small and peachy-gold, she was as soft and lusciously curved, and as feminine, as a blue-eyed freshly brushed Angora kitten.

"And you know Nikki, don't you, darling."

"How do you do, sir," Fish said. He felt more like an ox than ever in contrast to the casual elegance of the handsome man behind her. Nikki de Gradoff had patina. He was as tall as Fish, broad-shouldered, as Nordic as his bride, with clear blue eyes and smooth blond hair with a suspicion of a wave in it, sun-tanned, his English pin-stripe suit without a wrinkle. He had gloves, a stick and a Homburg hat.

"How 'je do, Finlay?" he said. His English accent was what they call "Oxford," with only the slightest trace of whatever Indo-European speech—unknown to Fish—had been his native language.

"Nikki's not staying, darling." Dodo took her husband's arm, her eyes proudly caressing. "I just can't get him to worry about the Maloney Trust. He thinks money's stupid."

"Not at all." Nikki de Gradoff smiled at her, and at Fish. "It's just that I don't know a damned thing about it, and you fellows do. I never had but one job in my life—and you know what happened to that, my darling."

He bent down and kissed her affectionately on the cheek.

"Don't worry your pretty head, sweet. That's what Finlay's for."

She went to the door with him. "Don't be too long, will you, love?"

When she came back her eyes were shining, her rounded cheeks flushed a warmer peach. "It's true, you know, Fish," she said. "Nikki had a job. In a garage, of all places! He got it in Paris—to support me!" She laughed delightedly. "It was very cute, and very silly. Because you see, we just ran into each other, quite literally, under a lamppost in the rain. I looked like a beggar, because I'd been antiquing with a friend and we didn't want them to think we were rich Americans. So Nikki didn't know I had any money at all, when he fell in love with me. It was fate, really. We'd never have looked at each other under normal circumstances. He was as sick of rich women as I was of impoverished nobility. And he got a job so he could ask me to marry him. It was terribly sweet. And when he found out, he was so upset. I had to bribe his concierge to find out where he'd gone . . . and go after him. Believe it or not."

7

She sat down in the shell-pink sofa against the mimosa, her face lighted with a warm glowing tenderness. Fish lowered his frame carefully back into the silver-blue satin.

"It's so sort of wonderful," she said. "I've had such rotten luck with my other husbands, and Nikki's perfect. He leans over backward to keep anybody from thinking the Maloney Trust was the reason he married me. That's why he's so determined not to know anything about it. Because you know how people are."

The smile on her lips dissolved, leaving her face as gravely earnest as a child's.

"Did you know that his first wife killed herself? It was horrible for Nikki. He wanted a divorce, but it was religion, or something—she was from the Argentine. Nikki was away. He felt terribly sorry for her, and he called her up on the phone and she started crying about the divorce, but he hadn't any idea she'd . . . do anything. Poor lamb, he blamed himself, of course. That's why he wouldn't keep anything she had, or take any part of her estate. It was terribly quixotic, I thought, but he says Americans don't understand honor, and I guess we don't."

She laughed merrily. "You can see how embarrassing it is, to have another rich wife, especially when you didn't know that's what you were getting."

Fish Finlay listened, knowing that when she got through with Nikki and got to her daughter this butterfly dust of happiness would dissolve like the mirage there on the terrace windowpane. He glanced over at it, moved slightly to bring it into focus, and sat motionless. There was a new figure in the center of his mirage. It was de Gradoff. He was moving quickly across the dining-room, oddly intent.

Probably forgotten something, Fish thought, glancing at the door de Gradoff would be coming through. But the door did not open. He waited a moment, and another. The door stayed closed, with de Gradoff behind it. Fish Finlay mentally lifted his shaggy brows. So Nikki isn't interested in the Maloney Trust. Nikki thinks money's stupid.

He sat forward as Dodo went blithely on.

"Nikki simply hates the idea of Newport, but I can't afford not to go there. Where my father got the idea—"

"Look," Fish said. "Why don't we go outside?"

"Outside? Whatever for?"

She looked down at the crisp fresh lace of the breakfast coat she was still wearing. "But darling, didn't you know? I'm not the outdoor type. Really!"

She got up, laughing. "Still, if you think this atmosphere isn't business-like, I'm happy to oblige. If it's not windy, that is."

Fish, listening intently, thought he heard a movement. He got up. "I'll see if it's windy." He went out and crossed to the balustrade, turned and glanced into the adjoining room. A door was closing noiselessly, leaving the room empty again. But the chances were there were other doors. . . .

He turned back. "It's not windy."

"Look, darling." Dodo de Gradoff laughed again as she came out. "If you're afraid somebody'll hear you, you can relax. I've sent both servants out on errands. Still, it is rather nice out, isn't it?"

She sat in the bamboo chaise longue he drew out for her and looked at him with sparkling amusement. "You're wonderful, you know." She tilted her golden head appraisingly. "I've been trying to figure out what it is that makes you so really attractive. You're not pretty, heaven knows, but neither was Abraham Lincoln. I suppose you're just so homely every woman knows you're an angel at heart. The girls must adore you, don't they?"

"I can get out of most places without being mobbed."

The sharp twinge he felt for an instant was in scarred tissue other than his leg.

She was still laughing at him. "That's what Caxson Reeves told me when he asked me to look you over—not that it mattered what I thought if he'd made up his mind, but it was a nice gesture. He said you 'inspired confidence.' " She made her voice gruff and let her eyelids droop. "Poor Caxey, he's like an old crocodile they won't let back to his native ooze. But he's sweet, really. You're the first person he's ever trusted with any of the Maloney problems. He said you were just what he'd been hunting for. Not too urbane, and very understanding . . . somebody he could depend on to take over for my daughter when her turn comes. *If* it comes."

Fish glanced at her. She was going cheerfully on. "Poor old Caxey, he's always been in love with me, after his fashion. But it's you I'm interested in. Why aren't you married? What do you do with yourself nights and weekends?"

"I've got a place in New Jersey," Fish said. "It used to be an old mill. I've got a couple of sheep and a few strawberries, and I plant stuff. Azaleas, mostly."

"Oh, no! *Pour l'amour de.* . . . Don't tell me!" She put her hand to her head in despair. "Just like my father! I can't bear it —"

She sat up. "Do you realize, Fish Finlay, that *that's* why I have to go to Newport every summer? Because my father got the mad idea of endowing that matchstick monstrosity of a house and grounds, because he thought those two horrible old gardeners Jan Vranek and Rob McTaggert were Nature's noblemen! Scheming old devils, is what they are. That's why

9

he endowed the place, so I couldn't sell it and kick them out of their job—both of which I would have done instantly, but believe me. So I'm stuck with the place. If I skip two summers, the whole works goes to the city of Newport as a public park. It's *monstrous*. It's *fantastic*. But, of course, the whole Maloney Trust—"

She broke off, smiling at him. "That's why I've sent Nikki and the servants out. I don't want anybody to know I'm a lady for a day. Not even Nikki . . . though it wouldn't make any difference to him. But I'd be ruined if my friends and creditors knew the truth. And it's *wicked*, Fish. The whole, entire Maloney Trust handed over to my darling daughter on her twenty-second birthday! Can you believe it! I won't have a hundred dollars a month that Jennifer Linton doesn't give me, six years from now."

"Four," Fish Finlay said mildly.

"Oh, my God, no! It can't be four!"

"She was eighteen last week."

"Oh, dear—and I forgot to send her a present." She smiled helplessly at him. "But Caxey said you're to take over *when* her turn comes, and I said *if* it comes. Because it's not coming, believe me. I'm going to break that Trust, Fish. But Caxey's told you that, hasn't he?"

"He mentioned it."

"Because it's an outrage, Fish," she said earnestly. "Father was out of his mind, stark, raving mad. He must have been, to write that kind of a Trust in the first place. And then to walk out of the bank and vanish into thin air—it doesn't make sense. All I'm waiting for is the legal seven years, and I'm going to have him declared dead and smash the Maloney Trust to smithereens. I've never believed my father just vanished anyway. I think he was killed and his body hidden, or something. He carried enormous sums of money with him. Why would he want to disappear, for heaven's sake?"

Fish shook his head. It was three years before his time that James V. Maloney had walked out of the bank at high noon one Friday and never showed up again. It would be seven years next October twenty-third.

"And if he did, that in itself would be plenty to prove he was out of his mind when he drew up that insane and revolting document. You know that's true, darling. It *is* revolting."

"I've never read it. Mr. Reeves won't let it out of his private vault."

"Well, it's fantastic. Here everybody thinks I'm rolling in wealth. Why, I wouldn't have a friend in the world four years from now. Except Nikki, of course. I wouldn't have married him if he cared about money. I'm sick of husbands who married me to get them out of debt. That's one thing I'm but really tough about. And Caxey thinks I ought to tell Nikki

10

about the Trust. He thinks it's because I'm afraid of my marriage that I don't. But that's wrong. If it was money Nikki wanted, he wouldn't have stood aside from his first wife's estate and he wouldn't have fallen in love with me in an old raincoat. Caxey lives for money and he thinks everybody else does . . . especially foreigners."

She lowered her voice, her eyes dancing again. "Do you know what he did?"

"Mr. Reeves?"

Dodo nodded. "He had a detective do a complete dossier on Nikki, the poor lamb. He doesn't know I know it, and I'm terrified Nikki'll find out. This absurd Frenchman gumshoeing around, asking my maid all sorts of questions."

Fish looked at her. "Are you sure? That it was Mr. Reeves, I mean?"

"Of course. Who else gives a damn who I marry, darling?"

"It doesn't sound like him, though."

"Well, it doesn't matter, of course. There's nothing about Nikki I haven't been told—by him or by his friends. You know, the ones that have their duty to do, however painful?"

She looked at him earnestly. "—You like him, don't you?"

Fish Finlay had a sudden sense of Caxson Reeves's bleak hooded gaze fixed on him *in absentia*. She was waiting, her eyes wide and serious.

He grinned at her. "No, of course not."

Dodo de Gradoff tossed her head back and laughed with delight.

"You're divine, Fish. Who said the American male had lost all gallantry? If I weren't old enough to be your mother—"

"Well, hardly," Fish said.

"I'll be thirty-nine my next birthday, if I don't forget it. With my child at Newport this summer I can't go on pretending I'm thirty-two."

Fish shook his head. "—Wait a minute."

"What do you mean?" Her sparkling gaiety vanished instantly.

"Your child isn't coming to Newport."

It came out quicker and flatter than he had meant it to. "Who says so? Of course she's coming."

He shook his head again. "She wants to stay at home and go to secretarial school."

For a moment she sat looking at him as blankly as if he'd spoken in Sanskrit. Then he realized it was not blankness. It was shock as if he'd picked up a stick and hit her across the face.

"I'm sorry," he said gently.

"Oh, no. It's quite all right." She got up and went to the balustrade. When she turned back after an instant, she smiled at him, too brightly. "But her *home's* in Newport, you know

11

—it's not in Virginia. You must be mistaken—or she's just being dramatic. If I had time, I'd run down and see her. Except that that wretched school's so far out in the country . . . and Nikki and I have to be in Paris. There's a tremendous costume ball; I've got to have a fitting on my dress. It's all so stupid, but we've promised."

She stood there a moment. "I'll tell you. I'll just call her and talk to her. There's no use going clear down there."

She started back into the living-room.

"I wouldn't call her, Countess."

"—Dodo." She corrected him with a smile. "You make me feel so ancient. Anyway, we're dropping that nonsense while we're in America."

She went inside, pulled a pale-blue telephone out from behind the mimosa, dialed and waited. "Oh, operator, I want to speak to Miss Jennifer Linton. I don't have the number. It's St. Margaret's Hall, Westminster, Virginia. I don't know, except that it's somewhere near Charlottesville. That's right. . . . Why wouldn't you call her?"

"She'll be in class, or somewhere. And she doesn't want to come. I wouldn't try to make her."

"Try?" Dodo Maloney laughed. "Listen, darling. For the next less than four years and for when I break the Maloney Trust, I'm the boss. It's me who says what Jennifer Linton does and doesn't do."

She listened. "Thank you, Westminster 604. Yes, I'm writing it down. Thanks a lot."

She was going on to Fish, not writing. "This secretarial school is Anne Linton's idea. Of course she wants Jennifer there. Who wouldn't? In another four years Jennifer's supposed to be a very rich young lady. Anne Linton's not the angel of light—"

She listened again. "Then tell them to call her. It's her mother. I really must speak to her. Yes, it *is* an emergency."

"I wish you wouldn't, Dodo," Fish said again. "Kids hate to be yanked away—"

"Look, angel. I know my child better than you do. It makes her important to be yanked, as you call it, and there's nothing she likes better than getting out of schoolwork. She loathes school. Anyway she's not in class, she's playing some crazy game. It's what Nikki says, American schools just make Amazons out of girls. That's been one of the child's problems. She's so enormous, and so full of adolescent antagonisms. She was a *grim* child. She hated Europe, and she hated me."

She turned back to the phone, her face lighting. "Darling! It's Mummy. How are you, lamb?"

The light died abruptly. "But it *is* an emergency, darling. Mr. Finlay's here from the bank. He has the fantastic idea you aren't coming to Newport with Mummy. . . ."

She was silent, listening to her daughter, her soft red mouth hardening, the cornflower blue eyes getting colder.

"Listen, my child," she said curtly. "That's ridiculous. If your friends aren't up there, you can make new ones. I'll *get* you some decent clothes. You're not going to any secretarial school and you're not getting a job. Understand that right here and now."

She drew a long breath and let it out again.

"Jennifer—be quiet and listen to me. You're *coming* to Newport. That's flat. It isn't just me and Nikki there. A cousin of Nikki's is coming over. He's just twenty-three and he's a love, really." Her voice sharpened. "And that's plenty from you, my lamb. Don't be such a rat, darling. You're upsetting me horribly."

She listened again, shaking her head at Fish. He turned to the window and looked out again. It was the scene he'd been sent up to try to avoid.

"Well, you'd better make up your mind to like it, darling," Dodo said. "Because you're coming, and no nonsense. Goodbye. Go back and finish your silly game. I'll see you in Newport in June."

Fish could see her reflected in the mirrored wall, her face stiff with stubborn anger and wounded pride. There was something else that seemed almost like compassion, struggling to soften and erase the other two.

"It's so stupid, isn't it?" she inquired lightly. "But I've promised Nikki. We had to have some attraction for his cousin, and I thought she'd love having a young man all of her own. But of course it's my fault, in a way. I shouldn't have let her stepmother take her away from me. And it shouldn't hurt— but it does."

"Why don't you let her stay?" Fish asked. "Secretarial school'll be good for her."

"And let her marry some bookkeeper?" she asked sharply. Then she smiled and put her hand on his arm. "Sorry, darling. Tell Caxey you did your best. And tell him that if my child stays in Virginia he's to cut off her stipend. We'll just see if Anne Linton wants to keep her for free. So run along, darling. Nikki'll be here, and I don't want him to see me looking like an old hag. Goodbye, darling."

At the door she stopped him. "Look, Fish." She was frowning. "Would you do something?"

"Surely, if I can."

"Go down to that blasted school and see the child. I don't want to be horrible to her, but make her see I'm her mother, not Anne Linton. I've got to have her in Newport. You can tell her I'm going to break the Trust if you want to. It might make her a little decenter. She was foul to Nikki when she met him last winter in Nassau. And do it soon, before she gets completely out of hand. Another summer down there and she'd let me starve if the Maloney Trust kept on. I'll call Caxey. Goodbye, darling."

Fish Finlay waited in the pale-peach and crystal foyer for the elevator. Another experience, no doubt . . . and one he'd be even gladder to skip.

CHAPTER : 2

He saw no reason to revise that opinion Friday afternoon when he came limping up from a culvert with a coffee can full of ditch water to pour into the boiling radiator of his pickup truck stalled on a presumed short cut in the backwoods and rolling green pastures of Virginia. The green Cadillac with a woman and two girls in the back seat, the only mobile unit he'd seen since he left the main road, hadn't even slowed down when he flagged it to ask the way to Dawn Hill Farm.

"Thought I was a plant hijacker, no doubt."

He grinned at the New Jersey license plates and the load of freshly dug azaleas in the old truck. They were the reason he was both late and lost. When his sister said she knew a man a couple of miles this side of Charlottesville, a stone's throw from Dawn Hill Farm, where he could pick them up dirt cheap, he should have known she meant a woman twenty miles the other side, nowhere near Dawn Hill Farm, and the reason they were only a little more expensive than usual was that he'd'd dug and balled them himself. The real folly, of course, had been to let the azalea woman tell him about the short cut.

"Twelve miles from Summerville Court House," she said. "A green and white mailbox. You can't miss it."

He'd give it another mile, Fish Finlay decided. Or if another car came by, he'd stay in the truck so they wouldn't see him limping. That was the trouble with his leg, he thought, knowing he was being a fool of sorts. Hypersensitivity, they called it. Other people lost worse than a leg in the war, didn't they? You're alive, aren't you? You've got a first-rate job, what are you beefing about? You just can't forget you were an all-Eastern end in your Ivy League days. Nobody gives a damn about your leg . . . it's your head that counts, old boy. Forget it. And behind the mahogany desk he did forget, and nights and weekends in his place in New Jersey. Only occasionally—at times like this, for instance—did it flash up into his conscious mind.

14

"Grow up, Psycho. Don't be a jerk. What's eating you now?"

Apart from the stalled engine, Caxson Reeves and the azaleas were the answer to that one.

"If you want Jennifer Linton to go to Newport, it's Anne Linton, not the girl, you'd better see," Reeves had remarked dryly when Fish reported his diplomatic failure. "And I'd make it as unimpressive and unofficial as possible. Didn't you tell me you wanted a Friday to go to Virginia and get some *bushes?*"

He made it sound like a load of stinkweed.

"Azaleas, sir."

"Then go get them and drop by Dawn Hill casually. Tell Anne Linton we have a serious problem. Keep your mouth shut about Dodo cutting off the stipend."

"You can stop that, can't you? It's a lousy trick. Or is that sort of thing why we call the Trust 'I. to M.'?"

That came out before Fish knew he was saying it. He flushed under the bleak eyes looking at him. "M. 5401" was the Bank's listing of the James V. Maloney Trust. "I. to M." was a top-echelon joke that Fish Finlay never should have heard and having heard never repeated. "I. to M." stood for "Invitation to Murder."

"I'm sorry, sir," he said.

"It so happens that the term 'Invitation to Murder' has nothing to do with the Maloney Trust as you know it, Mr. Finlay," Caxson Reeves said evenly. "It refers to a document that James Maloney drew up and signed the morning he walked out of here for the last time. It is concerned with the disposition of the Trust in the event of the death of both Dodo Maloney and her daughter Jennifer Linton before Jennifer is twenty-two years old. It also happens to be my business, not yours."

"I'm sorry," Fish said again.

"Very well." Reeves got up and locked the conference room door. "To get back to what is your business. I think it's time you know more about the Maloney Trust. But first—if Dodo wishes to cut off her daughter's stipend, there's nothing we can do about it. That's the way James V. Maloney wrote the Trust."

He looked impassively down at the empty chair at the other end of the table.

"He sat right there, and dictated to me."

He was silent for an instant, his eyes fixed on the chair.

"Jim Maloney was a bitterly unhappy man," he said deliberately. "It may be he was crazy. I never thought so. He knew he had the Midas touch. He parlayed a small inheritance into a large fortune. He married what you might call a girl of the people so he could have a large and healthy family. It was the only thing he wanted. He thought he didn't have it because it was God's way of making him pay for the Midas touch. Then he learned that it was only his wife's vanity and social ambition, and he learned too that Jennifer was the only grandchild he was going to have. Dodo had been through a blatant divorce and a damned unpleasant custody fight for Jennifer, and was embarked on another equally blatant romance. It was then, when he was sick of everything, that plants came into Maloney's life to remake it, through these two old gardeners at Enniskerry."

He nodded at the framed airview photograph of the Maloney estate at Newport that concealed the wall safe behind the chair where James V. Maloney had sat.

"That's why Dodo has the place there and can't get rid of it—except to let it go to the city of Newport. He endowed it, so she couldn't toss those two out of their jobs and their gardens."

He pulled his half-spectacles down over the bridge of his nose and sat gazing intently at the photograph.

"He was talking about Dodo and her daughter that day. A weed in rich soil takes nourishment from a useful plant. If the plant grows, it flowers quicker to make the best of what life it has. Jim Maloney thought Dodo was a weed. He gave her until Jennifer was twenty-two to prove she wasn't. His theory was that Jennifer, struggling against her environment, would flower into a useful life. He didn't put it that way, but that was the gist of it. Jennifer could sink or swim. When she was twenty-two, Dodo Maloney would get back from her precisely the treatment she'd given her. On that basis, it's been my job to help Dodo cut her own throat any way she likes . . . which she's done her damndest to do ever since I can remember."

He got up. "What contribution her fourth husband is going to make, I don't know. What Dodo told you this morning she's told me. I don't believe any part of it. As you know, I first heard about this marriage from a gossip columnist calling up to find out how much money she'd settled on de Gradoff. I'm skeptical of chance romantic meetings." A wintry gleam came into his eyes for an instant. "In my book, anyone pretending he has no interest in money is either a fool or a knave. And rather particularly, in the present case . . . in view of an item that came in the mail this morning, while Dodo was telling you her happy story."

He went to the end of the table and took the photograph of Enniskerry off the wall. He put it on the table, opened the safe, brought out a pale-blue airmail envelope and took a sheet of typed paper out of it.

"This is either in good faith, or it's a clumsy attempt to find out the provisions of the Maloney Trust. Not even my secretary knows them. I promised that to Jim Maloney. Dodo

16

knows them, but it's to her interest to keep quiet. Jennifer was told them on her sixteenth birthday. You know them. I'm getting older, and I don't think I've misjudged you."

He pushed his spectacles up in place and looked down at the paper.

"This is from our Paris correspondent. He says it is a 'friendly exploratory inquiry,' on behalf of an undisclosed principal, and in no sense a demand for money. The undisclosed principal wishes to know what progress we are making with our program for paying the outstanding obligations of the Countess de Gradoff's husband, Count Nicolai Hippolyte de Gradoff."

"He wishes to know what?"

"When we are going to pay de Gradoff's debts." Reeves's voice was as dry as the crackle of the paper as he put it back in the envelope. "I made a transatlantic call. Off the record, I was told that de Gradoff was heavily involved when his first wife died."

"Killed herself."

"I'm purposely restricting myself to what has been reported to me as fact," Reeves said quietly. "—To clear himself, de Gradoff borrowed a considerable sum on his interest in the first wife's estate. It is that sum this so-called 'friendly inquiry' is about. The undisclosed principal was given to understand that he was marrying a rich American lady . . . at which time the debt would be paid."

He put the letter in the safe, closed it and hung the picture of the many-towered mansion back on the wall. There was no ripple of expression in the dusty aridity of his face or in his voice when he spoke again. "Perhaps that is why de Gradoff appeared anxious to hear what you might have to say to Dodo this morning."

Fish looked at him soberly. "Do we have any program—"

"None. I have no authority to pay such debts. If Dodo wishes to do it out of income, that's her business. I advised the 'undisclosed principal' to take the matter up with her."

As Reeves gathered up his papers, Fish got to his feet. "One other point, sir—if I may stick my neck out again."

"Why not?"

"This French detective that Dodo—"

"You told me." He looked at his watch. "It would seem to indicate that there's a second 'undisclosed principal' making inquiries. But I have a meeting."

He went out leaving Fish Finlay standing there much the way he was sitting now in the stalled truck, the problem that seemed simple on the face of it complicated by a feeling of uneasiness he could not define. He looked at his watch. It was ten minutes to five . . . late to drop in on anybody in the mint julep belt in the rig he was in. He was aware suddenly that he was in honest fact procrastinating and had been all day. He could have got half as many azaleas and had plenty of time to get to Dawn Hill Farm earlier, if he'd wanted to.

"You don't want to let Dodo down . . . but you don't want to force the kid to go to Newport. Make up your mind, Finlay."

It was ten to one he'd passed the green and white mailbox without seeing it for the simple reason he didn't want to see it. He started the truck. He'd give the rolling landscape one more roll and the empty road two more curves, and then backtrack. It was around the second curve that he saw the boy perched on the white culvert down in the hollow. He rattled down, braked the truck, leaned over to ask the way to Dawn Hill Farm, and saw it was not a boy. It was a girl in a white shirt and green jodhpurs, her green jacket and black velvet cap in a dusty heap on the road at her feet, and it was about as miserable and dejected a little figure as Fish Finlay had ever seen.

He grinned, looking across the road up to the open field.

"Lost a horse, sis?"

Then he braked the truck sharply. He couldn't see the kid's face, just the top of her dark tousled head, but her shirt was badly torn and her fists clenched tight.

"You're not hurt?"

She shook her head. "I didn't have a horse." Her voice was strained, as tight as her fists. She raised her head then and Fish saw her face.

A feather of gold dropped from the wing of an angel there in the dusk. His hand stopped motionless on the door.

She wasn't a kid. She was a girl, or maybe not a girl but a dream half-dreamed, only seeming real there in the golden dusk . . . the heart-shaped face, moon pale, the wide-set stricken eyes, dark gray-green under thick glossy brows and long black curling lashes, full lips with no lipstick to hide their pallor, nothing to hide the intense unhappiness that shot like a poignant arrow through the futile armor of Fish Finlay's own unhappy heart.

She got up from the culvert and he saw her slim lovely body, high young breasts, girl and lost dream melted into one, as she stood looking at him for a moment of relief as poignant as her distress, and then picked up her jacket and cap and came over to the truck.

"Will you take me up the road as far as you're going, please?" she asked. She brushed off her torn shirt sleeve. "I came through the woods, that's why I'm such a mess. Some people dropped me, but they've gone. And I've got to get away." She looked at the load of shrubs in the back of the

18

truck. "Unless you're delivering those around here? I could wait if you'd come back. . . ."

Fish Finlay pulled himself sharply out of his trance-shock. "Sure," he said. "Hop in."

"Oh, good!" She ran around the front of the truck, yanked the door open before he could reach over to open it for her, climbed in and slammed it shut, an old hand at battered trucks.

"I'm so glad." She sank down in the broken springs and skinned her hair back. "I didn't know whatever I was going to do."

"Where do you want to go?" He knew he sounded churlish, but he couldn't help it.

"Westminster. About ten miles. Where are you going?"

"New Jersey."

"Oh, good. It's right on your road, this way."

She glanced at his earth-stained paratrooper boots and back at the plants.

"Those are azaleas, aren't they?"

"Right," he said, trying to start the damned engine again, with another hill to climb. She was waiting, taut till it started, and when she didn't relax, then he knew it was something else she was waiting for, as the truck made the grade around a steep bank of honeysuckle, dogwood above it. She turned her head painfully, looking across in front of him.

"Our house is up there, that's our lane. Oh, watch it, the frost boils are awful."

"Sorry." Finlay steadied the truck. It wasn't the frost boils. It was the green and white mailbox at the mouth of the lane. White with green stenciled block letters. Dawn Hill Farm. But it couldn't be. It wasn't possible. There must be another house up the Dawn Hill lane.

She was silent for a while, lost in her own unhappiness again, before she roused herself.

"Are you a gardener?" she asked. "I don't mean that. Gardeners are all so old. But do you work for one?"

"Like a dog," Fish said.

She glanced at him again. "Or maybe you're like my grandfather. He was a . . . a horticulturalist. But probably not, he was supposed to be crazy. My mother says so. He just disappeared one day."

Finlay kept the truck steady. There might be another house on the Dawn Hill Road. There couldn't be another girl living on it who had a crazy disappearing horticulturalist grandfather. *Snap out of it, brother.* It never was, it could never be. It was just an error in the golden dusk.

"My stepmother doesn't think so." Her voice was unsteady for a moment. "She thinks he just got sick of everything. But she loves gardens. My mother hates them. She says old men

19

plant trees, young men dream dreams. But you plant trees, don't you, or shrubs, anyway?"

"Or don't I dream dreams? Is that what you mean?"

"Sort of, I guess."

The maimed shadow of an old smile limped across Fish Finlay's homely face, rekindling the memory of far-off unhappy things that for one enchanted moment back there on the empty road he'd forgotten, and that the shock of her being Jennifer Linton had brought painfully back to him. That there'd been a time when dreams were his to dream, back when he didn't know an azalea from a privet hedge, and the brightest of them all had been another girl, a golden girl with amber eyes. And what he'd never told anybody, that it wasn't because he'd been an Ivy League end that he couldn't take his leg in his stride and had holed in, an old man planting trees. It was what the dream girl had said, as kindly as she could, about a golden girl tied to a junk heap: I'm a pig, darling. I've tried to be noble but I'm really not. We're just wrong for each other now. We couldn't ever have any fun any more. Not our kind of fun. Somebody'll come along, darling, somebody who loves to sacrifice. . . .

"No," Fish Finlay said. "I banished dreams."

To hell with dreams. To hell with sacrifice. His jaw tightened. The angel reaching sadly down picked up the golden feather in the dust.

Jennifer Linton was silent. He brought himself abruptly back to the job in hand and glanced sideways at her . . . the recalcitrant daughter of a lovely mother, granddaughter of old James V. Maloney, supposed to flower, if possible, scrabbling what nutriment was left in the shade of the lush luxuriant weed. Assistant Trust Officer Finlay's problem. He saw her again, simple and lovely, the aura of springtime in April about her.

The pale half-moon of her face was grave.

"You don't banish dreams," she said, her voice as grave. "They blow up, when you're not looking. They blow to pieces, right in your face." She laughed unexpectedly then and rubbed her nose quickly, like a child. "I know. It's what happened to me, just now."

"A dream blew up?"

"With a bang. I live with my stepmother, because my parents were divorced. My father was killed in a car accident, two years ago. And my mother . . . well, she can be. . . . Anyway, she said I had to come to Newport this summer. But I hate it, and she's so . . . so hard to get along with, anyway. So I wasn't going to Newport no matter how much of a row my mother made. I was going to stay with my stepmother. Then today I got a cable. I didn't have to go to Newport. My mother'd changed her mind from the other day when she

20

called me up . . . right when I was 6-2 in the match set for the school cup, so I had to lose by default. And she said, 'Go back to your silly game.' "

She laughed a little. "I guess it's funny, anyway."

"It wouldn't be to me," Fish Finlay said.

"Me either. Anyway, she changed her mind, and I didn't have to come to Newport. It was wonderful. That's why I'm in these clothes, I didn't take time to change. One of the girls' mothers was there with a car, coming down this way, so I dashed home. I thought Anne—that's my stepmother—would be as glad as I was."

"Wasn't she?"

Jennifer Linton didn't answer for so long that he glanced over at her and saw her still shaking her head, her lashes moist.

"I'm sorry," he said, disappointed some way.

"I didn't tell her," she said then. "There was a . . . a man there. An old friend of all of us. I sneaked in—kid stuff, I guess. You know . . . Big Surprise. He was there, talking to her . . . telling her how much he loved her, and how tired he was of waiting and . . . seeing her struggle, trying to hang on to the farm for . . . for somebody else's spoiled brat—that's me—when she ought to have a life and children of her own. I . . . I was just stunned, I guess."

She took a deep breath.

"I was so stunned I couldn't get out, and so I heard her say she loved him too but she wasn't going to break up the only home I had till . . . till I got myself a job and got squared away, just when I'd got myself together and had some confidence in myself and the fact that somebody really wanted me around." She paused a moment. "I just never thought about Anne getting married. I guess my mother's been married so many times I thought it was enough for everybody. And this man's terribly nice and has money enough to . . . I was just stupid. But it was a shock. You bear right at the next corner."

She was silent for a moment.

"So I'm going to Newport," she said, calm again. "It's funny. I get some money some day, and I've been planning all the things I'd do for Anne. Pay the mortgage on the farm, and that sort of thing. She's done so much for me. And here all the time she could have had . . . everything. I was just sick. And on the road, I was terrified somebody I knew would come along, and she'd find out I'd been home. She'd feel awful if she knew I'd heard. And she knows how I . . . I don't like this new husband of my mother's."

"Why not?" Fish Finlay asked.

"She thinks it's because my mother didn't even tell me she was getting married, this time, and one of the girls heard it

21

on a radio gossip program. But that's not it. It's what another girl at school told me about him. Her father's a diplomat in Washington. They're from the Argentine."

Fish Finlay concentrated silently on the road.

"This new husband was married before to a cousin of theirs. And she was supposed to have killed herself."

A sudden sharp chill froze the base of Finlay's spine.

"Supposed to?"

It came out more casually than he'd dared to hope.

"That's right. But the family doesn't think she did. This girl says they know, in fact—that she didn't kill herself."

Finlay's spine was not chilled at the base, it was stone-cold deep up into his cerebrum. "You don't mean—"

He caught himself. This was fantastic.

"It isn't me," she said. She spoke with a literal realism, so clear-eyed and without emotion that it made her seem at once both older and younger than he knew she was. "It's what the girl told me. She says they *knew* she didn't kill herself. She doesn't know how. It was just things she overheard."

Dear God . . . she can't possibly know what she's saying. He slowed the truck down, his eyes glued to the road.

"She said they fought like tigers to keep her from marrying him. Then when she died, they found out something. This girl isn't sure what. But they didn't want a scandal. Or maybe they didn't have actual legal proof. But they could see he didn't get anything out of it. And he didn't . . . not her money, or even her personal stuff. Not even her furs. This girl has a coat of hers. It's beautiful, but . . ."

She shivered a little, the only sign that she knew the meaning of what she'd said.

Fish slowed down again and looked around at her. There was no ripple on the opaque mask she'd drawn over her face since the naked moment back on the culvert.

"Now look," he said, as quietly and soberly as he could. "You don't seriously believe all this, do you?"

"I don't know," she said. "This girl swears it's the truth. My mother knows he didn't get any of her estate. But the story she's heard is different. I know, because I tried to tell her, in Nassau last winter, when she had me down to meet him. So I shut up. I was afraid, anyway. And he doesn't like me to begin with . . . any better than I do him."

"You didn't tell her—"

"I didn't even get started, really," she said calmly. "She cut me off with a lot of corny stuff. He'd told her his story and she believes it. He's smart."

"You haven't told anybody then."

"No. And I don't know why I'm telling you, except that I felt so horrible. And I'm glad I did, because you're prob-ably right. It does sound crazy. You see, I'm not worried about my mother, because she doesn't have any money to leave anybody. Unless something happens to me, before I'm twenty-two. Or unless she hasn't told him she just has income," she added.

As indeed she hasn't.

"Because she's funny about money. Terribly generous if it's something she wants you to have, not five cents if she doesn't. Like iron. Her last marriage went on the rocks over some fishing tackle. But maybe this one's smarter."

The wheeze and rattle of the truck intensified her silence and Fish Finlay's.

"I was going to tell my stepmother," she said then. "But she'd have worried. She wouldn't let me go to Newport now."

"She's be right," Fish said. "You mustn't go."

"And mess up Anne's life still more?" she demanded warmly. "How can you say that? Except that you don't know, of course. I haven't explained it very well. No. I've got to go. There's nothing else to do. That's all there is to it."

If Fish Finlay couldn't see it, he couldn't help hear it in the sudden passionate sincerity of her voice.

They were passing a service station, coming into the small town. She flashed up in the seat. "Oh, heavens, we're here already! What'll I do? What'll I tell them?"

He smiled a little in spite of himself. Suspected murder she could take. This was different.

"Oh, I know!" She flashed around toward him. "Oh . . . would you? Would you sell me a couple of your azaleas? The house proctor has a green thumb. I could tell her I went after them for her. Just one lie would cover it. I don't want them to call up Anne!"

"Sure," he said.

"Except that I haven't any money till next month. Or you could send the bill to the Bank. Mr. Reeves might—"

"Pay me later," Fish said. "I'll be back."

"Oh, wonderful! The brick gate right there. . . ."

He turned the truck in.

"We go left to the service yard."

Fish shook his head. "You hop out here. I'll take the trees, and find the old man to plant them."

He smiled at her and stopped the truck. She was out and around before he was. They met in front of the battered fender. Her eyes were shining as she put her hand out.

"I don't know how to thank you! Really, thanks *ever* so much!"

She turned and ran up the lawn toward the quiet mansion on the hill, and stopped, looking back, her eyes like breathless stars, their light transformed instantly to a new and lovelier compassion as she saw him limping back around to the other side.

23

"Oh . . ." she whispered. "That's why he's banished dreams."

She turned and ran on until she heard the truck rattle to a start. Then she turned and waved. *He said he'd be back.*

Fish Finlay had forgotten his leg, then and when he found the service yard and helped the old man unload the azaleas, all of them . . . all he had to give for a momentary dream he was sealing up in a heart where dreams were banished. Jennifer Linton was his job.

"She's not going to Newport." He said it out loud as he stopped the truck a moment at the end of the service lane. Suspicion was enough, whether the Argentine girl's story was true or false. The fact that there was that story settled it.

But he couldn't turn back and go to Dawn Hill Farm now and tell Anne Linton. Not with the passionate conviction of her protest still in his ears. There was plenty of time. Three months, practically. The de Gradoffs wouldn't be back home until the middle of June. He switched his lights on and turned the truck northward home.

Crossing the bridge over the Chesapeake he came into the rain. The long gray arms of the fog rose, swirling, beckoning him on, concealing a harsher surf-beaten shore and a golden sandal thrown back from the crest of a hungry wave, the infernal Rock and the grave fit only for a monster, as death and a motley crew assembled in Newport, faces yet unknown, and the hands of the gilded clock on the stable tower at Enniskerry moved silently, marking the hours.

CHAPTER : 3

Plenty of time. Three months, practically. The irony of his being that confident was slightly on the bitter side when Fish Finlay thought of it in Newport the last Friday in June.

It was around three o'clock when he got there and found the high serpentine brick wall Caxson Reeves had told him to look for, at Nantucket Avenue and Ocean Drive. He drove along it to the pink marble gateposts. Recessed in a niche in the front of each was a white marble urn of yellow marble flowers, with "Enniskerry" chiseled on the base, as if the place were already a monument, its mortuary elegance heightened by a dense somber screen of purple beeches swallowing up the driveway.

He drove past, needing time to adjust himself. He hadn't realized how small Newport was, a capsule compression of sharply stratified eras. The Jamestown Ferry lumbering along against the business-like back drop of the Naval Base, the narrow crowded streets of the colonial seaport town, the shabby gentility of the resort shops just before Bellevue Avenue became abruptly the stratum of the elite, with its wide emerald-shaded Victorian dignity and Italianate grandeur . . . and there he was at a dead end of pink brick wall and purple foliage. In front of him where the road turned was a parking place separated by a low stone guard from the jutting rocks, beyond them, stretching restlessly into the misty infinite, the blue Atlantic. He pulled in and sat there, at a dead end of his own, aware with a grim kind of humor that his April confidence had constructed it for him. . . . Finlay bolting back from Virginia confident that the Maloney Trustees had a vital and legitimate interest in the personal welfare of the Maloney heirs.

"We ought to call a first-rate private investigator in on this deal, sir," he'd said, briskly no doubt, at the end of his report, not noticing that Caxson Reeves's concentrated attention contained any element but interest. Until Reeves folded his half-spectacles and put them on the table, regarding Fish Finlay with bleak detachment.

"You've overlooked the only pertinent fact in the matter," he said dryly. "As Trust Officers we are not concerned with the safety of the Maloney beneficiaries. We're concerned solely with the safety of the Maloney money."

He stopped. Fish Finlay sat there blankly, until it occurred to him that Caxson Reeves had said all he intended to say.

"I guess I made a mistake."

"You did, indeed," Reeves said. "Show me where the Maloney money is in danger, and what a private investigator could do to remove the danger, and I'll be happy to authorize the necessary funds. There are none I can authorize to investigate Dodo Maloney's current husband . . . suspected by you of murdering his first wife on the slight strength of a morsel of schoolgirl gossip you've picked up. If there's nothing else . . ."

And there wasn't, except the slow burn under Fish Finlay's collar as he walked stiffly out of the room, until the end of May, when Caxson Reeves's secretary stopped him one noon.

"Is anything wrong with the Countess de Gradoff?" she asked, holding out a Maloney Trust expense sheet. "Look at this batch of transatlantic phone calls."

"I wouldn't know," Fish said. He took the sheet. The calls were listed for once and sometimes twice a week. The date of the first was what mattered. It was made the day Reeves had dressed him down for the slight morsel of schoolgirl gossip.

Then there was the local call last week, five days after the

25

de Gradoffs got home from Europe and went directly to Newport. It was from a friend of Fish's, Joe Henry on the city desk of the *Courier Graphic.*

"Hey, what's the revival of interest in old James V. Maloney?"

"Is there one?" Fish asked.

"Two inquiries this week . . . one a photostat deal. Why don't you come up and catch a drink and dinner and tell me about it?"

"Why don't I look at the file myself?"

"I'll have it out for you."

At six o'clock Fish was skimming through the Maloney file, which was mostly James V. Maloney's daughter and the custody fight over Jennifer, together with the two old gardeners at Enniskerry, a padded story of the life of a man with an iron resentment against personal publicity. The facts were few. Maloney had left the bank at high noon, a news vendor had found his hat stuffed into a Broadway trash basket, a week later his daughter reported him missing.

"Who got the photostat of this stuff?"

Joe Henry shook his head. "A Western Union boy picked it up. The other inquiry . . . his current son-in-law."

"De Gradoff?"

Joe Henry nodded. "Smith was the name he gave. Polly Randolph spotted him coming out. She was on the Paris edition when he married Dodo. She's around, if you've got a Maloney expense account to feed her on. Nice gal, red hair and green eyes."

As Fish watched the sea gulls wheeling, screaming among the rocks in front of him now at the end of Nantucket Avenue in Newport, he could see Caxson Reeves's parched immovable face at the end of the conference table when he reported the next morning.

"And maybe you'll think this is another slight morsel," he said. "But it isn't from a schoolgirl. It's from a society reporter named Polly Randolph you've probably never heard of."

"On the contrary," Reeves said evenly. "I know her very well. Her father jumped out of a window down the street in '29. Her uncle owns a good deal of the *Courier Graphic.*"

"She had dinner with me last night." Fish was seeing Polly Randolph then, as he described the scene in Tony's back room.

Polly Randolph regarded him appraisingly across the restaurant table. "But you people know all about Nikki de Gradoff," she said. "Or did something happen to the little French dick—wasn't his name Blum?—you had on his trail? At least we all assumed it was the Maloney trustees. Or aren't you in their confidence either?"

Fish grinned back at her. "I guess not." Repeating that, he thought he caught a barely perceptible twitch in Reeves's arid lids.

"Well, I don't know anybody else who'd be worried about Dodo," Polly said. "I understand little Blum had been working for the Argentine family until they called him off. However . . ." She shrugged. "Anyway, we gave the wedding the full treatment. Riches disguised in rags meets true love under a lamppost in the pouring rain. A month later, in comes de Gradoff's concierge with a story to sell. The rigged lamppost meeting, the phony flight from Paris when he found the girl was stinking rich. Nikki had forgot to pay the concierge for helping."

"Who rigged the lamppost?" Fish asked.

She shook her head. "Somebody who knew Dodo was a pushover for romance, no doubt. Who'd loaned Nikki money and saw that was the way to get it back, I imagine. He'd been going high, wide and handsome for a while after his first wife died. He was really down and out when Dodo ran into him . . . or vice versa."

"Did you know the first wife?"

Fish asked it casually. She went on eating for so long without answering that he'd begun to wonder if she'd heard him.

"You mean, can I prove he killed her?" she asked then, calmly. "The answer is No, Mr. Finlay. The same as I told the French dick when he was beating about the bush also. She took an overdose of sleeping pills and died. She was in Paris. Nikki was in a hotel near Dijon. He had a lady with him to prove it, also the hotel manager and staff. Being French, the police assumed an affair of gallantry. When Nikki admitted he'd wanted a divorce, they took the rest of it for granted, till her family stepped in. The body was exhumed, and showed nothing. And that was that. Or was it?"

She hesitated an instant, turned her head, looking Tony's back room over carefully before she turned back and leaned toward him.

"I've never told anybody this. It was the damndest thing that ever happened to me. I'm still not over it."

She glanced around again. The tables near them were empty.

"I was sent out to interview him right after the funeral. There was a rumor that the rake had reformed and was going to seal up the house with himself in it . . . something bizarre. I went out to the faubourg. He let me in and got me a drink. The servants were all busy, he said. We were in her little writing-room. We settled down for a heart to heart chat about life and love and the folly of it all. And I still don't know what happened."

She shivered a little and took another drink from her glass.

27

"He was talking: Could any pure woman ever love him again? How had he ever dreamed of divorcing an angel of light? I was a woman . . . did I think he was a monster?— All that crap, and I was ready with a touching reply of the same, when all of a sudden I heard myself telling him the truth. I was saying I'd always thought he was one of the most scheming, coldest, most utterly ruthless . . . I stopped before I said 'swine'. . . ."

Polly Randolph closed her eyes, a shudder running through her.

"It was just as if somebody else—or some thing else—was using my tongue, saying things I'd never even thought. I hardly knew the man. It was the atmosphere of the place . . . something. He had all her letters and stuff out, burning things in the fireplace. And just when I stopped, I saw all the dust on the table and I knew I was there alone in the house with him. There weren't any servants and hadn't been for days, because I remembered just then I'd noticed the hall was dusty. And he was looking at me looking at the dust, and I . . . I swear I thought he was going to kill me. I was petrified. I tried to get up, but he said 'Sit down,' and I sat. Then he started. Why did I say what I'd said? Why scheming? What did I mean, ruthless? Who had I been talking to? It was just like a silk stocking around my neck."

She shuddered again, her face pale.

"I don't know how I got out of there. I'll never forget that trek down the hall with him behind me. I truly never thought I'd make it. I knew he'd killed his wife, and he knew I knew it. I don't know how I did, but I did. And I knew that was why the servants weren't there. It was just as if some finger I couldn't see was writing it in the dust in her room. And if I'd turned up in the Seine with a suicide note in my pocket in the next couple of weeks, it wouldn't have surprised me. I was sick as a dog when I got home and I had cold sweat all over me when I saw him coming out of the office the other day. And what's he so interested in the Maloney deal for? Dodo must have told him all about her father. Three martinis and she sounds off on the dirty deal he gave her. I've even heard her say poor old Caxey Reeves murdered him."

"What kind of a dirty deal does she think she got?" Fish asked.

"She never specifies. She just gets a cagey look in her eye and says she's got everything she needs to break the Trust. Maybe Nikki's trying to help her. I suppose if Mr. Reeves murdered the old man you could establish undue influence, or something?"

Caxson Reeves had listened to that without a ripple of expression, waiting impassively for Fish to go on.

Polly Randolph shrugged her shoulders. "All I know is you won't catch me in Newport this summer. I've asked for Washington, heat or no heat. And you know, of course, I'm an overwhelming minority of one. Except for the first wife's family, and they won't talk. I tried to corner one of them in Madrid on my way back and he'd never heard of anyone named de Gradoff. Everybody else including Dodo thinks he's divine and that the family took him to the cleaners when he was helpless in the throes of chivalrous remorse." She shrugged again. "But I know if I were the Maloney trustees and I got even a whiff of that romance curdling, I'd see Dodo didn't have any sleeping pills within reach."

"Dodo does not take sleeping pills," Caxson Reeves said evenly.

"I'm just telling you what Polly Randolph said," Fish replied. "I still think an investigator could sound out the first wife's family."

"Who'd be happy to convict themselves as accessories after the fact for the benefit of the Maloney estate, no doubt." Reeves looked at him over his spectacles. "It is not my business as Trust Officer of this bank to accuse a client's husband of murder, Finlay. Dodo is trying to break the Trust. Just how long do you think it would take her to find out the Maloney Trust was paying someone to pry into de Gradoff's past, and to bring suit for damages? You're concerned with her safety and with Jennifer Linton's. I'm concerned with the Maloney Trust and the reputation of the bank. I—"

"You told me." Fish pushed his chair back to absorb the sudden resurgence of angry resentment. "As long as the bank and the Maloney dough are safe, that's all that matters. I guess that's the point of your 'Invitation to Murder' gag. You said it wasn't the Maloney Trust that was about, it was the reversion of the Trust in case both Dodo and Jennifer die. So de Gradoff, the hatchet man, can do somebody a big favor, can't he. While the bank sits tight and refuses to interfere."

He got up. "Sorry. I don't look at things that way. I've quit, sir. Unless you've already fired me. The bank's reputation and the Maloney money will be safer in other hands."

"That's hardly the way to help Jennifer Linton, is it?"

Reeves spoke on a dead dry level without raising his eyes.

"Don't be an ass, Finlay. I didn't get up and walk out when you suggested I may have murdered my oldest and closest friend."

"I was speaking for Polly Randolph and Dodo Maloney, not myself."

"I was speaking for the bank," Reeves said quietly. "Now, if you'll just sit down, I'll speak for myself. It's obvious something must be done."

29

Fish sat. Reeves reached for his briefcase.

"I've had this for several weeks." He took out a blue air-mail letter. "I don't know what its significance is, if any, but it disturbs me. It's a reply to my letter saying the Maloney Trust has no funds to pay de Gradoff's debts and referring the undisclosed principal to the Countess de Gradoff." He read the letter carefully before he put it back in the envelope. "The principal is still undisclosed. But he has withdrawn his inquiry. He trusts we will forget that any inquiry was made, and explicitly requests that no mention of the matter be made to any third party . . . particularly the countess."

"Meaning what?" Fish asked.

"I don't know. There's no inference the debt has been paid, or written off. I presume the undisclosed principal still wants his money."

"How does he plan to get it?"

"I've no idea. As he does not appear to be making de Gradoff a free gift of it, he must have a plan of some sort in mind. Another thing. Dodo is a creature of habit. When she changes, it's always been a sign of trouble. She's never gone to Newport an hour before she had to under her father's stipulation about the property. When she got here week before last, she chartered a plane and went directly up there. I want to know why. She was here in time for Jennifer's graduation, a full-dress occasion she'd normally love. She didn't go. Again, why? You tell me de Gradoff has been looking up the newspaper files. He has a very legitimate interest in his wife's father . . . why does he use surreptitious means to satisfy it? He could have come to me. Unless, as you say, Dodo's suggested to him that I murdered the man."

"Perhaps he knows there's the French detective tracking him."

Reeves glanced at him. "I'd bury that bone, Finlay," he remarked patiently. "You've given me opportunity to gnaw it. I've declined. Draw any conclusion you like . . . but silently, will you?"

Fish grinned. "Sorry, sir."

"To get back to Dodo. I haven't talked to her since she's been home. I understand you have."

"It was the day she got here," Fish said. "She wanted to know if she had a few thousand bucks lying around anywhere. She didn't. She then wanted to know if she could draw on her fourth quarter stipend. I said I was just your messenger boy and she'd have to ask you. She said she'd skip it and take a chance. She didn't say—"

Reeves's glance had sharpened. "—Take a chance?"

"That's what she said, sir."

"The damned fool."

"I don't understand—"

"No reason you should." Reeves was still irritated. He sat looking fixedly at the table. "I've had no experience with private detectives," he said then, abruptly. "I've had, however, a great deal of experience with Newport. It's not what it used to be, but it's still pretty much of a closed corporation. An outsider would get nowhere. We'd have to have somebody who could move on the inside track."

He was silent for a moment.

"It's a serious risk. Are you willing to take it?"

"Me?" Fish Finlay asked.

"You." Reeves nodded. "Go to Newport, find out what's going on."

"I'll be the rankest kind of outsider."

"I'll supply your credentials. An unattached male doesn't need too many. He must be presentable—which my sister says means he's in possession of a white dinner coat and doesn't spit on the floor."

"And has a normal complement of legs."

"Forget your leg, Finlay," Reeves said quietly. "Unless you're using it to escape the risk I was talking about. Because the bank and the Maloney trustees, as such, have no part in this. If Dodo, or de Gradoff, or your newspaper friend, anyone, finds out what you're in Newport for, you're finished here. That's the risk. You don't have to take it . . . but leave your leg out of it. If it comes to kicking de Gradoff in the backside, I expect you'll manage."

So it was Finlay or nothing. He was conscious of his leg again, sitting there at the end of Nantucket Avenue. Below him where the road turned was a Swiss chalet with two arcs of cabañas extending from it, like a dark prehistoric bird with brilliant multicolored wings stretched out along the glistening sands to catch the sun. The beach was empty now, but beyond the far arc of cabañas were the tennis courts, with half a dozen players out, their long brown legs flashing back and forth over the green composition surface. Pretty soon they'd be dashing down to the white surf feathering the sand. *Our kind of fun. . . .* The old dream girl with amber eyes crept out beneath the chinks in the shuttered places of his mind. If she'd said plainly, "I don't love you any more" and let it go at that, would he still be bleating about it? Or was it just the business of being put on the marked-down counter that made him shy away from every other girl who smiled at him, made her look like a sacrificial heifer, or a bargain hunter who didn't have what it takes to deal in first-class merchandise?

He got out of the car abruptly and went over to the guard rail. There it was back again, the old destructive formula of his lost confidence in himself. Its return had nothing to do with his leg and people playing tennis, and not much to do

31

with his being an outsider getting his first outside view of the closed corporation of Newport society, as symbolized by the cabañas and chauffeur-driven cars down there in front of the beach club. It was his suddenly changed perspective. What if he was wrong about the whole thing? And if he was right, what could he hope to do about it? All he was doing was cutting his own throat . . . which was, no doubt, what Caxson Reeves had been doing his devious damndest to tell him for the last three months, with all the double-talk about the reputation of the bank and the sole duty of the Maloney trustees. If de Gradoff had murdered his first wife. Reeves's French detective would certainly have found it out. If it was true and he hadn't been able to prove it, how could Fish Finlay expect to prove future intent to murder in time to stop it?

Reeves was presumably helping him. Fish grinned. Helping him to cut his throat, no doubt, just the way he admitted he'd been helping Dodo to cut hers for years under the stipulated terms of the Maloney Trust. But there was nothing he could do at this point but go on. It was a week before Jennifer Linton would be there. Maybe he could find out he was all wrong and get out before she came.

He went back to his car, too absorbed to see the shiny new blue convertible that came around the curve going toward the chalet, or see the dark-haired girl who was driving it jam on her brakes as she caught sight of his tall figure limping back to the gray sedan with the New Jersey license plate.

CHAPTER : 4

Fish Finlay turned in between the pink marble gateposts. It was curious, driving in through the twilight purple of the beeches on the actual ground level of Enniskerry, when the far sharper image of it in his mind was the black and white aerial photograph over the safe in Caxson Reeves's conference room, when Reeves had finally given in and started to help him.

"This is the stable." He put his forefinger on the clock tower of a long shingled building across an open courtyard from the turreted Victorian mansion that Dodo called a matchstick monstrosity.

"There's an apartment in it I can arrange for you to have."

The purple beeches were a sable rim in the photograph. Reeves's finger moved up to where the rollers broke with foam-filled crests on the rugged cliff and rested on a jagged black spot bisected with a thin white line.

"Here's the Devil's Chasm. A break in the cliff. The Rock,

32

the Maloneys call it. But there's no use loading your mind with old tragedies. Those were the bathtub-gin days. People tried to get Maloney to put a rail around it. He did board up the clock tower, but that was only to protect the shingle work."

The scalloped-shell road dyed mauve from the reflected light of the beeches hadn't shown in the picture. Bordered with purple-leaved begonias, curving gently back on itself to hide the house and inner grounds, it opened suddenly into a magnificent sun-flooded arc of sky and sea and lawn. The courtyard was a great emerald medallion of perfectly shaved, sharply edged turf, the drive a gleaming ivory frame around it. Directly across from Fish as he entered it was a low spindled balustrade set with marble urns of pink geraniums, concealing the terraced rose gardens down to the cliff. The stable was on his right. The hexagonal clock tower was centered in the high-gabled side facing the house, its shingles as intricately and delicately patterned as a bird's feathers, its molded cupola set like a feathered helmet wide at the brim to shield the gilded clockface under it.

The house across the medallion, shingled as intricately as the clock tower, had a curious air of summer stillness, no sound of human occupation and no sign of it except a long low foreign car standing under the porte-cochere. Fish's engine and the scrunch of his tires in the drive were like a tocsin sounding in a courtyard of enchanted sleep, making him more acutely conscious than ever of the embarrassment of his own position there. If the arrangements for the stable apartment hadn't already been made, he would have driven right on around and out again. He stopped in front of the porte-cochere and got out, his footsteps grating unevenly as he passed in front of de Gradoff's car. It was custom made, the draft he'd signed to pay for it exactly the amount of his own year's salary before taxes. It still didn't mean the man was a murderer, he thought ironically. He rounded the gleaming hood to the verandah steps, started up and stopped. "—Oh, I'm sorry."

Three people were facing him there, de Gradoff, a younger dark-haired man and a lovely black-haired woman with skin startlingly white in contrast to the sun tan of the two men, barefooted in shorts and sleeveless sport shirts. He'd obviously interrupted a first-class row. The arrogant flush on de Gradoff's face was mirrored in the sullen mouth and glowering brow of the younger man and by contrast in the woman's lacquered indifference. She wore a black linen dress and scarlet sandals, a black bag and scarlet parasol dropped casually under the bamboo chaise she was stretched lazily out on. Her dark eyes were leveled on Fish Finlay with total lack of interest. He might have been a harmless toad that had hopped up on the steps and would hop away in a moment.

Apparently de Gradoff did not recognize him.

"I'm Fisher Finlay, Mr. de Gradoff," he said. "Is—"

"I know," de Gradoff said, without moving. He was slumped down in a wicker chair, his bare legs over the arm. "The stable's over there." He motioned toward it. "My wife's not at home. The servants are busy."

One of them appeared, a thin sallow man wheeling a portable bar.

"I can take Mr. Finlay over, sir," he said. "If you'll serve yourselves, sir. Madam said—"

"He'll manage, I'm sure. What are you having, Alla?"

"G and T," the dark lady murmured.

"Scotch," the young man said. "On the rocks."

The servant stood there, his hand on the bar.

"Mrs. Emlyn said gin and tonic, Moulton." De Gradoff repeated it without emphasis. "Mr. Peter takes Scotch. Gin and soda for me. Just a touch of lime."

"Yes, sir." The man's eyes met Fish's for an unhappy instant.

"Thank you," Fish said. He turned and stepped back into the drive.

"That was stupid, Nikki, dear."

He heard Mrs. Emlyn's lazy voice before he was off the bottom step. But she spoke in French, which Fish, being an American, obviously could not be expected to understand.

"I shouldn't worry about that fellow Reeves's hired hand," de Gradoff said easily, also in French. "He won't be with us long . . . unless his hide's thicker than I think."

He added something Fish could not hear. He heard the burst of laughter that followed it as he got into the car.

"You'd be surprised how thick my hide is, friends," he thought pleasantly as he started around the ivory drive toward the stable. Their anxiety to get rid of him was all he needed to bring the situation sharply back into focus. They weren't being that insulting just for fun. He glanced in his side-view mirror. The lovely Mrs. Emlyn had bestirred herself to come to the verandah rail and was looking after him. He wondered. Mr. Peter was obviously the cousin aged twenty-three that Jennifer Linton had been summoned to entertain. Who was Alla Emlyn? And what was her interest in the Maloney Trust? De Gradoff's reply had pointed it up just as it pointed up his own concern. The hired hand routine was what Fish had given Dodo over the phone the day she landed in New York and had wanted to know if she had a few thousand dollars loose. Unless she'd passed it along, which was unlikely, it meant that Nikki listened in on phone calls as well as at keyholes.

He stopped in front of the hexagonal tower and got out

34

to open the trunk and get his gear. It was all to the good
. . . unless, he thought abruptly, they'd been at work on
Dodo. But they hadn't. He heard the gay toot of her horn as
she came in the beech tree drive. She saw him and swerved
toward the stable.

"Darling! What fun!" She threw the car door open and
rushed to him, arms out. "It's divine to see you!" She kissed
him warmly on both cheeks. "But where's Moulton? He's
supposed to settle you in."

"He's busy."

"Nonsense." Her eyes shot over to the porch. "Can't they
even pour their own poison, the lazy devils?"

In the brief incendiary flash, her laughter suddenly gone,
Fish saw her face. *Good God, what's happened to her?*

"But never mind, I'll take you up."

She was gay again, too gay, trying to conceal the taut lines
under the heavy layer of her peachblow makeup. She was
much thinner. The pearly lusciousness that was what he remembered about her was completely gone.

He picked up a couple of bags and followed her into the
hexagonal two-story hall at the base of the clock tower.
Central stairs led to a railed balcony level with the windows
on the three front sides of the tower. There were doors at
each end of the balcony and one in the center.

"Nikki's furious. He wanted Alla here." She stopped on
the stairs. "She's another cousin. Husband hunting." She
wrinkled her nose. "Marry a central European and you get
the whole family. And they're certainly realistic about life
and love. Alla married an Air Force major in Austria, he got
her out, got her naturalized and whoosh, off she went to
Reno." She laughed. "Couldn't stand being chatelaine of
Emlyn Appliances Inc, in Frisbie, Wyoming. But she didn't
stick him for alimony. Just a lump sum, plus her own jew-
elry he'd got in duty free as household effects. Smart girl,
Alla."

She went on up the stairs. "I knew her long before I met
Nikki. Peter's her nephew."

"Wife hunting?"

"Don't be funny, darling. Unless, of course, something
very *glamour* and very, *very* rich turned up. He might con-
descend."

She laughed again. "If it's Jennifer Linton you've got in
mind, relax, darling. She's not his type. And she's not rich,
my sweet. Not when I get through smashing up your old
Maloney Trust."

She went along the narrow balcony and threw open the
door at the terrace end. "This is your living-room, sir. The
whole thing used to be the hayloft."

Fish saw a large handsomely paneled room, open to the

steep gable of the roof, cool and pleasantly dark, with open casement windows filled with pink geraniums. The house was beyond them at his left, gardens to the right, and at the end, where the hay had once been brought up, a whole world of sparkling sea.

"It's wonderful, Dodo."

She was silent a moment. He saw the tired lines deepen in her face.

"I suppose it is," she said gravely. "It doesn't have a lot of happy memories for me. Bob Linton and I used it for a playroom. You can still smell juniper in the bathroom, I expect. Sometimes I think if it hadn't been for prohibition, Bob Linton and I . . . maybe we wouldn't have made such a mess of things."

She looked at the circular staircase in the corner. "That goes to the clock tower. Actually, all this is the gardeners' domain, not mine. They graciously permit me to use it sometimes. It was sweet of Caxey to ask me if you could have it, instead of asking Jan Vranek. The tower's still boarded—even when I promised Vranek you wouldn't climb after a few drinks. And don't go down to the Rock at night, drunk or sober. A friend of ours tried it." She shivered a little. "That was the end of our parties here."

She went over to the sofa in front of the dark paneled fireplace and sat down wearily. "It's funny, you know. It didn't depress me this way when Moulton was getting it ready for you, with old Vranek standing guard to keep us from committing sacrilege." She opened her bag aimlessly and let it slide off her lap onto the cushions. "Caxey said you needed a rest. I don't often think kindly of my father . . . but I thought he'd be rather pleased to have you here. He always felt so bitterly about not having any son of his own to go to war. And about my not having any."

She shook her head quickly. "But this is stupid. I guess the doctor depressed me."

"The doctor?"

"Didn't Nikki tell you that's why I wasn't home?"

Fish shook his head, watching her gravely, with rising concern.

"It's absurd, of course." She put her head back against the slip cover and closed her eyes. "It's maddening, actually. I just can't sleep any more. I can't eat. I'm so jumpy I can't sit still five minutes. I drink decaffeinized coffee and smoke hay with all the nicotine out of it. If I get to sleep, I have such nightmares poor Nikki's had to move out in self-defense. It's horrible."

"What does the doctor say?"

"Not a damned thing. Is my marriage successful? It's divine. How long has this been going on? Good grief, how do I know? It started in Europe, I guess, but I never had time to go to bed, anyway, so it didn't seem to matter. Then old Caxey started calling me up every other day, and I guess that worried me. All he was doing was waiting to hear me say my marriage was going sour, which it wasn't and *isn't*. Caxey's a ghoul."

She got up and moved impatiently around. "I guess it's my mother," she said abruptly. "She died of cancer. The doctor said if I was scared, I ought to go to a hospital for a checkup. But that really scares me. If I'm going to die, I don't want to know it. Or have Nikki know it. I don't want him to see a death's-head every time he takes me in his arms."

She jerked around to the mirror over the telephone table. "Just look at me, Fish! I'm horrible. This afternoon, I was crossing the street to my car, and right where I'd parked there was a chalk cross on the curb and 'Death' printed under it. I'm not superstitious, but—"

"Oh, nuts, Dodo," Fish said. "It was just some kid—"

"I know, but why was it right where I parked?" she asked sharply. "But it isn't that. It's my conscience, I guess. I've never told Nikki he won't have a penny if I die . . . and Jennifer'll be glad to see him starve. . . ."

She came back to him and gripped his arm. "What'll I do? Shall I tell him, Fish?"

He felt his arm stiffen under her grip. If she told de Gradoff, the death's-head would move to Jennifer Linton.

He stood there rigidly, not knowing how to answer her, when her hand relaxed abruptly. She was looking past him, her eyes widened, out of the window and across the courtyard at her own house. He turned. The stable loft was level with the second story of the house. Through the windows between its shingled turrets, flooded with sunlight, the master bedroom was like a lighted stage, and across it was the open door of de Gradoff's dressing-room. Or the room he was dressing in, fairly from scratch. With him was the lovely Alla Emlyn, in a black bra and black pantie girdle, pausing occasionally to talk to him as she brushed her long black hair.

Dodo's hand dropped from his arm.

"Well, bless me." She turned away, brows arched. "What was I saying? Let's skip it, shall we? I dare say he'll manage." She moved over to the door, not taking it as lightly as she pretended. "I'll go along. I ought to be there when—" She glanced at her watch. "Good heavens, I wonder what's happened to her? She promised to be here by four."

"Who?" Fish asked.

"Jennifer. You knew she was coming, didn't you?"

"Next week, I—"

"She changed her plans. She was going to stay with some South American friends in Washington, but she decided to drive Anne Linton and her new husband to New York instead to catch their boat to Europe. Anne's husband gave her the car for graduation. You knew Anne had copped herself a gold mine, I guess."

"Jennifer wrote Mr. Reeves."

"I should be pleased, I suppose, but I'm not." There was a waspish edge to her voice. "Now Anne can afford to keep my daughter, I won't have any control over her. She's only coming here to get out of Anne's way. Not because I want her to. You said not to make her come, so I began to feel like a dirty dog and say, darling, you can stay in Virginia. But not at all. She's coming, and will I lend her the money to pay off the mortgage on Dawn Hill Farm as a wedding present for Anne Linton, for the love of heaven. I could have killed her."

She laughed irritably. "I suppose, of course, I should have given her the car, instead of letting Anne's husband do it. But that thing of Nikki's cost all I've got to put in cars this year. He was so crazy to have it. Cars are the one thing he knows all about. He sat around New York three days getting a touring permit so he could drive it up here himself."

So he could look up the story of James V. Maloney, is what you mean, lady.

"Alla was in New York," Dodo went on. "He was going to bring her, but she decided to fly straight up with me and Peter. She adores Peter. I felt so rotten I didn't want to stay myself. And I don't know why I thought I'd feel better here. I hate the place. Sometimes I think I just come back to spite those two old monsters out there in the greenhouses. But then I think it's because I've lost something, and maybe it's here I'll find it. I don't know. But I was showing you the drains, wasn't I?"

She reached for the door next to the hall door, making a brittle attempt to be gay again. "This is your kitchen. I thought you'd like to get your own breakfast."

"Don't bother, Dodo. I'll find things."

He stayed where he was over by the fireplace while she went inside. Then, as she didn't answer, he waited a moment before an odd feeling of alarm made him start to go to her. As he did she came quickly out of the kitchen and closed the door sharply behind her. Her face was chalk-white under her makeup.

"Dodo . . . what's the matter?"

"Nothing, darling. I . . . I'm just losing my mind, I guess. But I . . . I've got to go now."

She opened the hall door. "If I could go to sleep! *Just once!*" Her voice rose hysterically. "It's driving me crazy. And that stupid doctor. He just looked at me as if I was lying to him. All he did was give me some sleeping pills. And I told him I'd never taken a pill in my life, not even aspirin. Nikki'll be furious. But it was Nikki made me go to the doctor, so he can't say I can't take what the doctor gives, can he?"

Fish looked at her blankly.

"Oh, I told you!" she exclaimed. "That's the way that wretched first wife of his killed herself. That's why he's so dead against sleeping pills. He raised hell the other night when Alla offered me something she uses. But if I don't tell him I'm taking them—"

She broke off, pushing her hair back from her forehead. "I don't know what's happened to me, Fish. I've gone all to pieces, all of a sudden." She shook her head quickly. "Just leave me alone a minute. I'll be all right. Go on and wash your face, and come over when my child gets there. Go on . . . please."

She pulled the door shut. Fish Finlay stood there, listening to her pacing back and forth on the balcony. Then he heard her go down the stairs and the car door slam. He went back and looked out of the window, his face grave, and saw her car reach the house. She got out and ran quickly around the black car and up the steps. He looked up at the front bedroom. The dressing-room door was closed. That pleasant interlude—casual rather than illicit, he thought suddenly—probably accounted for some of her distress. He started to turn away when Dodo flashed into the room from the other side. She stopped, balancing herself for a moment, before she threw her arms around the heavy post at the corner of the bed and clung to it, breaking away almost immediately as a maid in a black uniform and white apron came in.

He went across the room and stood looking out of the hayloft window at the end, trying to figure out what the hell was going on. De Gradoff's opposition to the sleeping pills, so in reverse of what had seemed to be the pattern. And he'd made her go to the doctor, she said. Fish sharpened his attention then, seeing de Gradoff strolling around from the back of the house, in a yellow sports jacket and brown slacks now. He glanced casually at Dodo's car and continued his stroll calmly down out of sight among the roses. He'd made her go to the doctor, but he was certainly controlling his impatience to learn the doctor's verdict, Fish thought.

As he reached down to get his bags and go find the drains, a glint of gold on the sofa caught his eye. He went over. It was a compact that had slipped out of Dodo's bag, and under it was a small green bottle with a black screw cap. He picked it up.

"One every four hours for sleep when necessary," the label read. "Dr. M. McNair." Under it was a red sticker. "It is necessary for your physician to authorize the refilling of this prescription." He unscrewed the cap and poured the twelve small capsules out into his hand. They were the mildest form of sedation the doctor could give her. She could take the whole batch at a gulp without serious consequences.

He put them back in the bottle, dropped it into his pocket, thought for a moment, went over to the telephone and picked up the book. Dr. Malcolm McNair, 24 Roger William Street, 684. He picked up the phone, heard a woman's voice and started to put it down when the operator came in, in front of the woman's voice dribbling steadily on about a dress sale.

He gave the number. Another woman's voice came on in front of the backdrop of the dress sale. "Dr. McNair's office."

"Does Dr. McNair have evening hours?"

"By appointment. He's in tonight. He could see you at 9:15."

"I'll be there. Put me down, please."

He put the phone back quickly before she could ask his name, and stood there with his hand on it. Caxson Reeves might know Dr. McNair and give him a green light to ask questions and get answers. But if the voice of the anonymous woman could filter through the old-fashioned phone system, so could his, no telling to whose ears.

He got his bag and went through into the kitchen. Dodo had been far more upset coming out of it than she had been looking across the courtyard at Nikki and Alla Emlyn. He looked around. There was nothing he could see that could have upset her. He crossed the room and looked out the window over the sink. Below him was a vegetable garden, trim weedless squares enclosed with fruit trees neatly cordoned along iron pipes. Up beyond them, behind a high screen of lilac trees, were the greenhouses, the stronghold of the two old monsters, Vranek and McTaggert. He could see them now, perched on stepladders with orange-handled clippers, pruning a vine or tree espaliered along the inside of the roof, caught in the rays of the sun through the squares of glass opened high for ventilation.

They looked more like gnomes than monsters, in their dusty blue denims and brown derby hats, slow-moving, methodical little men minding their own business in their own domain, hardly worth Dodo de Gradoff's bitterness. But the whole setup was fantastic, of course, and bitterness hardly cares what food it eats.

He heard a car come in then, hidden behind the lilacs, and saw one of the gardeners put his clippers down and lean out through the open square of the glass roof. Fish picked up his bag again and went through into a small foyer and on into a bedroom with a bath. He washed up and changed his shirt in concentrated silence, thinking about the dilemma that had faced him when Dodo wanted to know if she should tell de Gradoff about the Trust. What would he have done if the view of Nikki and Alla Emlyn hadn't distracted her? Would he have said, "Don't tell him?" Would he, in other words, have said, It's okay if de Gradoff kills you, as long as he doesn't hurt Jennifer? Was that what he had in mind?

He shook his head and took a final swipe at his rusty short-clipped thatch, catching an unaccustomed full-length view of himself in the mirror on the bathroom door. He might not have patina, but at least he was a far cry from the driver of the battered truck in April in Virginia. He grinned in spite of himself as he went out into the hall and down the stairs.

The woven cedar fence between the stables and the rim of purple beeches hid the blue convertible in front of the greenhouses from view on the ground level, just as the lilacs had hidden it from the kitchen window when Jan Vranek leaned out to look down at the disappointed face of the dark-haired girl behind the wheel.

"Oh . . . I've missed him again!"

She looked up and saw the dour face peering down at her.

"Oh, Mr. Vranek! Hello! I'm looking for a friend of mine. A girl said she saw a New Jersey car come in here to Enniskerry. But you've forgotten me, haven't you. I'm Jennifer Linton." She opened the car door and got out. "May I come in and see the flowers?"

The two old men looked at each other in wooden silence.

"Mr. Vinlay at the stable," Vranek said.

The other nodded and went on with his work. Jan Vranek climbed down the ladder and trudged dourly along between the benches to the girl looking delightedly around her in the greenhouse door.

CHAPTER : 5

How do you greet people who've just been as offensive as possible? Fish came around Dodo's big car and crossed in front of de Gradoff's sleek black car considering the problem with detached interest. But it was academic. Dodo was there alone, with Moulton putting glasses and a fresh thermos of ice on the bar.

"Darling . . . welcome to Enniskerry!"

She came gaily over to the steps, hands out, and bent forward to kiss him lightly on the cheek. "Did I leave my compact and pills at your place?" she whispered. He brought them out of his pocket. She closed her hand over them and slipped the pill bottle down her bra as she put her other hand in his arm to lead him across to the bar.

"Nobody's down yet."

"Two of us are, darling."

Alla Emlyn and Mr. Peter came from somewhere around the verandah that flowed like a pleasant river of shade around the house.

"Alla, darling, this is Fish Finlay. Nikki's cousin Mrs. Emlyn, Fish."

"How do you do, Mr. Finlay. . . . Fish, if I may call you that. I've heard such charming things about you."

Alla Emlyn's dark eyes raised to his were alight and mocking, not mocking him but Dodo, as she managed to convey to him that he and she, not the others, were basically akin. "I'm sorry we were all too flagrantly unclothed to receive you properly when you first came."

"But you're really clothed now, aren't you, darling?" Dodo remarked.

In the lacy shadows cast by the fretwork gingerbread cornice of the verandah, her peachblow makeup was entirely convincing. Mrs. Emlyn was indeed clothed, from mid-calf to only slightly below the demands of normal decency. A chiffon stole covering her dazzling white arms and shoulders that slipped when she gave her hand to Fish was drawn gracefully up again as she moved to include Mr. Peter in the circle.

"And Nikki's cousin, Peter de Gradoff."

"How do you do, sir?"

Peter's handshake was not cordial, but it was civil. His accent was neither so polished as Nikki's nor so charming as Alla Emlyn's, and his eyes, dark like hers, were sullen, like banked furnaces full of hostile fire. He was a handsome devil, Fish thought; fine profile, cleft chin, full arrogant lips, like the Belvedere Apollo.

"Where's Nikki?" Mrs. Emlyn settled herself lazily in the bamboo chaise, lifting her chiffon skirt to let it fall in graceful folds over her slender legs. "And where's that beautiful child of yours, Dodo? Peter's utterly mad to meet her. Look at him."

She laughed as Peter shot her a sullen glance.

"Who'd like a drink?" he asked curtly.

"Fish would, I'm sure." Dodo said it easily, but there was cobalt fire in her own eyes. "And you can relax about Jennifer, Alla. She doesn't pretend to be a beauty. Scotch and soda, Fish?"

"Every girl's a beauty, by definition." That was de Gradoff, at the bottom of the steps.

"If she's rich," Peter said under his breath, in French. It

was audible only to Fish and Alla and presumably understood only by Alla.

Fish took the glass handed him. "Thanks." *They're pushing Mr. Peter to bracket the Maloney dough and Mr. Peter won't be pushed.* He carefully kept the new cordiality he felt for Mr. Peter from showing in his voice as he looked back at Dodo, her face alight, going to meet her husband.

"Darling!"

"I didn't know you'd got home, my sweet." There was an overtone of coolness in the way he kissed her that wasn't audible until he said, "I thought you were still over with Finlay, whose charm I am very happy to admit." He said it without a smile. "Sorry, Finlay." He glanced over at Fish. "But I've really been rather anxious, you know."

"So sorry," Fish said. He caught Dodo's startled surprise. It was probably the one sure way to get him out, he thought, as he saw Dodo's surprise change to instant flattered delight.

"Oh, don't be silly, sweet," she said gaily. "Actually, there's nothing wrong with me. Dr. McNair said so."

"Then I hope he gave you something to make you sleep," Mrs. Emlyn's remark had an edge of bitter interest.

"Not a thing, darling."

Dodo spoke too brightly and looked too quickly at her husband. Fish, watching de Gradoff over the rim of his highball glass, wondered. Did he see the blue dragonfly swoop with which de Gradoff picked it up, or did he imagine it?

"I'm relieved about that, of course." De Gradoff turned abruptly to Fish. "Mrs. Emlyn and I aren't in agreement on some things," he said stiffly. "I'm opposed to the use of the barbiturates. She hasn't had my exceedingly bitter experience with them."

"Well, you're sufficiently on record, Nikki, darling." Alla Emlyn yawned lightly. "A record we're all a little tired of hearing, if you'll forgive me."

She smiled at him quickly. "Oh, I'm sorry, Nikki," she said, with genuine warmth under the cream-smooth surface of her voice. "I shouldn't have said that. I know you're psychotic about sleeping pills. We'd all be, if we'd been accused of the murder of a stupid woman with them."

There was a moment of silence there on the porch. Then Dodo laughed.

"What a thing to say! When I feel so bloody rotten and the doctor says there's not a thing organically wrong with me. . . . Where's that incredible tact of yours gone to, Alla, dear?"

She laughed again. But an extraordinary thing had happened. As light flashes more swiftly than sound, thought flashes more swiftly than light. Fish Finlay saw the flash of

43

the thought in Dodo's mind. And de Gradoff saw it. He moved toward her. For a split fraction of an instant she drew away from him. He stopped abruptly, and for another instant so brief that Fish was not sure he hadn't only imagined it, he saw the blue dragonfly dart in de Gradoff's eyes again, the thing that Polly Randolph had seen, and that Fish Finlay now did not have time to put a name to before it was gone. De Gradoff took the other half-step to Dodo and took her face in his hands, raising it to his.

"No, my dearest," he said tenderly. "You're not turning against me. That I couldn't bear." His voice was low and richly intimate, and to show he didn't believe that anything at all had happened he smiled, almost boyish in his appeal, before he bent down, kissing her lightly, so that she flushed and laughed, happy again. He turned then, one arm pressing her to his side, and smiled at the rest of them, with just a touch of self-deprecation.

"Of course," he said candidly, "it's so wise of Alla, really. I'd assumed that Finlay must have heard all that. If he hasn't, he will, here in Newport. So it's much the wisest for us—"

The measure of the undersurface intensity of what had happened there on the porch was the shock with which they heard the sudden voice calling gaily from the driveway. "Hi there, Mother!"

The blue convertible had come cautiously through the purple beeches to reconnoiter. Vranek must be wrong, Jennifer Linton told herself. It couldn't possibly be Mr. Finlay from the bank. There must have been two New Jersey cars on Nantucket Avenue. Then she saw the gray car standing in front of the stable, stepped delightedly on the gas and brought the blue convertible to a stop, facing her mother in front of the porte-cochere, seeing people there, her mother and Nikki standing together, their backs to her. It was the first time she'd ever been happy arriving at Enniskerry.

None of them on the porch, not even de Gradoff, apparently unperturbed, had heard her come. It took a moment even then, before they turned, curiously slow-motion, for the shock of Jennifer Linton herself.

"Great heavens . . . she *is* a beauty! Peter—look at her!"

Fish heard Alla Emlyn's quick whisper in French as Dodo turned and saw her daughter.

"Jennifer! *Baby!*" She stood motionless for an instant. "Why, *Jenny* . . . *you've grown up!*"

Fish Finlay got to his feet, not knowing he'd done it. He stood there, holding his glass, looking at Jennifer Linton coming up the steps, her mother's arm around her, Dodo's face transformed with light, Jennifer's shining with inner excitement, glowing and lovely, like the sickle moon in the evening sky, a subtle radiance around her. *She's like a marsh iris,* Fish Finlay thought. *She makes Dodo look like a painted marigold. And I'd forgotten her. I'd forgotten what she looks like.*

He stood there half-dazed, trying to remember the other girl, and seeing only the tousled hair, strained gray eyes and white face, the torn shirt and green jodhpurs. That was the picture of Jennifer Linton that had stayed in his mind. He'd never in the wide world have recognized this as the same girl. Maybe it was the navy-blue dress. Or the lipstick. Her hair was still short—Capri cut, his sister called hers—and the dark curls flecked with gold where the sun touched. The thick glossy brows he remembered now, and the long curling black lashes, but her gray eyes were darker, dancing with light. But it was the sum total of all of them, and something else that was inside her shining out. She wasn't pretty, she was beautiful, and fresh as dew. Even Mrs. Emlyn looked faded beside her and hard as brand-new railroad spikes, Fish Finlay thought, coming out of the fog, seeing Nikki spring forward with all his old-world charm intact.

She hadn't even glanced at Fish. She didn't recognize him, either. But that was what he wanted, wasn't it? That was when he glanced at Peter de Gradoff and saw him leaning casually against the bar, the picture of a young man contentedly adjusting himself to the pot of gold now he'd seen the rainbow that came with it.

She was speaking to Mrs. Emlyn now, with the opaque but polite reserve cultivated by the present generation of young ladies' schools. It was his turn then.

"And Mr. Finlay, darling," Dodo said.

"How do you do, Mr. Finlay," said Miss Linton. *He thinks I don't recognize him. He thinks I've forgotten him. That means he's never told my mother he met me.*

"He's that creature your banker, darling," her mother said.

"Oh, really?" A demure and charming smile allowed itself to light Jennifer Linton's face a moment. "I always thought you were old, Mr. Finlay. Old like Mr. Reeves."

"Why, Jenny!" Dodo said, laughing.

"It's the way I feel, Miss Linton," Fish said. She hadn't even recognized his name as her Assistant Trustee.

"It's the way your letters always sounded." She smiled and turned to Peter de Gradoff, the delight and amusement she'd been holding in check flashing through, her gray eyes dancing, dazzling all of them. "And you must be Nikki's cousin Peter. Mother told me you'd be here."

"Hi there Jennifer." No old-world charm from Mr. Peter. But even Fish Finlay, reluctant to give the handsome devil his due, saw that Peter hadn't expected to be that devastating that fast.

45

Fish put his glass abruptly down on the bar. He'd better get the hell out of here. It wasn't Peter who made him sore; it was de Gradoff, and the ironic complacency in the amused smile he filtered across to Mrs. Emlyn. Her own face was expressionless. Fish saw it through the lazy cloud of smoke from her cigarette, and saw her eyes move over to him, quietly dissecting. He'd certainly better get out.

"I've got to get along, Dodo," he said.

"What about that drink, Jennifer?" Peter asked.

"No, thanks. I've got to unpack."

Jennifer had changed her mind about sitting down, and got up at once as Fish came across the porch. "We're going to the Randolphs' tonight, aren't we, Mother? I met Polly down town."

She was not looking at Fish, but she saw him stop a second.

"Oh yes, of course. Fish, I forgot." Dodo put her hand on his arm. "I meant to tell you. They'd love to have you come with us."

"Yes, do, Finlay," de Gradoff said stiffly. "Take my place, will you?"

Dodo smiled archly and dropped her hand from Fish's arm. "You will come, Fish, won't you?"

"Sorry," Fish said. "I've got a date," he added, as Dodo smiled again.

"We'll see if you can't break it," she said. "Come along, Jenny. I'll take you up. Moulton'll bring your bags."

Fish went down the steps, aware of Alla Emlyn's dark scrutiny following him, all hell getting set to break loose inside him.

Mrs. Emlyn watched him, listening to Dodo's and Jennifer's steps across the Aubusson carpet until they reached the stairs. She put down her cigarette.

"You're stupid, both of you." Her voice, no longer lazy, froze the complacent smile on Peter's face. De Gradoff's eyes were already cold.

"That's girl's in love. The man's here in Newport. That's why she was so late getting here. That's why she was so breathtakingly beautiful when she came up those steps. It wasn't you, Peter. And you'd better do something and do it quick, my love."

She turned sharply to Nikki.

"Finlay's nobody's hired hand. You're crazy. And he's not here for any rest. He didn't say ten words while he was here and he had one drink and left half of it. He's watching us . . . *believe* me . . . and with that face I couldn't tell once what he was thinking. You'd better both take a lesson, you're transparent as children. But you're right about one thing, Nikki. Get him out of here—quick, if you can."

She rose swiftly. "This date of his tonight . . . I'd find out who it's with if I were you, Nikki. And you're going to the Randolphs'. Your creditor's going to be there. And you'd better see that he doesn't talk to Dodo before I talk to him. And Polly Randolph. You remember Polly Randolph, Nikki. She's the newspaper girl who really *believes* you killed the lady from the Argentine. Have you thought how extremely unpleasant it could be for all of us if Finlay's date's with her?"

CHAPTER : 6

The shadows dwelling among the high-pitched beams of the loft crept down as the sun gathered its last lingering robes across the ocean, and closed slowly in around Fish Finlay, sitting hunched forward on the sofa.

What the hell. He straightened up and reached into his pocket for a cigarette, his mouth still full of the bitter fruit of another empty dream. If he hadn't come to Newport . . . if she hadn't come . . . he might have gone on deceiving himself. He was in love with her, and had been since the moment he saw her on the empty Virginia road. He knew it now, and the impact of knowing it had shattered all the cauterizing reserves he'd built up for himself. His cigarette glowed a small fitful light in the lonely darkness as he began to pick up the pieces and put them painfully together again. There was no question of hope, no dream, no reaching for a start, no sense of loss, as there would have been if he'd reached and failed, only a profound personal hell his heart had betrayed him into, that his head had had nothing to do with. A bell ringing somewhere inside of it only gradually focused itself into present reality. He became slowly aware that it was the telephone, and when it kept on ringing he went across the room through the dark and picked it up.

"Hello . . . Mr. Finlay?" A woman's voice was remote in his ear. "Fish, this is Polly Randolph. Remember me?"

He jerked himself back into the world around him. "Oh, hello, Polly. I heard you were here. I thought you said nobody was going to catch you—"

"They weren't, dear, but they did. My uncle. He's the stockholder who got me my job. One of the granddaughters is making her bow tonight. It's a family deal."

"Well, watch it," Fish said.

"Believe me, I shall. And I want to see you—I've got something to tell you. But right now I'm calling for an admirer of yours, Mr. Finlay. She wants you to come. She just called me

47

and explained all about you. I didn't tell her we'd met. She said you had a date but maybe you could be persuaded."

"Dodo, I expect."

Polly laughed. "I promised not to tell. Anyway, this date of yours must be horribly wrong side of the tracks, Fish. Everybody else is coming to the Randolphs', including a man from Mars already out in the guesthouse. But please come, Fish."

"Okay," Fish said.

Polly Randolph laughed again. "Dear heavens, it's not that grim. There'll be oceans of champagne and plenty of good honest whiskey, if you need an anesthetic."

"Sorry. I'll be happy to come. What time?"

"Around eleven. I'll be looking for you. Black tie'll do."

He put the phone down. An anesthetic wasn't what he needed, it was a monumental drunk, first class. Except that he wasn't a free agent and the clock in the shingled tower was striking eight. His date with Dr. McNair was at nine-fifteen. He had to find some place to eat, and to be on the safe side he'd better avoid all bars, public and private, now and later. He switched on the light to blot out the laughing lips and dancing eyes of a girl with glossy thick eyebrows and the gold-tipped gamin haircut that materialized in front of him whenever he relaxed his guard, and went through the kitchen across the narrow foyer to dress and get under way. As he took off his coat, he caught another view of himself in the mirror on the door, surprised to find he looked much the same. A little beaten up, maybe, but not much. It was the only advantage of a corrugated mug like his. Nothing showed through. There'll be a lot of people there, he thought. Maybe he wouldn't even see her. At least he wouldn't have to stick around and watch her dance with Mr. Peter. He could come home and get blotto there.

"—So that's the way it is, darling." Dodo rose lightly from the bench in front of the dressing table in Jennifer Linton's room. "I've just never told Nikki about the Trust . . . I don't want you to."

Jennifer had given up trying to unpack and was sitting on the foot of the bed, listening gravely.

"You'll promise. Please, Jenny."

"All right, Mother. But I don't know why the point should ever come up, do you?"

"No, darling. Unless—"

She came over and put her arms around Jennifer's waist. "You're really enchanting to look at, my child," she said smiling. "You don't know Newport as well as I do. There'll be men of all ages trying to marry you, my pet, with their mothers and daughters and aunts and cousins trying to help them. You'll be surprised at the chances they'll give you to tell

48

them just how much money you can count on the day you're married. Unless you're very smart, you won't even know they've asked you until you've told them."

Jennifer laughed. "Well, you don't have to worry about that. I'm not interested in men."

Dodo looked at her sharply. Jenny laughed again.

"Relax, Mother. All I mean is I already know who I'm going to marry, if—"

Dodo's lips tightened, her eyes beginning to shoot fire.

"Here we go again," Jennifer thought desperately. "I'm a stupid fool. But she was being so sweet. I should have known it wouldn't last."

Her own storm signals started to rise. She hadn't come here to be pushed around. Then she remembered what Anne Linton had told her: Don't lose your temper, angel. Just laugh, and Dodo'll come around. Try it once and see.

"Now you listen to me, Jennifer Linton," her mother was saying.

"*You* listen to me." Jenny laughed and kissed her mother's cheek. "Let's you and me refuse to quarrel, Mumsy, dear. And don't you worry. I know exactly what I want, and he's nobody you'd be ashamed of, truly. I knew it was him the first time I met him. I adore him, and I've only seen him twice. So please, Mamma, be on my side, just once, will you?"

"Oh, of course, baby." Dodo's lashes were moist. Then suddenly she laughed. "But what in hell am I going to do with Peter, darling?"

"Oh, we'll manage Peter." Jenny laughed. Then she fixed narrowed eyes on her mother. "Dodo de Gradoff, were you trying to rig me into marrying—"

"Of course not, darling. Don't be silly."

"Because if you were—"

"But I wasn't."

"Well, the rest of them are," Jennifer said lightly. "I knew it in my bones. But don't worry. I'll be an angel—to Peter, to Nikki, to everybody. I'll go to all the parties. I'll do everything. But I'm *not* going to marry anybody I don't want to. Is that fair, Mrs. de Gradoff?"

"Perfectly, Miss Linton."

Dodo laughed more happily.

"And there's something else, Mother, I've been wanting to say," Jenny said, suddenly very earnest. "It's about the Trust. Don't worry. You don't have to try to break it. There's plenty for both of us, and you'll always need a lot more than I do. You're used to it, and it doesn't—"

"That's sweet, darling . . . thank you. But . . . this man you're—"

"Don't worry about him." Jennifer's eyes danced.

"That's what they all say, darling." Dodo turned away

abruptly, the lines suddenly deepening in her face. "But . . . thank you, Jenny. And I'd *like* us to be friends."

She smiled quickly. "We've really got to hurry, dear. We're dining at the Clam Bake Club before the Randolphs'. You'll promise not to do anything silly, Jenny? This man . . . he's not already married, is he?"

"No, Mother."

Mr. Vinlay is a bachelor, Miss Yennifer. She'd been sure he wasn't married, but she hadn't really known till Mr. Vranek told her.

"How did you meet him?"

Jennifer laughed. "Just like you and Nikki, except it wasn't a lamppost."

"Oh, no!" Her mother's distress was so patent that Jennifer's eyes widened. "Oh, darling! That's pretty dangerous. Those things don't happen—"

"It happened to you and Nikki."

"But that's different. Promise you'll be careful. Promise you won't run off and marry him."

"I won't. I promise you I won't. And you won't tell anybody, will you? Not Nikki . . . not *anybody*."

"I promise, Jenny." Dodo took her daughter's face in her hands and kissed her lightly. "It's fun having secrets with my own child." She laughed happily. "And you could be right about Peter. He certainly brightened when he saw you. So did Alla . . . for a minute. And you'll probably change your mind fifty times before the summer's over. I did the summer I married your father. You rush along and dress, sweetie. If you'd like a maid, just ring."

Jennifer closed the door and stood there, her hand on the knob, her face sobering. There was something very wrong with her mother. She looked awful, so awful Jenny hadn't dared ask about it. And the business about the Trust, and about the lamppost. *She doesn't believe in Nikki any more,* Jenny thought; *not really, in her heart.*

As she stood there she became aware suddenly of the doorknob under her hand, and looked down at it, puzzled. The doorknobs all through the house were crystal, or had been. But this was silver-colored metal, with a push latch in the center. She opened the door softly and looked around the balconied hall. All the others were crystal.

She closed the door. It was three years since she had been in Newport. Lots of things could have happened . . . except that the house was not supposed to be changed at all. The porch furniture was all her mother had been allowed to modernize. She looked around at the familiar pieces in the room, that had been the fashion when her grandfather bought the house. They were still there. But something was different.

She went across the room and looked at the long windows

50

opening out onto the porch on the sea side. That was it. It wasn't the windows themselves but the wrought-ironwork outside them. It was very lacy, the same pattern as the fretwork of the cornice under the eaves, and it hadn't been there before. She unlatched the window and opened it, and stood there looking, still puzzled and not very happily, at the white-painted iron bar inside across the two ironwork wings. Her face brightened suddenly then and she lifted the bar, swung one of the iron wings open and looked out over at the stable. There were no lights there. She stepped out, slipped off her shoes and went along the porch in her stocking feet until she could see down in front of the clock tower. His car was still there. Maybe he just didn't like being dragged along to parties, but if one of the Randolphs called him up. . . . She got her shoes and hurried back inside.

It was then that she saw something else was different in her room. There were two telephones there, and she'd never had even one before. Her mother must really be planning for her social life. She laughed as she looked up the Randolphs' number, picked up the phone on the ivory desk in her sitting-room, and put it down at once. It was an extension, and Mrs. Emlyn was talking on it, in some language Jenny had never heard before. She went over to the other phone, in the alcove on the table between her twin beds, and picked it up tentatively.

"Number, please?" the operator said.

She gave the Randolphs' number, her face shining. An outside phone all of her own! Her mother must really think she'd grown up.

"May I speak to Miss Polly, please?"

She waited, looking around the room, disturbed again. It wasn't till she'd put the phone down—Polly was wonderful. "I'll be delighted to invite your trustee, Jenny. You're a smart girl to cultivate him. I swear I'll never tell"—it wasn't till then that the small seed of doubt began to grow.

The outside phone wasn't her mother's idea, because her mother hadn't thought of her as grown up until she saw her getting out of the car. She glanced at the lock on the door. It was an inside lock. The iron bar on the window was inside. She could lock herself in . . . *and lock other people out, and have an outside phone if she needed one.*

She got up slowly, her lips suddenly dry. Somebody must think. . . . It went through her mind quickly then: it's Mr. Finlay. That's why he's here. He hadn't believed the story when she told it to him. He did, now.

She moistened her lips and swallowed, her throat dry. It made it different, some way. She believed the story, especially after what she'd learned in Washington last week—it was the reason she'd hurried to Newport—but it had slipped

51

out of her mind in the excitement of finding him there. Or it wasn't that it had slipped out, exactly; it was just that most of the time it didn't seem real. It was more like a frightening dream, or something she'd seen at a movie, not really a part of her own life. Until something like the portrait in Washington, or something like the changes in her room, brought it all sharply back again. And if Mr. Finlay believed it. . . . She caught her breath, startled at a soft rap on the hall door.

"Who's there?"

She went over quickly. It was stupid to go to pieces like that.

"It's Elsa, miss. The maid."

"I'm sorry." She opened the door. "I didn't mean to lock you— Oh! Aren't they lovely!"

The maid had a spray of white butterfly orchids in her hand, her gaunt face flushed with pleasure at the pleasure in Jenny's.

"Mr. Vranek, miss. He sent them over specially for you." She held out another orchid. "He said I was to give this one to your mother, in case you felt she'd have to have one, too."

"Oh, don't!" Jenny caught herself before she laughed. Her mother's was an enormous frilled purple cattleya, handsome in itself, but blowzy, bosomy-lush beside the exquisitely delicate waxy spray that was for her. It wasn't funny, of course. It was just the shock that old Mr. Vranek, so earthy and heavy-footed, could think of that kind of sophisticated malice. Because it certainly wasn't accidental. She'd half-forgotten, till then, how virulently he and her mother hated each other.

"I mean, it won't go with the dress she's wearing," said Miss Linton tactfully, as she took her own. "They're lovely, Elsa. I'll thank Mr. Vranek in the morning. Why don't you keep that one?"

"Oh, thank you, miss!"

Jennifer closed the door and stood there with the butterfly spray in her hand, her eyes widening soberly as she looked from the lock on the door across to the iron lace grille over the windows. Mr. Vranek. He was in charge of the house. He'd be the one to make the changes. And they'd taken time. It wasn't any spur of the moment deal to get wrought iron the same design as the fretwork under the eaves and on the other gate at the end of the second-floor porch. Stubborn and stolid as he was, he wouldn't go to all that trouble and expense without knowing the reason for it. So they were all in on it, and had been for quite a while. And all of them were there protecting her. For a moment she had a sort of watery feeling of relief inside her. Then she swallowed, her throat suddenly dry again. Protecting *her*. But her mother. . . . They didn't care what happened to her mother. The gardeners hated her. And Mr. Reeves. . . . Even Jennifer knew how fed up he got with her, and indignant at things she did. And Mr. Finlay would have to do what Mr. Reeves told him to do.

She went to the dressing table and sat down, her face as waxen-pale as the spray of orchids.

"And I promised her I wouldn't tell Nikki about the Trust. The one thing I could do that. . . ."

She put the orchids down and looked at herself in the mirror, her cheeks suddenly burning hot.

"It's not right. I won't do it. I *will* tell him! They're not going to—"

She flashed up as she heard her mother's voice calling her out in the hall, and dashed over to the door.

"Sorry I'm not ready, Mother. Go ahead. Ask Peter if he'll wait and drive with me."

Dodo came fragrantly down the stairs. "Where's Nikki?"

"Gone to see if your Mr. Finlay won't come along with us. Nikki's afraid he was rather rude." Alla Emlyn turned. "Oh, you're wearing them, after all."

Dodo, stopping at the hall mirror, leaned forward to catch the light on her necklace of star rubies set with diamonds. "Aren't they glorious?" She laughed with delight, unaware of the sudden bitterness in Alla Emlyn's dark eyes watching her. "Really, they're fabulous, Alla!"

"That's why I wonder if it's safe to wear them, dear," Mrs. Emlyn's voice was lazily inquiring. "There's sure to be an awful mob there tonight."

"But Nikki said—"

Dodo broke off as he came across the verandah.

"Finlay got away, I'm afraid." He came on into the hall. "Oh, lovely!" He laughed, suddenly gay. "My darling! She's such a child! Can't resist a new toy."

Dodo's face clouded. "But you said it would be all right to—"

He interrrupted her, playfully firm. "I said all these people tonight are your friends, not mine, my sweet. *You* know them. I don't want the blame if anything stupid happens." He picked up her blue mink stole as she stood, hesitating. "But if my darling's going to be unhappy if she doesn't wear them, . . ."

He laughed, putting the stole quickly around her, dropping a kiss lightly on the top of her golden head.

"Of course they're my friends," she said, happy again. "It's ridiculous to worry."

Nikki glanced at Alla. She turned away with a faint smile.

"Where's your lovely child, darling?" she asked casually, pulling on her gloves.

53

"She wants Peter to drive with her in her car. So let's go, shall we?"

Nikki glanced at Alla again, whistling a lilting bar or so.

"Precisely, my friend." She spoke in neither English nor French. "Don't forget . . . it's Peter *and* the Wolf you're whistling. We'll see who she dances with the most."

"I wish you two would stop babbling in unknown tongues," Dodo said irritably.

"Alla just said how very well you look tonight, my sweet." Nikki took her arm. "And not too much champagne . . . and early home to bed, my girl."

"Right. Because I'm really going to sleep, tonight." Dodo laughed again, pressing her evening bag to make sure she had the pills Dr. Malcolm McNair had given her securely in her own possession.

CHAPTER : 7

It was half-past ten when Dr. McNair opened his consulting room door for his last patient.

"I hope you're sicker than you look," he said, his glance resting on Finlay's white dinner coat. "I've had a long day." He watched him crossing the reception room. "Sorry. Leg bothering you?"

Fish shook his head. "No, Doctor. And I expect you'll throw me out no matter what kind of a day you've had. I'm here about a patient of yours. These are the only credentials I can offer."

Dr. McNair looked silently at the cards in the billfold Fish handed him.

"I'm the Assistant Trust Officer under Caxson Reeves for the James V. Maloney Trust. I'm staying in the stable at Enniskerry."

"I know Mr. Reeves."

"I would have asked him to call you, but your telephone system here sounds pretty leaky. So I took a chance. On its lowest level, I guess what I'm asking you is to commit a breach of professional ethics. I'm worried about Mrs. de Gradoff."

There was nothing he could put a name to in the pale-blue eyes probing him across the desk.

"I don't even know how to explain it to you without saying more than I have any business to say at this point."

He saw the slow burn incandescing in the doctor's tired face as he pushed his chair back.

"In other words, I'm to violate my ethics but you don't intend to violate your own." Dr. McNair got up. "I was out at 3:30 for a delivery this morning. Mr. Finlay. My dinner's on the back of the stove. My wife wants to go to the Randolphs' too."

"I'm sorry, Doctor. I don't blame you for being sore. But my position isn't quite the way you stated it. Will you give me five minutes? Or can I come out and talk to you while you eat?"

Dr. McNair sat down. "I'll give you five minutes."

"Thanks. I got here this afternoon. I'd seen Mrs. de Gradoff three months ago. I was appalled today at the change in her. She told me she'd been to a doctor because she couldn't sleep or eat. The doctor told her there was nothing wrong with her and if she was afraid of cancer she ought to go to a hospital for a checkup. She dropped the bottle of Nembutal you gave her out of her bag—that's how I got your name. She also told me that her husband is violently opposed to the use of sleeping pills. His first wife—"

"She told me that."

"She said, also, that you acted as if you thought she was lying about her symptoms."

"About the cause of her symptoms," Dr. McNair said evenly. He looked steadily at Fish. "Let me ask you a question. Did Mrs. de Gradoff tell you I advised her to go into the hospital for a week, to see if her symptoms wouldn't disappear?"

There was no mistaking the irony in his quiet voice.

"It was surprising how many IV-F's with hypertension cleared into I-A's in the course of a week's observation during the war, Mr. Finlay."

He got up again. Fish stayed where he was. "You mean Benzedrine, Doctor, or—"

"Or caffeine derivatives, or any of a number of things? I didn't say so. Nor did I say Mrs. de Gradoff was lying when she said she never took a pill in her life. But I can't overlook the obvious just to please Dodo Maloney.There are too many sick people for me to worry whether Dodo can sleep or not —much as I'm indebted to her father. I used to edge turf and chop poison ivy at Enniskerry after school. He loaned me the money to go to medical school. Dodo wouldn't know about that. I signed a note payable to James V. Maloney five years from graduation. When I paid it, in full and on the exact day, Mr. Reeves sent the canceled note back with a check for the entire amount—Maloney's way of helping people help themselves."

He smiled faintly. "That's the reason I haven't thrown you out, Mr. Finlay."

"Let me ask you a hypothetic question, then, Doctor," Fish

said. "Could anyone, with such symptoms, be taking something of that kind, with no knowledge of it?"

Dr. McNair took out a pack of cigarettes and lighted one slowly.

"I suppose you know what you're saying."

"I told you my position was difficult," Fish said.

McNair's eyes rested on him a moment. "It's possible. If there's such suspicion, the patient certainly should be in the hospital."

"How could that sort of thing be taken?"

The doctor's face was impassive. "Is the question still hypothetical?"

"Yes."

"In a martini before dinner. In coffee after. A quarter grain would do it. The effects are cumulative. The nervous tension built up would keep one awake, even without additional dosage."

"Then let's take Dodo Maloney. If that was happening to her, would her symptoms be what you observed today?"

Dr. McNair nodded. "It's possible. But aren't you forgetting that she's been burning the candle at both ends for twenty-five of her forty years?"

"You'd never have guessed it in April, Doctor. She wouldn't burn to a raddled stub in three months, would she?"

"She'd better go to the hospital," Dr. McNair said quietly. "I'm afraid I took for granted a lot of natural wear and tear she'd refuse to admit even to herself. With a new husband, something to boost her—"

Fish shook his head. "She wasn't lying. She's too scared. But she did lie to her husband about the sleeping pills you gave her . . . knowing how opposed he is to them. So, if she takes an overdose, it's certainly no fault of his. He didn't even know she had them. And you'll testify that you thought she'd been taking Benzedrine or something. The overdose will be put down to accident or fear of cancer in a distraught mind. It'd be a neat setup, Dr. McNair."

McNair got up. "I'll see if I can get her in the hospital." A profound weariness sagged his shoulders. "I can see her at the Randolphs'." He went with Fish to the door. "There's one thing. All the Nembutal I gave her wouldn't hurt her."

"Is there something she could take with the Nembutal that would . . . and that wouldn't be traceable—twelve hours later, say? I might as well tell you, Doctor. A rumor about the first wife's death is what brought me up here. Nothing but barbiturates was found when they exhumed her body."

"We'll get her in the hospital," McNair said quietly.

"Could anybody with knowledge of a substance of that sort get hold of it, Doctor?"

56

McNair looked at him. "There's nothing I know of that you can't get if you've got the money," he said bitterly.

Fish Finlay found a place to park and followed a giddy group of the very young through open gates onto a rose-colored carpet into a fairyland of laughter and music. The carpet was a velvet gesture thrown handsomely across the paved courtyard to the crowded doorway under a Palladian window lighted by a spangled crystal chandelier like a pend-ant jewel. Through the lace brick wall on either side, Japa-nese lanterns, strung maypole fashion in undulating ribbons of flower-colored light, made the gardens into rainbow-roofed pavilions. Clusters of people moved among tables set in concave wings on the lawn. He followed the chattering group, young and buoyant—not a care in the whole bloody world, he thought—grinning as he waited behind them, abruptly startled then to hear one of them lower her voice to the careless lad beside her.

"I hope mother's not stinking drunk when she gets here. I'll simply die."

He glanced at her. She was a lovely little thing with golden hair and wide blue eyes.

"You help me keep her away from daddy and his bride. Oh, Miss Randolph, hello! Oh, mother's just fine, thank you."

Fish saw Polly Randolph, laughing and holding her hands over her ears as the whole young crowd saw another crowd their own age and broke into delighted screams.

"Did I shriek when I was their age?" She held out her hand. "It's so nice to see you." Her green eyes lighted with amusement. "You look very distinguished, Mr. Finlay, Olym-pian in fact. The line's breaking up so the grandchild can dance, but come along and meet my uncle and aunt."

The youngsters were filing decorously past the handsome white-haired man and his handsome purple-haired wife in the receiving line.

Polly took his arm. "I told the de Gradoffs you were com-ing as my guest."

"Nikki?"

"No. The ladies—Emlyn, Dodo and Jenny. Uncle, dear, this is Mr. Finlay, Caxson Reeves wrote—"

"Of course . . . how do you do? You're at Enniskerry. Charming fellow, de Gradoff." He turned to his purple-haired lady. "My dear, Mr. Finlay, a friend of Nikki's."

"So good of you to come, Mr. Lindley. Nikki's a delight. Dodo's very fortunate. Darling. . . ." She turned to Polly's cousin next to her. "Mr. Lindley. An old friend of Nikki's."

"Oh, really. Why did you ever let him marry that absolute moron? Oh, darling. . . ."

Polly drew Fish out of the way. "You see." she said dryly. "The majority opinion. Don't worry about Dodo's I.Q. Dodo's second husband belonged to my cousin, and now she's bright bitter green on account of Dodo's new red necklace. She's got a perfectly good replacement around somewhere. There he is, over by the bar. The lady holding him up, or vice versa, was the D.P. in that shuffle. It's all to the good, though. It's making nonalcoholic monogamists out of all their kids."

They went out onto a broad terrace. Across it, between graceful nymphs on a marble balustrade surrounding it, was a sunken garden floored over for dancing, the filmy dresses of the girls bright as butterflies under weaving rainbows of light playing softly over them.

"Shall we get a table near or far? Joe Henry told me you'd tossed your dancing pumps into a rice paddy in Korea, but you might have a proprietary interest in watching the show. There's no doubt who's the belle of the Randolphs' ball." As the music stopped she said, "See the clutch of white coats? Or is it a pride . . . or merely a pack?" She laughed, nodding at the crowd of men of all ages converging on the marble steps nearest them across the terrace. "The Stag Committee doesn't have to worry about Jenny. Do you see her?"

Fish Finlay saw her. He'd seen her before the music stopped, her dark head radiant about her slim bare brown shoulders, swirling in a misty cloud of scarlet, as lovely as the spray of white butterfly orchids in her hair. Courtesy of Mr. Peter? He looked around for him. He was at a table at the corner of the balustrade. The lovely little golden-haired girl was with him, her eyes darting about among the older people . . . . hunting her mother, no doubt. Peter was ignoring her, watching Jennifer and the pack. Proprietary, Fish thought. Polly had put the right word to the wrong man.

"Do you know Peter de Gradoff?" he asked her.

"I do," she said curtly. "And I don't know what in heaven's name Dodo's thinking about. But let's get out of everybody's way."

She'd been keeping him there so Jennifer could see he'd come. And she hadn't even turned around. "Let's go through here." She maneuvered him forward toward the other side of the garden. Miss Linton couldn't help see him there.

"Hi there, Polly! Oh, hello, Mr. Finlay!"

The music started, she was off in a swirl of stardust, with Polly Randolph looking after her a little blankly. *Well, I'll be damned. The little rat. Her first Newport party and she's just making sure she had a man on tap if Peter ditched her. And I fell for it. Me . . . promoting romance.* She glanced at Fish. *No wonder the poor guy looks bewildered. He must think I'm bats.*

58

She laughed and took him by the arm, steering him toward a table at the edge of the Japanese lantern pavilion. "Mr. Finlay," she said, "you deserve a drink. Champagne, or Scotch?"

A small nervous waiter with a tray of highballs balanced on his hand, his eyes darting expectantly around, saw them and rushed forward.

"Scotch," Polly said.

"This side, madame." He whirled the tray around with a flourish. "And for M'sieu' Finlay? Good evening, M'sieu' Finlay." He bowed with another flourish, his Gallic mustaches bristling with satisfaction.

"Good evening." Fish took a glass.

"A friend?"

"Not that I know of." He looked around at the waiter and shook his head. "I don't recognize—"

"Oh, *quick!*" Polly exclaimed. She tried to edge past him, but it was too late. A woman in a splotched print dress, with hennaed hair and a thin ravaged face with startling patches of rouge on it, rather more than three sheets to the wind, swayed forward and caught her by the arm.

"Polly, darling!"

As she backed Polly Randolph into a table, knocking the glass out of her hand, Fish moved on a little, looking out at the lights of the fishing boats, lonely on the dark horizon of the ocean.

"Such a shame the poor child has the Linton mouth." A woman's voice off to his side was gently sympathetic.

"She could be cross-eyed with all that beautiful Maloney money, dear."

"Her mother looks simply awful. Such a pity. Just look at her over there. And she's as high as a kite. That's Nikki with her."

Fish glanced around. Polly Randolph had heard it. She was suddenly paler as she tried to free herself from the woman in the splotched print, now in the weepily earnest stage.

"Yes, I know, darling," Polly was saying desperately. "I know you'd be wonderful, writing my stuff. You'd be ever so much better than I am. But I don't *have* an assistant, darling. Please go back to your table, dear."

The antiphonal voices kept coming brightly in. "That's his cousin Mrs. Emlyn. My dear, he's coming over . . . I knew he saw us."

Polly's free hand flew out and gripped Fish's arm. "Look, darling!" Her taut voice had risen. "You can have *my* job. Just the minute I'm through with it, it's all yours. I *promise* you. Now *please*, dear . . . I'll be more than—"

"Oh, Mother dear!" The lovely little blond child was there

59

at the woman's side. "I've been looking for you, Mums. Let's go sit down, shall we? I'm sorry, Miss Randolph."

"It's all right, darling."

"Polly's promised me her job on the paper. . . ."

It's like being a dress extra in a movie extravaganza, Fish Finlay was thinking . . . nobody tells you who the stars are, you haven't read the script, you've no idea what's going to happen. He shook off an uneasy sense of catastrophe that seemed to be building up inside him.

The woman wove gently away with the little blond girl, nobody else paying any attention to her. Polly's fingers bit into his arm. He looked around. De Gradoff was a good distance from them.

"Take it easy," he said. "You don't have to be afraid of the fellow here." He pulled out a chair for her at the nearest table and sat down facing the garden scene. "He's coming, all right. Alla's dropped out."

"They were all on the other side of the house. I've been trying to avoid him."

Polly shifted her chair to watch de Gradoff's casual progress, and leaned toward Fish. "Joe Henry and I've been doing some research for you. Item One: the Western Union boy mailed the photostats of the Maloney file to Mrs. Arthur Emlyn, Enniskerry, Newport, R. I."

Fish nodded. "Do you know her?"

"Somewhat. Item Two is: she was the lady at the hotel near Dijon the night Nikki's first wife—"

Fish put his glass down. "You said it was an affair of gallantry?"

"I said the French police said it was. My guess is a good clean alibi, only."

Her green eyes moved past de Gradoff to the big crowded table, all very gay and noisy, where Dodo de Gradoff, in the center of the crowd, was gayer and noisier than any of them.

"Dodo's certainly tied one on tonight. She doesn't usually drink too much. And do you see at the table with Mrs. Emlyn, behind Dodo? That's the man from Mars I told you is staying in my uncle's guesthouse."

The man was a hunchback, with a grotesquely enormous head.

"My cousin's guest—which means my cousin owes him money. A lot of people do."

"Does Mrs. Emlyn?"

Polly shrugged. "She's being terribly nice to him, isn't she? He's a fairy godfather to the improvident rich, tides them over when they're strapped. Strictly on the up and up, incidentally. It's just the way he buys his way in. He's horrible to look at but very kind, I'm told. I don't know him. Alla called him three times today before he got here. I thought you might be interested."

She glanced casually back to where Nikki was being detained by another group. "He's watching us. You wait . . . I'm going to fix him," she said coolly. "And where's your friend the waiter? That wretched woman knocked my drink sky-winding."

Fish looked around. "Here he is."

The little man put fresh glasses in front of them, each time with a flourish. With which flourish he put the note down, Fish could not have told. It was there beside his glass on the table as the little man moved off.

"Peculiar," Polly remarked.

"Very."

"It's a piece of an order blank from my aunt's kitchen."

Fish unfolded the torn slip and read the hastily scrawled message.

"All is prepared. I will attend Monsieur at his quarters after the ball. Be silent. It is necessary to be of the discretion of the most great."

There was no signature.

"Public or private?" Polly asked. "Nikki's watching you, by the way."

Fish looked up, uneasiness stirring again in the back of his mind. De Gradoff was looking the other way.

"Private, I guess. I'll let you know." He put the note in his pocket, glancing around for the little man. "Who are these people . . . the waiters?"

"The caterer brings them. He seemed familiar. But most waiters do. You run into the same ones everywhere, now that nobody can afford a real staff. I go to so many of these routs that I recognize them quicker than I do the guests." She shook her head. "He escapes me, though."

"Nobody and nothing escapes the charming Miss Randolph. It's absolutely impossible. Our delightful friend is deceiving you, Finlay."

Nikki de Gradoff was at the table, urbane, handsome, more than at ease, smiling at Polly, his blue eyes lighted with amusement. "May I sit down?"

CHAPTER : 8

He drew a chair over from the next table.

"If this is an interview, Finlay, I advise you to watch it." He looked at Polly, one brow quizzically lifted. "Have you told him about our famous tête-à-tête, Miss Randolph? But

61

it's been a long time, hasn't it? Are you still convinced I'm . . . what were all the things you called me?"

He put his head back and laughed heartily. "I'd never been so flattered, Finlay. Here was a young lady of the press come to interview me. The servants were out, which I concealed from her. It's so boorish, to have to repulse eager young women. And, bless me, I discovered Miss Randolph thought she was going to have to repulse me."

Polly Randolph's cheeks were hot. Fish brought his knee sharply against hers and saw her relax a little.

"I shouldn't imagine Miss Randolph had any personal concern, de Gradoff," he said coolly.

"My dear Finlay, when a lady invites herself to my house on the pretense of an interview and attacks me, verbally of course, and then turns tail and runs as if the devil were after her, what am I to think? She'd come there prepared to be either a friend or . . . a foe. I was deficient in effort, no doubt." He smiled at her. "I had no idea what an imaginative young lady she was. Her uncle tells me I'm not the only victim of her extraordinary gift for what he calls making things up out of whole cloth. But I do hope by now you've absolved me of serious . . . misdeeds, shall we say?"

He made a gesture of dryly amused deprecation.

When Fish looked at Polly Randolph he was startled by the guileless wide-eyed wonder in her face.

"Misdeeds? I haven't an idea what you're talking about. Did I accuse you of misdeeds, for heaven's sake? I don't recall it if I did." She smiled at him. "It couldn't be that the guilty flee when no man pursueth, could it, Count de Gradoff?"

De Gradoff moved to settle himself in the spindly gilt chair, smiling at her, amused again.

"You seem to have forgotten that day at my house, Miss Randolph."

"Not at all. We just don't seem to remember it the same way."

A cautious light flicked on in his suddenly watchful blue eyes. She picked up her glass as if dismissing the whole thing, and put it down abruptly.

"All right," she said. "I *was* frightened. I might just as well admit it. But it wasn't you. It was your friend who frightened me."

"My friend?" de Gradoff was puzzled. Fish felt the warning nudge of her knee against his. "What friend?"

"The woman who was there."

"My dear Miss Randolph." He laughed again. "There was no woman there. Except yourself, of course."

"Look, darling." Her brows were arched. "It doesn't make the least difference to me. I've never mentioned it to anyone.

62

I never gossip . . . not for free. I'm saving up till I get a column of my own. So you don't have to be cagey with me. I shan't tell Dodo."

He was not frowning at her so much as making a serious effort tinged with caution to try to understand her.

"I'll admit you *acted* as if she wasn't there." She laughed. "That's what confused me so. I couldn't figure out what the hell was going on. You didn't even look at her when she came in from the garden with the basket of carnations."

"Carnations?" de Gradoff asked slowly.

"Carnations, darling. You know. Flowers. Very fragrant. I waited for you to introduce me, because she obviously wasn't any servant. She put the basket on the table and started looking for something. A letter . . . because you must remember when she looked at the ones you had on the coffee table, before she went over to the desk and started writing one."

It seemed to Fish Finlay that something was changing behind the smiling mask of de Gradoff's face.

"She seemed so unhappy about the dust all over everything. I hadn't noticed it until she kept looking at it. That's when I realized you didn't have any servants in the house. It all seemed so odd. Especially when she started talking to herself . . . silently, she didn't say anything aloud. That's when I got really scared. I thought you'd both lost your minds, and it scared the living daylights out of me. I just wanted out. I was almost fainting. It was so hot, with the room all closed up and the fire burning. And the smell of carnations always makes me a little sick."

She sniffed lightly. "I can almost smell them now. I really can, as a matter of fact. Somebody's perfume, I guess."

De Gradoff leaned forward. "This woman, Miss Randolph . . . what did she . . . look like?"

Polly laughed a little. "She hasn't changed too much, has she? Except for the way she's got her hair done. I didn't have any trouble recognizing her when she came in with you and Dodo this evening."

"Oh!" de Gradoff sat back a little. He was still puzzled. "My cousin Alla . . . ?"

"Oh, no. I know Mrs. Emlyn when I see her. She wasn't with you tonight when you came in, she was back with the Davises. I mean the woman. . . . Look, you know who came in with you, for heaven's sake. The woman with the red-gold hair, sort of sherry-colored eyes, quite a long neck, lovely looking. . . ."

She raised up a little in her chair. "I don't see her now, but I saw her a little while ago with some other people, looking at Dodo's rubies. But that's what alarmed me at your house that day. It was silly, I know."

63

De Gradoff's face was the curious color of coffee with skimmed milk in it. She smiled at him.

"I don't know what misdeeds you thought I was accusing you of. But I'm glad you told me, because Dodo's an old friend of mine. I'd be awfully uncomfortable if you thought I was carrying a judgment seat around with me. Good Lord!"

She laughed and pushed her chair back. "I know you'll excuse us now, I want Mr. Finlay to meet—"

De Gradoff did not seem to be hearing her. He had got up and bowed, and he went off holding himself stiffly erect, like a man afraid to look to either side to see who might be walking with him.

Polly Randolph moved her chair forward again, her eyes fixed on him.

"So I make things up out of whole cloth, do I? Let's see how he likes that one. But what's happened? He's different. He isn't the least worried about me any more. Or he wasn't."

"Not when he came over," Fish said. He added gravely, "I wish to God you'd left it that way. Why did you—"

"I'll tell you later. It's something—"

She broke off as some people came to the next table, and lowered her voice. "You don't have to worry about me. I'm leaving early in the morning. They're sending me abroad to cover the fashion shows. As long as I'm here, believe me, I'll—"

She stopped short and looked quickly behind her. "Oh, darling!"

Jennifer Linton was standing a yard from them, still poised in the act of taking the last step, arrested there as motionless as one of the marble nymphs on the balustrade. Her lips were parted, her eyes wide, shifting from de Gradoff going stiffly erect into the house over to her mother hysterically gay at the large table.

Polly reached out her hand. "Come and sit down, Jenny."

Fish Finlay jerked himself out of a slow-motion universe, his awareness of her so vividly intense for an instant that it blocked out everything else around him. He moved over abruptly to de Gradoff's chair, holding his own for her.

He looks as if he'd like to cut her throat, Polly thought, a small new light dawning.

"I . . . don't know what to do," Jennifer said soberly. "I asked Peter to get Nikki to take my mother home. She never used to get drunk like this."

"Don't be brutal, darling. She's not drunk, she's just high. And she's probably declined to be taken home."

"Somebody ought to make her go," Jennifer said quietly. "I don't dare ask her. There'd be a scene with me. She looks awful."

She turned to Fish, the color seeping into her cheeks. "Could you—"

"Let me." Polly got up quickly. "You two stay here and keep my place. I can get her upstairs at least. Don't get up, Fish."

She slipped lightly away. He's mad about her too, only she doesn't know it, the little dope, she thought, enormously pleased. The abominable Peter was nobody for Jenny to know.

The silence at the table hung in a breathless balance. For Fish Finlay it was almost unbearably lovely. For Jennifer Linton . . .

"You like her, don't you?"

"Very much." His voice sounded far away and not his own.

I don't know why I thought he could ever be in love with anybody like me. She managed a crippled smile as Polly Randolph looked back at her across the garden.

"Oh, the little idiot," Polly thought. As she laughed and shook her head at Jennifer, she caught sight of Fish's little friend the Gallic waiter tray balanced, poised alertly, eyes darting around to spot an empty glass. He was about two feet from Alla Emlyn. Polly Randolph stopped short, her green eyes saffron with excitement, and flashed back towards Fish. But he was entranced with the girl beside him. What she'd remembered would have to wait.

I can't ever tell him now, Jennifer was thinking wretchedly. I'll just have to go on pretending I don't remember him. The rainbow castle she'd built in the springtime was a miserable heap of rubble that left her heart numb, buried beneath it. She could see in his face the light for Polly still kindled. It lingered there even when he leaned forward a little to speak to her. Her eyes were dark pools of misery she was too young to conceal, vivid in her pale otherwise expressionless face.

"Don't take it too hard, Jenny," he said. "Your mother's no higher than lots of others."

Her eyes widened, her lips parted for an instant. She'd forgotten her mother. Then she swallowed quickly, as the other thing came back to her. "It's not that," she said. It was what she'd heard standing there behind him and Polly before the springtime castle began to dissolve. "It's something else. Polly shouldn't have said all that to Nikki."

She turned and looked over her shoulder, the way Polly Randolph had looked that night in Tony's back room.

"I know where she got all that stuff," she said, very quietly. "It was a portrait at a one-man show at the Berdan Galleries in Washington, last week. The carnations . . . everything. Some friends of mine from Argentine—"

Fish looked up as she broke off suddenly. A waiter was coming to the table with a small silver salver in his hand.

"Miss Randolph?" He bowed and held it down for Jennifer to take the blue envelope on it.

"Miss Randolph's over there," Fish said. "In the green dress, by the yellow rose trellis on the porch."

He'd had to look to find her. She'd bypassed her mission to Dodo apparently, or decided it was no go. Then something, a sort of alert excitement, in the way she was looking over at Mrs. Emlyn and the hunchback still at her table, sharpened his glance. Unless it was the little waiter, hovering behind them, that she was looking at. He glanced back at Dodo, still high in the treetops of cloud-cuckoo-land.

"It's all right, Mr. Finlay," Jenny said unhappily. "I don't see Nikki anywhere now, but maybe he'll come get her." She moved her chair. "I just can't sit and look at her, that's all. I'd go home but I have to wait for Peter. Could we go somewhere else? Maybe we could get us something to eat. I'm hungry."

"That's a good idea," Fish said. "I'd be glad to stretch my leg." It was the first time he'd ever said it without thinking.

"It doesn't bother you to walk, does it?" she asked, just as naturally.

"Not at all."

They moved back across the terrace.

"There are lots of nice people around," she said, as if he might not have noticed it. "You don't hear them. Food's on the other side. We could take our plates down to the fishing platform. There's just surf and rocks down there. I'm just not used to so much racket yet, I guess."

"That's a good idea, too."

It seemed wonderful, in fact, to Fish, caught in the delusive enchantment of having her alone with him just a little longer before the pride of white-coated, nimble-footed young lions surrounded her again.

If only they hadn't taken so long to get their food at the handsomely laden buffet. Or if halfway there the boy he'd seen with the lovely little golden-haired girl hadn't stopped them.

"Jenny, have you seen Skunky's mother any place?"

"She was around looking for Polly Randolph a minute ago, son," a man passing them with two plates said over his shoulder.

"We'll see if we can find her," Jenny said. The boy went on.

"Why not leave her be?" Fish asked.

"Because Skunky's worried. Sometimes her mother does awful things."

How long was it? Fish could never remember. He seemed

66

to be moving in a golden haze in which time no longer existed, looking with Jennifer, with an elaborate pretense of being casual, for the blond child Skunky's mother. Until they found her, and the horror wiped out all the loveliness.

They'd quit looking and got themselves each a plate of food and a cup of coffee. The stairs to the fishing platform were cut in the solid rock, winding down between masses of rugosa roses naturalized in the stony soil, softly lighted on each side with double rows of Japanese lanterns dancing in the breeze from the ocean; the stars, golden bees on the velvet of the night, emerged as he and Jennifer left the garden, talking, so they wouldn't surprise anyone else taking refuge on the steps. It was where the steps curved for the second time among the roses that Fish, taller, saw—before Jennifer could see it— the concrete platform built out over among the jutting rocks like the base of an unfinished watchtower, a single iron-pipe waist high around it for a guardrail.

He saw that, but saw it only in the instant flash of the horror that made him stand, shocked motionless, for a split second, and then shout, and shout again, as he dropped his plate and coffee cup and ran, sprang forward down the winding steps, shouting to stop the woman there at the rail . . . knowing, before he shouted the first time, that it was already too late. The moving arms and, for an instant, the billowing green skirt caught in the offshore wind, before the monstrous white maw of hungry surf closed over her, swallowing her, dragging her out of sight . . . and then, before Fish could reach the bottom and dash across the flattened rock to the platform itself, tearing off his coat, the surf rising again, hurling her back in its terrible white arms, dashing her with mighty force against the black jagged rocks.

"Oh, don't, Fish! No! You'll kill yourself!"

Jennifer was behind him at the iron rail, clinging desperately to him.

"You can't! It's solid rock down there!"

He dropped his hands onto the rail as the long grating roar dragged, withdrawing, over the black barnacled rocks protruding savagely through the surf, swirling the frail limp figure in and out of the pitch-black crevices between them.

"Oh, God, I've got to get her . . . it's Polly!"

He gripped the rail in the maddening frustration of utter helplessness as he saw the great wave came back empty-handed, and break. From under its white crest a single feather of spray lifted a golden sandal and tossed it up onto a cluster of black mussels clinging to the rocks where it caught and held and stayed.

"The Coast Guard!"

He heard the shout from behind him and feet were racing back up the carved stairs.

67

He turned then, slowly, white-faced, to the woman in the splotched print dress holding on to the iron pipe, her body swaying gently back and forth against it.

"She's gone now, isn't she?" she asked in a childlike voice. "I pushed her. She said I could have her job when she was through with it. She thought it was going to be a long time. But it wasn't."

She moved her head, looking vaguely back at the roses densely clothing the rock. "Voice?" she called. "Where are you, Voice? I did it. You said it wouldn't hurt her."

She weaved back around, looking down into the boiling sea.

"Polly's gone away, now. Maybe the little black man caught her. He was waiting for her. He's gone away, too. But there won't be any trouble about the job. Everybody heard her say I could have it." She held the rail, her head drooping. "Poor Polly. She looked so surprised."

She's mad. The woman's mad.

Her knees bent slowly, her hand loosening on the rail. "I'm dreadfully tired. Polly shouldn't have been so . . . so. . . ."

She sank gently down on the platform.

Something soft, tenaciously binding, clinging to Fish's legs, seemed to take away any power to move or think as he stood there. He looked stupidly down. His legs were wrapped in a scarlet pall. It took him a long moment to draw himself back into awareness. It was the folds of Jennifer's scarlet skirt, whipped around him by the wind. He brought his eyes slowly up to her, standing there motionless, his white coat clutched in one hand, her face as white as it but alive as her eyes were alive. They were pitchy luminous black as she turned to him, her lips moving silently before she could make a sound.

"No!" she said. "She didn't do it, Fish!" She gripped his arm. "Oh, I knew Polly shouldn't have told him . . . she should never have told Nikki what she did!"

CHAPTER : 9

"She didn't do it, Fish!"

"I *saw* her, Jenny."

It was all he had time to say before the rock steps were filled with rushing feet. What followed was a nightmare he still hadn't waked from, how much later he had no idea when he opened the clock tower door and went slowly up-

68

stairs to the living-room in the loft. It had been pitch dark, down on the platform. Now the frail dawn was breaking, only the planets still lanterns hung to light the new day's way into a stinking world. Or was it? For the poor liquor-sodden woman who'd done it, maybe the world was greatly kind where it could have been greatly cruel.

He'd seen them take her out of there. Was it the speed with which they'd got her neatly past the two unsuspecting cops directing traffic outside the gates? Or was it the instant silent recognition of what had to be done and the well-bred ease with which they did it? All of it had staggered him, still taking the count for the thing itself, stunned still more by Jenny's flat insistence that what he'd seen happen had not happened at all.

The woman hadn't stirred as the two men lifted her, out cold. She'd wake up this morning in a shaded room, doctors and nurses around her, a brace of high-priced legal talent guarding the door . . . wake up with what, if any, memory of it only they and God would ever know.

He stopped halfway up the stairs, tired, bone-tired, his leg nagging. He couldn't see Polly Randolph any more or the hell of white surf and black rock . . . just the golden sandal lodged in the black mussels, and the woman in the splotched print peacefully unconscious on the concrete floor. But he could see himself as Polly's uncle and the three other men in white coats got to the platform . . . taking his white coat out of Jenny's hand, putting it on, reaching down for his bill-fold that had dropped out, putting it in his pocket, telling them quietly what he'd seen and what the woman had said.

They lifted her then and Fish saw a gleam of emerald and ruby. Her long full skirts had covered it before. It was an elongated leather-covered flask set with jewels, a braided green and red thong around the neck. Colonel Randolph bent down and picked it up without a word. And all the while the gold slipper was lying there in the mussels on the black rock.

"Mr. Finlay wanted to go over after her." It was the only thing Jenny said.

"Sheer suicide," Colonel Randolph said curtly. "No swimmer could live down there."

The lights of the Coast Guard cutter raked the platform minutes later, but no one was left there but the gray-faced old man, Jenny and himself. The others had gone, discreetly silent, up the steps through the roses, never a word spoken, only a glance and heads nodded in exchange.

The music was still playing under the weaving rainbow of light, the floor over the sunken garden still filled with dancing forms. The tables under the flower-colored lanterns were full of laughing people, the waiters still passing by with their silver trays still laden. It struck Fish with traumatic impact as he came back into it from the lonely surf-beaten hell on the fishing platform . . . nothing changed, he thought, until he looked at Polly's uncle, shoulders rigidly erect, his head up, only his face gray as old death, and recognized the Spartan remnant of what Newport had once stood for . . . and still did, he thought then, remembering the girl they called Skunky.

"I'll ask the police to go around to the guesthouse, Finlay. Will you please meet them there." Colonel Randolph nodded his white head toward the rose arbor behind them and turned to Jenny. "If you'll kindly go and find Skunky, Jennifer, and take her to the old nursery. Stay with her till I find her father. I needn't ask—"

"Don't, please, sir." Jenny touched his arm quickly, the tears springing to her eyes. "I'll find Skunky." Her head was up too as she went off across the garden full of people. Fish stood a moment, bracing himself. *I guess I'm not a thoroughbred.* He looked around for an instant. Dodo's place at the table was empty. Alla Emlyn's hunchbacked companion, the fairy godfather of the improvident rich, was still at the smaller table, sipping a glass of champagne with Polly's cousin from the receiving line. Fish saw Peter de Gradoff, dark and handsome, and saw Jennifer's head with its coronet of butterfly orchids and her scarlet dress moving toward the little golden-haired girl who was with him. He turned away, sick for an instant, and went through the rose arbor to find the guesthouse.

The two policemen they'd brought in from the gate were already there.

"The dame's wacky. She's been wacky for years. But she's never done anybody any harm before."

"Except the time down on Mill Street."

"Well, she was in bad shape, that night."

They nodded to Fish as he came in, and the younger of the two got up and shut the door hard after him. "You'd think they'd have the decency to stop all that racket and get the hell out," he said.

"Well, they don't want to start a riot," the older man replied. "That's not the way they do things."

He looked at Fish. "You're Mr. Finlay, the eyewitness? I called the lieutenant. I hear you were on the top of the steps. They tell me you *saw* her shove Miss Polly over the rail, like she said she did before she passed out. They say you and Miss Linton both saw her."

"Miss Linton didn't see it. She isn't tall enough to see over the bushes on the rocks. It was all over by the time we got to the bottom."

"They oughtn't to let a screwy dame roam around loose

70

when she's drunk," the younger one said. He looked tough, but he was the one who was upset.

The older policeman nodded. "It's sure bad, right at the beginning of the season and all. But like you say, it's lucky we got an eyewitness that saw it. You're at the Maloneys'? The lieutenant'll want to see you, I guess."

The lieutenant saw him down at the fishing platform. There hadn't been much for Fish to add. He left when the waiters were beginning to bring around scrambled eggs and bacon. The music had gone and most of the guests . . . and Jennifer. He'd waited for her, but she hadn't come. After that he got his car and drove around to the Coast Guard Station.

"You better go home, Mac," the kid with the earphones at the radio sending set told him. "Get yourself a slug and turn in. You're dead and don't know it. We'll let you know when we find her. It's hell, but there it is, I guess."

Fish went heavily on up the clock tower stairs, along the balcony hall to his door. Inside he stopped short, abruptly alert. Someone else was in the room. The furniture, the tables and chairs loomed, magnified in the misty yellow light seeping in through the open windows. Then he saw the black huddled mass on the sofa. His hand went to his pocket as the little waiter flashed into his mind. He'd forgotten him entirely. Asleep, he thought. He put his hand in one pocket, then in the other. They were both empty. The note was gone . . . dropped out, probably, the way his billfold had done when Jennifer had his coat, and blown out into the surf. He reached for the light switch and stopped motionless as a cold finger touched his spine. He stiffened, listening intently. There was no sound except his own breathing. The mass on the sofa was as silent as it was motionless. He took a quick step forward, his throat dry. The dark mass was a quilt covering a small inert figure. His hand shot out to wrench it off, and stopped.

"Well, for the love of God and the forty-nine angels," he said.

It wasn't the little waiter, dead. It was Miss Jennifer Linton, sound asleep. But for one ghastly hairbreadth fraction of an instant, the shadowy half-moon of her face on the cushion had been so pale, so still, that fear leaped with a knife at his heart. His violence was the reaction of a relief too intense to control.

"I ought to break her blasted little neck."

He reached for the lamp on the table at the end of the sofa, to wake her without scaring the living daylights out of her, and stopped as he saw a light on in her mother's window on the upstairs porch across the courtyard. Her blinds were drawn. His own weren't, and there were other windows over there. The goldfish bowl was a two-way stretch. But it was fairly light outside now, anyway. Only the high-pitched dark-painted beams gave the loft the continual sense of darkness. The point was to get her up and out of there before everybody, not only her mother, was awake to see her.

"Jenny. Wake up." He put his hand down and touched the quilt over her shoulder. She woke, not in a series of dopey stages, but at once, her eyes wide open and clear. It took only an instant for her to adjust herself to where she was, before she brushed the quilt aside and pivoted around, reached for her slippers at the foot of the sofa, wriggled her feet into them, pulled her blue wool bathrobe around her legs, sitting up and regarding him with no self-consciousness whatever.

"I was asleep," she said.

"So I observed," said Finlay. "In the wrong place. You've been home. Why the hell didn't you stay there?"

"I would have if I'd known you were going to stay out all night," she said, promptly and with spirit. "You needn't be so cross about it. I made you some coffee, if you'd like a cup."

"And what do you suppose your family—"

"They can't see in the dark, can they? I didn't turn the light on except in your kitchen."

She stood up and tied her robe sash around her middle. She looked about ten, with her tousled curls and her shiny washed face and the lipstick gone. It made it easier for Finlay in one way, harder in another, Especially when her voice softened and she said, "I'm sorry you're angry."

"I'm not angry. Just . . . concerned."

"I know. I shouldn't have come," she said simply. "But I . . . I wanted to know, about Polly."

"They haven't found her."

"I'm so sorry," she whispered.

"All right. Just go home and go to bed, will you?"

It came out more sharply than he meant it, and she drew back, surprised.

"I'm sorry, Jenny," he said less abruptly. Then he relaxed and smiled at her.

"Look. My first duty is to protect the honor of the Trust Department of the Merchants and Mechanics Bank and Deposit Company, 25 Broadway, New York, New York, and of the personnel thereof. Now if you wish to roam around strange men's apartments in the bleak gray dawn, in a wrinkled old wrapper tied around you like a potato sack, that, Miss Linton, is your affair. But in view of my stainless past and my exalted position in the world of finance, I must beg you not to compromise me any further. Now will you get the hell out of here? I'd also like a little sleep."

72

"Well, all right." She smiled gravely at him. "If you want to go to sleep, I'll go. I just thought maybe you'd. . . ."

She hitched her bathrobe sash tighter around her and went to the door. He watched her, his whole insides melting like warm jelly. If he could only keep her there forever. . . . But if de Gradoff, or any of the others, saw her. . . . He looked over across the courtyard. The lights were still on. He turned back as he heard the click of the latch as the door closed. But she hadn't gone. She'd opened the door and closed it again.

"Mr. Finlay," she said soberly. "Could I ask you something, without . . . without. . . ."

She came to a stop and stood looking at him, hesitating. "I don't want to be unpleasant, or anything, but. . . ."

"Go on."

"Well, it's this. Had Polly had very much to drink, before. . . ."

He shook his head. "Why?"

"Because I've been wondering." Her eyes rested steadily on his. "I've been wondering how *he* got her to go down there. You don't suppose he wrote her that note the waiter—"

"Oh, Jenny." He crossed the room to her. "Look. You're dead wrong, Jenny. I *saw* what happened. You couldn't see it, because you couldn't see over the roses on the rocks. But I could. I saw it happen . . . believe me. It's horrible, but it's the truth."

She shook her head.

"You just saw her . . . going over. I know it was horrible. But you don't know Skunky's mother. I do. She . . . she wouldn't hurt anybody."

"But she did. Maybe she didn't mean to, Jenny, but she did. You didn't see her in the garden, when she had hold of Polly. That's when Polly said she could have her job . . . just to get away from her."

"But . . . that's the point," Jenny said evenly. "That's just what I mean. Everybody knew she did crazy things when she'd had too much to drink . . . and when she went around telling everybody Polly'd promised her her job, that made her just a natural to blame it on."

Fish shook his head. "I saw her, Jenny."

"All right." She took hold of the doorknob again. "Do you remember what she said? 'Poor Polly, she looked so surprised.' But Polly *knew* her. She wouldn't just stand there looking surprised and let herself be pushed over. I don't believe it, not for one minute I don't. But if something . . . if something hit her that surprised her, and she was dead before she knew it, she'd go on looking surprised, and it'd be easy to push her over then."

He shook his head again. "The way you calmly talk about

73

people murdering each other makes my blood run cold, Miss Linton."

"Well, mine ran cold when Polly was trying to scare Nikki," she said warmly. "Describing his first wife in the room with the carnations, when she was already dead. . . . That's what she got from the portrait in Washington. And Nikki was scared, all right, but it wasn't a ghost that scared him. But if you think I'm crazy. . . ."

She opened the door again. "And anyway, they can tell when they . . . find her, can't they? Whether she was drowned? If they do an autopsy. And it wouldn't be fair to Skunky's mother if they didn't. Well, I'm going now. You better get some sleep."

At the stairs she turned back. "I'd planned to sneak in the backway, Mr. Finlay. But the Maloneys defend the honor of the Maloney guests even as they defend their own . . . so I'll walk straight in the front door with no subterfuge whatever."

She took one step down and turned again. "You know, it's very stupid for us to go on pretending we don't know what I'm talking about, Mr. Finlay," she said gravely. "Even dangerous. Did you think I wouldn't notice all the locks you had put on my door and windows? So thanks, Mr. Finlay. And thanks again . . . the azaleas were the loveliest anybody's ever seen."

Her eyes were shining and her cheeks touched with color an instant as she smiled at him, before she turned and ran quickly down.

CHAPTER : 10

Fish Finlay stood in the doorway, punch drunk, trying to absorb the accumulation of shocks Jennifer Linton had produced with no intent to shock and with a simple sanity and quiet logic that was the most confounding shock of all. That she'd recognized him was the least. He'd been aware of her basic acceptance of him ever since Polly Randolph had left their table. Pretense, if any, had been a purely surface gesture, with no attempt to deny that each knew perfectly well what everything was all about.

But the locks. . . .

Did you think I wouldn't notice all the locks you had put on my door and windows?

Caxson Reeves, of course. Reeves had been six jumps ahead of him all the way, letting him maunder around the edges, picking up what he could, while he was taking positive action behind his back, acting with one hand, protecting the bank with the other. And abruptly the light that had flickered once and vanished, hidden under the basket of his own stupidity, gleamed bright and clear. The little waiter with the waxed mustaches, who knew him by name and whom Polly Randolph had vaguely recognized, standing over there, when he last saw him, by Alla Emlyn's table. . . . A whole series of unrelated incidents he hadn't even been conscious of observing until then fell into place in his mind, and Caxson Reeves's French detective emerged as bodily intact as if he were there in the room, as he'd said he'd be as soon as the ball was over.

He put his hand in his pocket, forgetting that the little man's note had gone with the offshore wind.

So where is he? He looked around the room as if he expected him to pop out with a flourish. He'd probably been here. And Fish hadn't come directly home himself and young Miss Linton had arrived in her pajamas and bathrobe. Fish grinned and looked at his watch. The little man, no doubt, had assumed another affair of gallantry, and with Gallic delicacy and a discretion of the most great had withdrawn, for the time being. Which by now was a quarter to six. Even discretion needed sleep occasionally. Even Finlay needed it, aware of it again as he was aware that now he had a glimmering of Caxson Reeves's arid New England hand in there helping him he felt suddenly better about the whole thing. Or he did until he moved abruptly back onto the momentarily forgotten ground that Jenny Linton had dug up and seeded with the small teeth of the twin dragons, suspicion and grave doubt.

He scowled as he took off his coat and went through the kitchen to the bedroom, pulling at his tie. Granted her original assumption about de Gradoff, what she'd said about Skunky's mother had an appalling logic.

That made her just a natural to blame it on.

Except that Finlay had seen the whole thing. Or had he? What would he say on the witness stand?

Can you swear of your own knowledge that Miss Randolph was alive when you saw her pushed over the iron-pipe rail?

I saw her arms moving and her golden sandals under her green skirt blowing in the wind.

He ripped his shirt open and pulled it off. He was bone-tired. His head wasn't working. I saw her, didn't I? He put it forcibly out of his mind. The autopsy would tell—if they had an autopsy.

He set the alarm clock he'd brought with him for half-past eight, got into his pajamas and lay down, pulling a quilt over him. A couple of hours' sleep would clear the miasma. But

75

somehow, on the hypnagogic beachhead between waking and sleeping, he knew the thing he'd been unconsciously rejecting. He must have spoken it aloud, he heard it so clearly spoken.

Jenny knows what Polly knew . . . or what Polly said without knowing what it meant. If that's why Polly died. . . .

He passed then into a disordered dream filled with a dream's intangible sweating horror, a cresting sea tossing what he knew was a framed portrait of a woman but that, every time he struggled through the pitchy night to seize and look at, was nothing but a black mass of barnacle-encrusted mussels, their shells open to hold a small sodden slipper that he knew was dead because once he'd seen it alive and shining. Off somewhere, a bell was tolling, calling him out to sea, beyond the jagged rocks. Bees were buzzing among the carnations strewn on the waves. He struggled up through them, aware at last that the tolling bell was the clock in the tower. The buzzing of the bees was the telephone in the living-room. He barged blindly up and across the room, shaking himself loose from the clammy hold of the dream, through the kitchen, still only half awake, until he picked up the phone and Joe Henry's voice hit with the impact of an ice-cold shower.

"For God's sake, what happened?"

Fish told him. "The woman was drunk, probably crazy. I don't know her name . . . but I saw her do it."

"Her name's Winton." Joe Henry added evenly, "It's her family's name that counts here."

When he spoke it then Fish caught his breath. It was a name fabulous in the economic conquest of the frontiers of America. All he'd heard her called was "Skunky's mother."

"That's why everybody clammed up. Randolph was on the phone for half an hour. 'Tragic and all that, but no help for it.' They still haven't found her. Look, Fish . . . you're sure? You're dead sure?"

Was he?

"They ought to do an autopsy," he said.

"By God they will, Randolph or no Randolph, and to hell with the family name," Joe said. "I just can't get it, Fish. I loved that gal. I can't believe that's the way it happened. Listen. I'm sending a man up. He'll bring you a letter she wrote me from D.C. last week. About a portrait. I sent a guy to the gallery to get a shot of it. He found a bowl of fruit and some dead seafood in its place. The portrait's gone and nobody'll say what happened to it. You stick at it, Fish. If the so-and-so killed her, we'll draw and quarter the bloody bastard."

Fish Finlay put the phone down and stood with his hand on it for an instant, picked up the phone book then and turned to the yellow pages. The third caterer he called was the one who had served the Randolphs' party. It was the caterer's daughter answering.

"I think I know who you want," she said at last. "If there's anything wrong you'd better speak to my father." She was obviously disturbed.

"Not a thing," Fish said. "It's entirely personal. I just want his name and address."

She hesitated. "His name's François Beyle," she said. "He lives at a rooming house on Thames Street . . . the Azores. We don't have a phone for him."

"Thanks."

He warmed up the coffee Jenny had made for him and cooked some bacon and eggs. He was putting his dishes in the sink when the phone rang again.

"This is long-distance," the operator said. "Do you want me to try Hubbard 2-6200 for you again?"

"Try what?" Fish asked blindly.

"Is this 6229?"

"Right."

"Well, somebody there called that number last night."

Fish sharpened to attention.

"Whose number is it?"

"We're not allowed to give that information."

"Look." He spoke as amiably as he could manage. "I was on a big party last night. Would you mind telling me who I called this time?"

The operator laughed. "You called the United States Government Collector of Customs, Port of Boston, Mass. *Brother*, you *musta* been blind!" She laughed again. "I'll just cancel it, okay?"

"Thanks," Fish said. There was obviously some mistake, but it was too late to tell her so. He glanced ironically at himself in the mirror as he put the phone down. Detective Finlay. He grinned, went out into the kitchen for another cup of coffee and came back into the living-room with it. The tumbled quilt was still where Jenny had pushed it, the imprint of her dark head still on the cushion, the shadowy sense of her presence there weaving a soft web of enchantment around him, until, as he put his cup on the table and reached down to touch the cushion, the alarm clock rang stridently from the table by his bed. He straightened up.

"Okay. You don't have to remind me. I haven't forgotten. I'm still the Maloneys' hired hand."

He picked up the quilt, took it into the bedroom, shut off the alarm and put the quilt on the other bed. He turned on the radio to see if he could get the local news, but a gust of wind slammed the bathroom door so that he didn't hear the bulletin that was released while he was under the shower.

CHAPTER : 11

A shaft of sunlight shooting amethyst and gold across the dark wall of the purple beeches caught Jenny's new car in a dazzle of chromium and shining blue. She stopped outside the porte-cochere an instant, pride and pleasure chasing away the shadows she'd brought with her from the stable across the courtyard.

"Isn't it beautiful?"

She took a step to see the gleaming side of it, and stopped short, the shine in her eyes fading. The white-walled tire of the right front wheel had bitten a hole in the perfect turf that edged the scallop-shell drive. She caught her breath sharply.

A childhood fear from her mother's long-standing quarrel with Mr. Vranek flashed vividly back to her. The chewed-up turf was one of the things they'd battled most bitterly about. She went over and looked at it. It was an accident, but after the spray of butterfly orchids. . . .

"I should have put it in the stable," she thought unhappily. But Peter had already been hard to manage and she didn't want to be alone there in the dark with him then, any more than she wanted now to be responsible for setting off another incident in the long-drawn battle between her mother and the greenhouse. So far her mother hadn't even mentioned the gardeners.

"I'd better go explain to him right after breakfast."

She picked up the skirt of her robe and wiped off the condensed salty moisture on the door frame, leaning over then to look at the speedometer. It was her first car and last night the figures had a special charm in the special excitement of waiting for the first thousand miles. They read "999.9," and they wouldn't be all nines again for nine thousand miles, she'd thought, with Peter turned moody and unattractive, hardly waiting for her to switch off the engine before he was out. She looked at her nines again and her face fell abruptly. The speedometer read "1034.7."

She straightened up, flashing her head around to the rut her wheel had chewed in the edge of the turf. "Somebody took my car." They'd taken it 34.8 miles and cut the turf besides. She slipped across the leather seat and tried the brake. It was jammed on, so tight she could hardly release it. She sat there soberly a moment. "That's very funny," she thought.

"I bet it was that Peter." She was angry then. "He has no right to take my car."

She glanced up at her mother's windows, flaming red-gold in the rising sun. In the windows between the bulging turrets where the sun hadn't struck there were lines of pale cold yellow through the closed slats of the venetian blinds. Her anger changed to sudden sharp anxiety. She slipped out across the sea-moist leather seat, closing the door softly, and hurried back under the porte-cochere to the porch. Halfway there she remembered that the front door of Enniskerry was locked and chain-bolted, and hurried around the verandah up the back stairs the way she'd come down. She put her hand out to open the iron grille at her windows and stopped. Her mother's lights were false cold yellow at the front end of the porch, more apparent in the pearly softness of the young day still clinging under the broad overhang of the roof where the searching sun hadn't yet found it. The windows between, the empty guest room, Nikki's bedroom, were quiet the way windows of empty rooms and rooms where people are asleep are quiet.

And her mother hated bright light. Unless. . . . It seemed a long time ago that Polly Randolph had left the table to go persuade Dodo to go upstairs, but it hadn't been, actually, and maybe her mother wasn't . . . in any shape to turn the lights off.

She let the grille go and tiptoed softly along the heavy woven-hemp carpet on the verandah floor. Part of the light came through the windows of Nikki's dressing-room, through the door there open into her mother's bedroom. She got to it and stopped short. Her mother was crying. She caught her breath. She'd never heard her mother cry before, and never heard anybody cry that way, the edges flaring up torn off in a sudden frenzy that was almost like the howl of some creature beyond the pitch of nervous endurance. She took a swift step forward and froze stiffly where she was.

Nikki's voice came through the window. He was with her, trying tenderly to comfort her. His voice was raised only for her to hear it above the storm of her own.

". . . Won't let them take you, dearest. There's nothing wrong with your mind. I don't know why the doctor thinks you need observation."

Jenny had started to slip back, her cheeks hot at seeming to spy. She stopped again.

Observation?

"He just spoke to me a moment, but I saw him in Randolph's library talking to Reeves."

Mr. Reeves? Jenny hadn't known he was at the Randolphs'.

"Can they all be trying to use Jennifer against you some

79

way, dearest? Is that why this fellow Finlay's up here? He's had her over there all night with him in the stable. He can't be making love to the child. . . . Not unless he's an unmitigated swine, my darling."

Jenny moved quietly away from the window, her jaw tight, her eyes ominous pitch-black.

And I thought for a minute he was being so sweet to her.

The tender flypaper poison of his voice seeping through her mother's nerve-wracked sobbing infuriated her. She slipped back and yanked open her iron grille, pushed the screen in and closed them both, and stood there trembling in her own protected room. What good were locks and bars, she thought passionately. That's not the way he does it. He hasn't the guts. He gets crazy women to take the blame. Snaky-sweet, driving her mother crazy, too. . . .

It was a jumble of incoherence, but she knew exactly what she meant. She flashed over to her dressing table, drew her lipstick across her mouth and ran her comb through her hair, and went quickly to the door, pausing to take a deep breath and relax so he wouldn't see she was angry. She slipped out into the hall, where the sun was sending thick shafts of jeweled light through the Tiffany window around the flattened central turrets, and stopped, her heart in her mouth, as she heard a stealthy whisper of feet in the narrow backstairs passage beyond the door next to her own, standing a little ajar. She turned and pulled it open, startled, but in a different way, at the equally startled and startling figure of Elsa, the maid, her big bony frame wrapped in an old padded-silk dressing gown, her hair tied in a blue net.

"Oh, I'm sorry, miss. I was going down. . . ." She turned to creep back up again.

Jenny stepped into the passage and drew the door to. "What's the matter, Elsa? Don't you feel well?"

"It's nothing, miss." She stopped, clutching at the neck of her robe. "It's . . . just sometimes I can't stand it . . . just not every night. All the noise comes up through the fireplace. I asked him to let me move my room back with the other servants, but he said she'd be all right pretty soon. He's so considerate, miss. He won't let anybody stay up with her. He says it just makes her worse. But he just never gets any rest himself. But he can sleep late in the morning. He just doesn't *know* that I never get any rest."

She kneaded her big hands desperately. "He says it makes her worse if anybody comes in when she's like this. And I know it does, because she gets terribly angry. She threw a book at me one night. He's the only one that can quiet her when she . . . she's like this. I . . . I just don't know what to do. I wanted to leave, but he asked me not to, on his account. He needs somebody he can trust not to talk about it."

She took another backward step. "I was just going down to get a cup of tea."

"All right, go on," Jenny said quietly. "You go and make me some coffee, would you, while you're down? You can just put it on my table. And you move into one of the back rooms right now and go to sleep. I'll tell Moulton, and I'll speak to Mr. de Gradoff. I'm sure he just doesn't understand, and now I'm here I can help with my mother. I could always run up and get you, if we needed you."

"Oh yes, miss!"

The torn edge of the woman's voice reminded her sharply of her mother.

"Well, that's the way we'll do it, and I'll have my coffee black," Jenny said. "And maybe we could have some toast, do you think? You just bring your tea upstairs and drink it in your new room."

"Oh, thank you, miss." She smiled back, pathetically grateful, picked up her robe and started down the stairs.

Jenny watched her a second, and looked up the crooked flight of stairs going to the third floor. "Of course, she believes it. She can't see the lights, upstairs," she thought quickly. "And she's really honest. That's very good . . . for him."

She went out into the hall and glanced up again at the beamed walnut ceiling. The stairway to the third floor was back in the corner turret, winding elegantly around the inner service stairs she'd just come away from. Of course, nobody'd see the lights, unless they were outside, or outside her own room on the porch. Not even Mrs. Emlyn or Peter in the guest rooms just to the right on this floor. The bulging turret between her mother's big dressing-room and her bath would cut them off. Nor could anyone hear. The doors of Enniskerry were solid walnut. Not much came through them. Their windows would be open, but the roar of the sea would swallow the sound from her mother's room, except up the fireplace flue to Elsa's room.

She went quickly round the spindled balcony rail and stopped at her mother's door an instant before she knocked, straightenening up and relaxing, arranging her face into an inquiring blank for whatever appeared. She was aware instantly of a sharply different quality of sound or silence through the polished door as she knocked again.

"Oh, gosh, Nikki, I'm sorry. I didn't know you were here. I just saw Mother's light."

He was there abruptly, not pleased, opening the door sharply, prepared to rebuke an interloper, Elsa probably, and Jenny there in her blue wool robe and pajamas was clearly not who he expected to see. It took an instant for his arrogant disapprobation to dissolve and reassort itself in the face

81

of Jenny's apparent surprise and apology. He had on a heavy black silk knee-length dressing gown, his silk pajama legs only a little rumpled. The glaring lights in the room behind him were gone.

"What is it, Jennifer?"

He opened the door a little wider, not arrogant, merely a man whose privacy had been disturbed by an intrusive step-daughter old enough to know better.

It was so genuine that Jenny drew back, unsure.

"I'm terribly sorry. I . . . I saw my mother's light. I wanted to—"

"I'm afraid she's trying to get some rest, my dear. Later, if—"

"No. Let her come in, Nikki."

Jenny heard her mother's voice suddenly sharp. The old childhood pattern was before her. "What-does-she-want-now?" it demanded, with an overtone of "You-let-me-talk-to-her, I'll-see-that-she-does-as-she's-told." It was there so clearly, and with it the rest of the pattern, that the old agonizing fear of her mother's anger dredged blindly up out of the past, the way the rut in the turf had dredged up the fear of another row with the gardeners. For a moment it held her in its irrational grip, erasing all the years in between, until she caught herself shrinking under de Gradoff's intent blue eyes. He stepped back and opened the door, confident again in some odd way she could instantly sense, aware he'd seen she was diminished and that her mother was antagonistic to her again. She swallowed and slipped past him into the soft peach-shaded light of the room, that didn't need light, now the day was all around them.

Her mother was sitting bolt upright against the peach faille bedrest, her eyes almost glittering bright through the red-dened lids and hollow circles under them, her mouth hard, her cheekbones splotched with anger.

She believes him. She believes I'm against her. Jenny could see it instantly. She braced herself and went over to the side of the bed. It was littered with picture and fashion magazines. A couple of novels, the pages crumpled, were caught under the peach velvet comforter kicked down to the blanket rail at the foot of the four-poster bed.

"Mother, I've been over at the stable," she said simply, and saw her mother's taut fingers jerk the rumpled edge of the peach linen sheet. "Nikki's told you about Polly, hasn't he?"

The freezing awareness of her mistake clutched her even before she felt the small vivid mushroom of silence that ex-ploded in the room around her. Nikki's voice was the flash of light coming instantly with it. "Polly? Do you mean Polly Randolph? What about her? What should I know about her?"

She steadied herself against the side of the bed. A light

flashed too in the recesses of her own dark conviction. *He knows.* But her mother didn't. She was waiting, taut, but not because of Polly.

"She's dead, Mother. She was drowned, tonight. Mrs. . . . Mrs. Winton pushed her off the fishing platform at the Randolphs'."

"Oh, no!" Her mother's lips framed it without sound. The angry splotches on her cheekbones vanished, leaving them bloodless white. "Not Helen Winton . . ." she whispered. "Oh, Jenny . . . *she wouldn't!*"

"Mr. Finlay saw her, Mother. We were taking some food down to eat on the steps. He saw her from up the bank, and she told us both she did it. I . . . I thought Nikki knew."

She forced herself to stop and turn and look at him, standing there, watching her so intently that his eyes did not react to her turning for an instant. Then he was frowning, not understanding why she thought he knew.

"Because one of the men who took her up was talking to you when you were waiting at the gate for your car. That's why I thought you knew. I saw you all from the nursery window. They've taken her to Shepherd's Vale, Mother."

"Oh, how awful." Dodo covered her face with her hands and bent her head forward. "Poor, poor creatures," she whispered.

"And I went over to Mr. Finlay's. I thought he was back. I thought he'd know whether they'd . . . found her. But he wasn't home, and I thought I'd wait, he wouldn't be awfully long, and he'd want some coffee. So I made him some, but he didn't come and I went to sleep on his sofa. He didn't get there until just a few minutes ago. And I didn't stop to think how it would . . . upset him, to find me there. . . . when he was already dreadfully upset, about Polly. But you'll explain to him for me, Mother, won't you? Because it's sort of . . . embarrassing."

"Silly, darling," her mother said gently. "Forget it. Fish isn't the kind of person that—"

She broke off, a faint flush seeping into her drawn white face.

"He'll understand perfectly," de Gradoff said. Dodo flashed him a grateful glance that Jenny saw wiped out everything he'd said about Fish Finlay himself.

"He's hardly likely to take advantage of a thing of the sort," de Gradoff added. His manner implied that he easily might, and Jenny felt her cheeks tingle.

"It's just if anybody else saw me, is what I mean, Mother," she said quietly. "They haven't found Polly yet."

She blinked back the tears that had sprung into her eyes.

"I just feel so awful about it," she said unsteadily. "What . . . what'll they do with—"

"With Skunky's mother?"

It was curious for her own mother to put it that way, and somehow it erased all the dregs of the old pattern from her mind.

"They'll keep her at Shepherd's Vale, Jenny. Under . . . observation."

Jenny felt her voice tighten as she said it and saw the color seep out of her lips, leaving a white line around them as her eyes moved, drawn in a sudden panic past Jenny to her husband, her fingers twitching the hem of the sheet.

"You mustn't let it upset you, Dodo, dearest."

Jenny stiffened at the soft caress in his voice again.

"Mother," she said quickly. "Could I stay here and just . . . just talk to you a little while? I . . . I hate to be alone."

"Surely, darling." Dodo's voice was firm again. She nodded a little at Nikki. "You go and get some rest . . . please, dearest."

"Jennifer had better go. You'll be all upset again, my darling."

This is sort of a battle. She thought it suddenly. Her back was to him, but she could feel that he was winning. In a moment her mother would make her go and let him stay.

"Or why don't you come down to my room, Mother?" she said quickly. "I've got some coffee—"

"Oh, wonderful." Dodo pushed back the sheet and silk blanket cover. "Give me my slippers, darling. I feel so horrible about poor Helen Winton. And poor Polly. I just can't bear it."

She was putting on her velvet robe.

"Polly was so excited about my rubies."

She looked through her dressing-room doors. They were lying in a pool of deep wine-bright light on the dressing table, four pools of wine-colored light, their own and the three images of them in the triple wings of the mirror. Jenny steadied herself, her hand on the bedpost, aware of another smaller silence mushrooming when de Gradoff stopped suddenly, moving toward his own door.

"I wouldn't have thought she'd be interested in them," he said easily. "Most women only like jewels they'd look well in themselves."

"That's what she said, you know." Dodo paused, tying the ribbon at the neck of her robe. "She said she was terribly surprised anyone with reddish-gold hair could wear them."

"Come along. Mother. Our coffee's getting cold."

Jenny opened the door and waited, not daring to look at the silence again where her stepfather stood. She could feel it spreading out, cold, terribly cold, and terribly dark. Then with a self-possession that surprised her she said, "Polly just wanted something interesting to put in her column. She

84

was phoning her story in to her paper when Peter and I got there."

"Oh, but she promised not to use it," Dodo said confidently. "I told her it was off the record. See you, darling."

She said it to Nikki without turning back as she went into the hall. Jenny followed and closed the door, her heart still tight in her breast. She could feel him standing there, motionless, behind it. The palms of her hands were clammy moist and very cold.

CHAPTER : 12

It was half-past nine before Fish found the Azores on Thames Street. He'd passed it several times, but the Portuguese funeral parlor on the corner, its window full of flyspecked tinsel trappings of gaudy death, threw him off, and he didn't look up to see the neon sign with the flowing purple arrow pointing to "Rooms, Day or Week," around in the weed-grown dead end, littered with shells, that extended to the jetty between two piers, where the fishermen were swabbing out their empty boats. He turned his car in. The building was a long starkly barren clapboard-sided former warehouse, built on barnacled piles over the water. The rickety porch had another neon sign over it, and three women on it, like bundles of old laundry dumped in rocking chairs, waiting to be picked up.

"Does Mr. Beyle live here?"

One of them looked up at him and nodded her black head back at the door. Inside was another woman, vigorously scrubbing the linoleum on the stairs, her face flushed, her black eyes bright in contrast to the lilies of the field outside. He asked for Mr. Beyle again, and through the torrent of words he thought were angry until she laughed he gathered that Mr. Beyle occupied Number 7 on the floor above. She moved her scrub bucket aside for him, still voluble about something, presumably about the tracks on her clean steps. There was a set besides the ones he was making, the faint trace of them continuing in front of him along the shining strip of linoleum on the second floor. They ended at the door of the room with a polished brass "7" on it. Mr. Beyle must have just come in himself.

He raised his hand and knocked. There was no answer. He could hear someone moving inside the flimsy door, and knocked again. Then he knocked louder and tried the door. It was locked.

"Mr. Beyle!" he called.

He heard steps then. A key turned in the lock and the door opened. It was not the little waiter. It was a workman in blue dungarees and blue denim hat, with a thin weather-beaten face and sad faded blue eyes. He looked at Fish, shook his head and walked past him down the hall back to the steps, leaving Fish alone in the open door of Number 7.

"This whole blasted town is wacky," Fish thought, hearing the woman below sound off volubly and violently and then laugh, ebulliently good-natured, as her pail grated out of the way again. He went into the room. It was as spotless as the halls, cheap and garish pink and purple, but scrubbed to the bone. Any evidence that it was the room of the little French waiter was not externally visible as he glanced from the neatly made brass bed with the violent pink spread and pink-shaded drop light over the head of it to the wash-bowl and wavy mirror. Until he looked at the pot-bellied chiffonier against the wall beside the door. Propped on the starched pink runner was a framed motto, elaborately inked in many colors. It was in French, no authorship ascribed, and none needed. He translated it.

"Discretion is the shell of the oyster guarding the priceless pearl within."

The good two inches of decorative flourish at the end of it were so precisely like the flourish of the silver tray in the Randolphs' garden that he grinned and pulled up a chair to wait. He noticed then that the bottom drawer of the chiffonier was not closed straight, in a room in which everything else was cameo-clean and neatly ordered. The oyster-shell of his own discretion opened perceptibly. He leaned down and pulled the drawer out. He frowned and pulled out the one above it. The drawers were a mess. It was clear from the way the underwear and shirts in them were folded that that was not their normal state, furthermore that they had not been that way long . . . not long enough to wrinkle the fancy striped shirts, size fourteen, and flowered shorts that were side by side with a pile of waiter's starched white dickeys with built-in white ties . . . on and off with one flourish.

He went over to the cupboard built out in the far corner of the room, its flimsy door papered lazarus blue and purple, the same as the walls. Somebody had been in a hurry there, too. Two black suits with the cleaner's wrappings partly torn from them were pushed at a cockeyed angle on the broom-handle rod. A coat, a gaudy French version of an English tweed, was on the floor, the pockets turned out. Even the small highly polished shoes were jumbled together as if they'd been kicked impatiently aside.

Fish stood there looking around. If the workman in the dungarees had found what he'd been hunting, it must have

86

been fairly small. His hands had been empty as he came out. Fish looked at his watch. Actually, except for the fancy motto on the potbellied chiffonier and the fancy message no longer in his possession, he hadn't much to support his conviction that the waiter was, in fact, the French detective Blum. Except that Dodo and Polly both had described him as absurd. But Polly hadn't recognized him. Or had she? He suddenly remembered the impression of excitement she'd given him when he pointed her out to the waiter who had the message for her. She'd been looking over at Mrs. Emlyn's table, with the little man hovering near it. And if he was the detective, he certainly hadn't recognized Polly either. She was in evening dress, of course, and he mightn't expect to find a newspaper reporter he'd seen in Paris there in Newport. "It might all be another bust like the long-distance call you so avidly traced an hour or so ago, my friend," Fish Finlay told himself.

He'd look like a damned fool if M. Beyle came back and found him there pawing through his dresser drawers. It would be worse if the voluble wench on the stairs demanded an explanation for his being there. He crossed the shining clean floor and closed the door of Number 7 quietly behind him. As he did, he noticed that the door of Number 6, just across from it, was slightly ajar. Halfway down the hall he heard it squeak, and looked back. A blonde in a striped house coat had stepped out, but she skirted modestly back. He went on, relieved to find the stairs empty of the scrub bucket, and the three depleted babes on the stoop the only other hazard outward bound.

It seemed strange that François Beyle, if he was only a waiter, would be out that early when he'd worked so late the night before. It wasn't until he drove away from the Azores and out of the milling chaos of Thames Street that it occurred to him that a waiter would have to have a regular daytime job too. That was probably what the scrub lady was trying to convey, in her flood of Portuguese volubility. He grinned and drove down Bellevue past the library, with its magnificent fernleaf beech in front, looking for a place to park.

The thing to do would be to go to the caterer's and find out more about M. Beyle's daily routine. But the only parking place he saw was behind him. He went on to make a right turn and come back along the cross-street, stopped to wait for the traffic light to change, and straightened up, blinking sharply at the man in the old yellowed panama hat and old-fashioned cream-colored poplin suit, narrow-legged trousers two inches above his ankles, a walking stick in his hand, crossing the street on the green light a couple of cars ahead of him.

It couldn't be. But it was. The clothes were strange, but there was no mistaking the saurian profile and the patient droop to the shoulders of the Vice-President and Trust Officer of the Merchants and Mechanics Bank and Deposit Company. The impulse to sound his horn or lean out the window and shout surrendered to discretion's pearl. Hired hands didn't sound horns or shout at Caxson Reeves. He was headed Fish's way, and Fish leaned over and ran down his window. But Reeves turned then, and went up the steps of the white clapboard hotel on the corner. By the time the light changed he was inside. Fish drove on and turned the corner, grinning at the sudden warm lift to his spirit.

Whoever'd think I'd be that glad to see the old lizard! He parked his car in the first place available and got out. Ten to one, the little waiter had a job here at the hotel, and Reeves. . . . There was a side door. Fish hurried up the steps, and slowed down then as he pushed the door open, his exuberance diminished abruptly. If Caxson Reeves wanted him there, he'd have said so. He hadn't even told Fish he was in Newport. It wasn't a question of time either, not if he'd had time to go to his sister's and haul out the rig he was wearing.

Fish let the door bang shut behind him. The hell with that stuff. This business of being a hired left hand not knowing what the executive right hand was doing wasn't funny any longer. It was like his going on pretending he didn't know what Jennifer Linton was talking about. Even she saw it was stupid . . . and dangerous. And if Reeves had cast him in the role of blind assistant to his French detective—and no wonder the little man knew his name and recognized him when he saw him—then Reeves could hardly object if Fish tracked him down too in the process. He grinned and went through another door into another hall. He'd tell Mr. Reeves it was line of duty. That'd fix the crafty old alligator.

The place was a dark maze of narrow passages and closed doors. He'd obviously come in the wrong way. Another tack brought him out to the serving end of a dining-room, very empty, no waiters, French or otherwise, in sight. Next to the dining-room was a small dark bar where a man in shirt sleeves was polishing glasses, listening to the radio turned on quietly behind him. Beyond it was a constricted passage leading into the main hall. Fish started through it and stopped abruptly. There was a window in the wall opening into a small cubbyhole where the reception desk was. What stopped him was Caxson Reeves's voice.

"Will you ring Mr. Durban's apartment, please? Tell him Mr. Reeves is here."

"Mr. Durban's waiting in the lounge."

Fish stepped discreetly back into the bar, the interior dimness concealing the flush creeping uncomfortably up the back

88

of his neck. The fact that Reeves might have other interests than the Maloney Trust was acutely vivid to him. He would have preferred to fade quietly back into the street and avoid the sardonic scrutiny from under the drooping lids, but it was better to stick it out in case Reeves had seen him in the car, as he probably had. There wasn't much he missed.

"Want something, Mac?" The bartender asked.

"A milk punch, if you've got one handy."

"Have to get the milk. Only take a second."

"Okay."

Fish sat on a bar stool. "Line of duty" . . . very funny. He was wondering what he could say if Reeves walked in, when he heard a deep voice, and heavy footsteps with lighter ones coming through the hall toward the central staircase. He shifted uncomfortably on the leather stool as he heard Reeves's voice then.

"I'm not unwilling to discuss it, except in public, Mr. Durban," he was saying, in the familiar dust-dry tones. "You have my address if you wish to come at three o'clock. It isn't possible for me to discuss it in your apartment, however private it may appear to be. I'm sure you'll appreciate my position."

"Certainly." Mr. Durban's accent was precise if obviously foreign. "I'll see you at three. I know nothing of the acoustics here and nothing of my neighbors. I checked in from the Randolphs' very late. The situation there is most unhappy."

"I'm sure it is."

"Most unhappy. And I think I rather need a pick-me-up. Will you join me?"

It was cool in the bar, but Fish's hand went up and wiped off his forehead. He waited.

"No, thank you. I'll see you at three, sir."

Fish got out a cigarette and lighted it, breathing normally again as he listened to one pair of footsteps diminishing, the other, heavier, coming closer, until it was in back of his stool. He heard the deep voice again.

"Anybody in attendance here?"

"He'll be back in a second," Fish said. He looked around, and gave an involuntary start as he saw the man beside him.

"I'm sorry," Mr. Durban said. His smile was ironic but not unpleasant. "I'm rather horrible at first sight."

Mr. Durban was the man from Mars, the hunchback with the grotesquely enormous head, the fairy godfather of the improvident rich, that Polly had pointed out sitting with Alla Emlyn at the Randolphs' party. He smiled at Fish again.

"Don't let it disturb you. I'm used to all sorts of reactions."

"Sorry," Fish said. "It was very rude. The bartender's gone to get some milk to make a milk punch. Would you have one with me?"

"I'll be happy to," Durban said. "I've never had one."

"They ease your conscience, if you have one, about drinking early in the morning. Also your stomach."

"I doubly need one, then."

He got up on a stool and bent his huge head, listening to the radio as the bartender came back with a bottle of milk. He nodded to Durban familiarly.

"That fellow you were talking about, sir," he said. "The one they found his body this morning?"

"Have they identified him?" Durban asked calmly.

"Yes, sir."

He shook up the bottle of milk and took off the cap.

"It came over the radio a few minutes ago. He was a waiter, they said. His name's François Bailey, or something like that. He lived at a Portuguese hangout down off Thames Street. The Azores, they call it. He was working on the Randolphs' party last night, but nobody knows when he left, or if it was the tide carried him out over to the Island. I was talking to a Coast Guard fellow in the service yard just now, helped haul him out. He said he was drowned, all right, a lot of water in his lungs. Figured he was sampling the Randolphs' chamagne on the q.t., I guess. What are you going to have, sir?"

"This gentleman has offered me a milk punch," Durban said pleasantly. "From the man's description I thought at first it was someone I knew. But I was mistaken."

"Who did you think it was, sir?" Fish asked quietly.

"Just a man who did some work for me once," Durban said. "But it was a long time ago, and in another country." He smiled. "And besides, the wench is dead. That's a line from one of your English poets, is it not?"

CHAPTER : 13

Fish Finlay found a telephone book in the office next to the bar and turned the yellow pages again for the address of the Randolphs' caterer.

"The Coast Guard plane spotted him." The bartender had explained to him. Durban had lost interest when he heard the little waiter's name. "They thought it was Miss Randolph, the sea gulls were making such a row out on the end of the island. The plane's still up looking for her. This fellow I was talking to out back said there was one of her slippers got caught up on the rock. It's funny how little things like that get you, isn't it?"

Fish nodded and went to find the telephone book then.

The shop he was looking for was just off Bellevue Avenue on John Street, a small gold stencil on the window discreetly announcing the premises of Jean Paul Lanson, Caterer, Open 9 to 3, Or By Appointment. He stepped into a clean bare room with a fine tiered wedding cake in a glass case. A desk with two chairs stood by a curtained door. The curtains moved and the sallow anxious face of a woman of about forty appeared.

"Not the police again," she said. She looked at him with weary desperation. "My father's very ill."

"I'm not the police, Miss Lanson," Fish said. "I talked to you early this morning. My name's Finlay."

"Oh yes." She came on into the room. "I had to tell the police somebody called. I hope I didn't make a lot of trouble for you, too."

"Not so far."

Her drawn face relaxed a little as he smiled at her. "It's been awful, Mr. Finlay. We just don't know what to do." She gave the impression of wringing her hands without moving them at all, searching his face with a pathetic need of some kind of understanding. "Are you a friend of Mr. Beyle's?"

"In a way. I came to see your father. I have an idea that Beyle was something besides a waiter."

She looked almost sick. "Are you . . . from the government?"

"No. I work in a bank. I have nothing to do with the law or the police. I just think maybe the little guy got a pretty raw deal."

"Oh, I'm so glad you've come, then!"

She went quickly to the front door and pressed the latch to lock it. "We're just out of our minds. Sit down, will you? Let me run up and tell my father. His ulcers flared up. If he was Mrs. Winton, he'd be in a hospital where nobody could worry him." She added it bitterly as she hurried through the curtains. When she came back in a moment, she pulled a chair up to the desk and pushed her hair back from her anxious face.

"Father always trust the wrong people. I told him we'd be ruined if it ever got out. But he would do it. Mr. Beyle was discreet. Father's friend would never have sent him if he hadn't been absolutely trustworthy. And look what happened. It's simply ruin, Mr. Finlay. Nobody will ever come to us again when they find out father let a detective in with his waiters to spy on them. And we've worked so hard." The tears were running down her sallow cheeks. "We've just bought a brand new trailer kitchen with all the latest equipment."

"Maybe there's something we can do," Fish said soberly. He took out his pack of cigarettes, offered her one and lighted it for her.

"I've racked my brain ever since I heard them describe him over the radio this morning," she said. "It's not only the customers. We couldn't sell the business—good will is our biggest asset, and there wouldn't be any left—but we could scrape along on what we've saved. But the government . . . I don't know what the penalty will be. Maybe prison even. My father—both of us—knew his union and social security cards belonged to somebody else."

"Have you told the police?"

She shook her head. "We lied to them too. That's part of father's upset. Lieutenant Bestoso's a good friend of ours. Father wanted to tell him everything. But he's a policeman first. You see, father doesn't believe it was an accident."

"I don't either," Fish said. "And you can't go on lying, can you. The social security and union cards are a matter of record."

"I know. And the real François Beyle will have to have them back before he can work again. He's an old waiter of father's. It'll make terrible trouble for him too. I told father that from the beginning."

The tears were springing up again.

"Beyle's real name was Blum?" Fish asked.

"Oh, you've heard of him, then? We never had, till father got the cable, from an old friend of his in France—one of the really great chefs, father was apprenticed to him. He said the renowned Ferenc Blum was coming to Newport. It would be a distinguished honor for my father to assist him. It didn't sound like a customer to me." She smiled a little. "Father cabled back, and got a letter. M. Blum was a world-famous detective, on the track of a 'black-hearted devil incarnate.' I burned the letter this morning or I could show it to you. The family who retained him first had given up, but M. Blum was convinced there would be another 'victim.' He told father's friend the whole story over a bottle of wine one night, and the old chef recognized the victim's name. He'd known the family in his old days in New York, at the Ritz. He'd lost touch during the war, but they were Newport people, so he wrote here. He got a letter back from a connection of theirs who said he'd retain M. Blum to go on with it, if it could be done absolutely *sub rosa* . . . with this person's name and connection never under any circumstances appearing."

Fish Finlay nodded. He knew the name and connection. *The reputation of the bank. The sole duty of the Maloney trustees.* "When did all that happen, do you know?"

"We didn't hear about it until M. Blum found out that his
92

. . . quarry," she hesitated before she spoke the word, as if it had some disturbing meaning for her, "or the victim, or both, were going to be in Newport for the season. But the arrangement had been in effect for some time . . . since October, anyway."

Or practically from Dodo and de Gradoff's meeting under the lamppost in the rain. The marriage had been in October. Finlay, the hired left hand, hadn't appointed himself till the April following. "You didn't know the names of the people—"

"Oh no." Her face had the same expression of perturbation he'd noticed when she hesitated before. "They purposely didn't tell us, except to assure my father they were old customers of his. That's really what made him take M. Blum on his staff. Because a waiter can be right in people's pockets and they never see him. I did my best, but father's very simple in some ways, and sentimental about old friends—"

She broke off abruptly, her uneasiness suddenly acute. "That's why he read the note, Mr. Finlay."

"The note?"

She nodded. ". . . That took M. Blum to the fishing platform. That's really why father's so terribly upset. And I won't let him tell the lieutenant. It'll just make everything that much worse. And Polly Randolph's dead anyway. . . ."

Fish waited, silently intent.

"One of the other waiters found it on his tray that he'd set down for a moment while he got more champagne. It was just a sheet of paper folded over and marked on the outside for M. Ferenc Blum. Of course the waiter didn't know who Ferenc Blum was, so he brought it to father in the pantry. Father thinks it was premonition made him open it. I think it was Old Devil Curiosity, myself. Because father'd noticed how excited M. Blum had got all of a sudden there, when he'd been terribly down in the dumps for the last two or three days. He was even more excited when father gave him the note . . . very cocky, very pleased with himself. He asked where the fishing platform was and what the word 'deal' meant. Father was amused . . . he told him both and forgot all about it, he was so busy—until this morning."

"What did the note say, Miss Lanson?" Fish asked quietly. "Your father probably remembers it, doesn't he?"

She nodded. "It was very short. It said: 'I've been expecting you for a long time, M. Ferenc Blum. I still believe we can do a deal, you and I. Say nothing, but meet me at the fishing platform as near one o'clock as you can.' " She closed her eyes a moment. "It was signed 'Polly Randolph.' It . . . it's just so awful, Mr. Finlay. That's why father didn't think anything about it, then. He did her parents' wedding . . . he just can't believe—"

93

"But he's right, Miss Lanson," Fish said gently. "Miss Randolph wouldn't—"

She broke in with a kind of renewed despair. "But you look at it, Mr. Finlay. We'd assumed it was a man M. Blum was after, but he never said so. Polly Randolph lived in Paris. She wouldn't be the first black sheep in the Randolph family. She'd never expect my father to read a note addressed to someone else. And God knows she'd never expect Helen Winton, drunk, to follow her down there. I haven't a doubt that seeing her there is what put the idea in Mrs. Winton's befuddled mind. Because M. Blum was already dead . . . his watch was broken at six minutes past one."

Fish Finlay felt a slow dry crust forming on his tongue. *Maybe the little black man caught her. He was waiting down there.* He could hear the childlike, blood-chilling voice of the woman weaving back and forth against the pipe rail. He'd taken that as an alcoholic hallucination, never for an instant dreaming it was the literal truth. There was in fact a little black-clad man down there, or had been until the cresting waves swallowed him.

"She knew there wouldn't be anybody else down on the platform," Miss Lanson was going on. "She was the one who showed her uncle all the poison ivy under the roses. A girl sitting there would be sure to touch it, and the girls' arms bare in their evening dresses. So her uncle had a thick white rope put across to bar the steps. And who else would know about the blackjack?"

She caught herself quickly, her face paling. "Oh, I shouldn't have said that. We were told in confidence. Don't say anything, please . . . unless Lieutenant Bestoso tells you, too."

"All right." Fish hesitated, and pushed back his chair. There was no use arguing with her. He got up. "I think you'd better tell Bestoso about the note."

"And have everybody think father reads their letters and runs to the police? No, Mr. Finlay. And if Polly Randolph didn't do it, it's better not to tell them. They'll see it just the way father does, now that M. Blum's dead. They'll think Helen Winton's killing Miss Randolph just cancels the whole thing."

It was precisely what they were supposed to think, Fish Finlay thought grimly. There was cunning behind all of it. Miss Lanson was right. It was the way the police were bound to read the note.

"Will you do one thing for me?" he asked. "Check with your waiters, and find out which one of them brought a message in a blue envelope to Polly Randolph. He might know who gave it to him to deliver."

"I will." She followed him over to the door. "This seems to be what always happens when you try to help somebody."

94

"Isn't it the truth," Finlay said. "But there ought to be some way for you to let the police know what Blum was doing without ruining yourselves. What about his records? Somebody thinks he kept some. They've already gone through his stuff at his rooming house. But I have the idea he wouldn't just have left them around, with all his passion for discretion. You've got a safe, haven't you?"

Miss Lanson shook her head. "There's nothing in it. I looked this morning. All I know is that he typed a long time night before last. On my typewriter, with some old blue onion-skin paper I had. I know he made a copy, because he brought one sheet of carbon paper out and burned it in the garbage pail. He hated to do it. It was still good, and he was full of little economies. He had a long envelope in his pocket when he went out. But you'd better give me your phone number. I'll call you about the other waiter and anything else I can find out."

Fish gave her the number.

"That's Enniskerry stable, isn't it?"

He waited, and relaxed. She was too involved with her own difficulties to make the connection between Enniskerry and his special interest in Ferenc Blum.

"We've got a worse problem," she said. "Worse because it's immediate. The police expect us to make the formal identification for the inquest."

"I can help you out there," Fish said, and she brightened for the first time. "I know a man who can identify him as Ferenc Blum. And I'll damn well see that he does it," he added doggedly. The Lanson reputation was as important to them as the bank's was to Caxson Reeves.

"Oh, thank you!" she said. "And thanks for everything. I feel so much better I can't tell you. If you ever give a party, and we're still in business. . . ."

"I'll remember that."

He walked back to Bellevue Avenue and stood on the corner looking in at a window of artificial flowers. Artificial flowers, in a town that was a gardener's paradise of the most great. He realized then that it was a large bowl of carnations that had caught his eye. De Gradoff's voice the night before, and Polly Randolph's, echoed in his ear.

"Carnations?"

Carnations, darling. You know. Flowers. Very fragrant."

They had some significance in terms of the first wife whose death the Argentine family had retained Ferenc Blum to investigate. They'd then called him off, leaving a black-hearted devil incarnate free as a bird to hunt another prey. And the Lansons were facing ruin because they'd innocently tried to help out. He glanced back at the shop, saw a police car pulling up to the curb in front of it, and started down the street to pick up his own car over behind the hotel. On the corner he stopped, looking both ways carefully before he crossed, grinning to himself without amusement. The surprising thing really was that he hadn't been included in the scheme that had liquidated Polly Randolph and Blum. De Gradoff, seeing all three of them there at the table, must have realized the possibility that Polly and Blum had told him more than they in fact had. And taking precautions at street crossings wasn't going to help. When his turn came, it would be something as neat and unpredictably opportunist as the fishing platform, with somebody else to take the blame, as Polly was supposed to take it for Blum and Mrs. Winton was already taking it for Polly . . . with eyewitnesses as unimpeachable as James Fisher Finlay present, no doubt, to make it foolproof.

But it wasn't foolproof. He quickened his uneven pace to his car, two things Miss Lanson had told him fusing themselves in a sudden and simple solution of the whole thing. Blum's excitement at the Randolphs', and his message to Fish —"All is now prepared"—meant that he had found the salient fact he needed to complete his case. The message was clearly spur of the moment. That bracketed the salient fact in time and place. The report he'd typed on the thin blue paper the night before the party, when he was still down in the dumps, would bracket all the rest of it: the identification of de Gradoff, of Ferenc Blum himself, the reason he was in Newport, what was behind his being there, what he'd found out, what the keystone fact was that he was looking for and found the next night at the Randolphs'. If it wasn't stated in so many words, it would have to be so bracketed that it ought to be easy for the police to work out. It was that simple. All Fish Finlay had to do was get Caxson Reeves to turn over the report to them. The reputation, honor and prestige of the bank would be pristine and unimpaired, the personal welfare of the Maloney heirs fully assured, and Finlay could go back to New York and forget he'd fallen in love with a girl young enough to be his granddaughter, the way he'd forgotten it in April when he came back from Virginia—until June when he saw her a second time in Newport. Out of sight, out of mind.

A dull pain in the pit of his stomach made him look at his watch before he set out to find Caxson Reeves for the showdown. It was twenty minutes past twelve. The pain was nothing, he hoped, that a large fresh-broiled lobster wouldn't cure. He got out of the car, started into the hotel and decided to call Jenny Linton first, just to see if everything was all right. He crossed the street to the drugstore there.

"I'm sorry, sir. Miss Linton is out." It was Moulton answering, adding, as he recognized Fish's voice, "She and Mr.

Peter have gone to play tennis at the Casino, sir. They're going on to the Chalet for a swim and lunch at half-past one, sir."

Fish put the phone down. He tripped clumsily coming out of the booth, and flushed as the girl at the soda fountain looked startled and then distressed.

"Ham and cheese on rye," he said curtly.

"Plain or toasted?"

"Plain."

He wanted then to tell her he was sorry, but couldn't think just how, and a moment later he forgot it as a lime-green parasol open above a graceful figure in black caught his eye across the street. He watched the woman turn up the front steps of the hotel, close the parasol and go inside. Mrs. Emlyn was probably lunching with Durban before his conference with Caxson Reeves at three o'clock. He went back to the telephone booth, got the book and looked up Reeves's number at his sister's.

"Who's calling, please? Oh, Mr. Finlay, Mr. Reeves left a message if you called. He's lunching at the Chalet, he'd like you to join him at one o'clock."

And watch Peter and Jenny swimming and having lunch together? No, thank you, Finlay thought. He stood there staring at his hand on the book, picked it up and found another number. The Lansons' line was busy. He went back to the counter and started on his sandwich, looking across the street again. Mrs. Alla Emlyn was coming out of the hotel, Fish put his sandwich down and picked up his plate and coffee cup. "I guess I'll take this to a booth. I'll take this, too." He picked up a magazine, went across the room and sat down, his back to the door. In a moment he heard it open and the click of the high-heeled lime-green sandals. He put his hand up to his head and bent over the magazine.

"May I have a glass of water, please."

He looked over. Mrs. Emlyn was taking a couple of aspirin out of a box in her bag.

"Headache?" the girl asked sympathetically, and Fish cringed at the second nasty brushoff she got for giving a damn what happened to the human race.

"No," Alla Emlyn said sharply. "It's just the sun. I'll have a cheese sandwich toasted and another glass of water. At the booth."

At his booth, no doubt, Fish thought. But not by design. She wouldn't have snapped at the counter girl if she'd known anyone she knew was there. He saw her face then. She looked as if she had worse than a headache. Her whole lovely ivory-white façade was caved in, in some odd undefinable way, and she was too concentrated on the evils, or the anxieties, of her own universe to notice any other around her. *She looks raddled. If it was anybody else, I'd think she was scared as well as sick. Or just scared sick period.*

She came to the booth next to his and sat down, facing him, not seeing him, and sat looking down at the table, not seeing it at first and then aware of it and wincing with distaste as she pulled a paper napkin out of the container and brushed the table off. She moved to let the girl put her sandwich and water down.

"How much is that?"

"Twenty-five cents. The water's free."

She fished in her bag. The girl went back to the counter holding two dimes and five pennies in her open palm, the curl of her bright red lips expressive.

It was then that Alla Emlyn saw him across the scarred edge of the wood partition between them.

"Why, Fish! How divine!"

CHAPTER : 14

It took her a full moment to make it appear divine, a much longer, much less adroit moment than Fish would have expected her to take, before she rose gracefully, her sandwich, glass of water and lime-green impediments all, the way women manage, in her hands.

"May I join you? I hate these places but I'm in a frantic hurry. Don't get up, darling, it's too close quarters to be polite."

She slipped into the seat across from him.

"Why aren't you at the Chalet? I'm sure Dodo expects you."

He closed his magazine and smiled at her. "Why aren't you?"

"I've got a touch of the sun. And it's so crowded there on Saturday." She took a bite of her sandwich. It was clear she still had not had time enough really to compose herself. "You're going to the dance tonight, I suppose, aren't you?"

Fish shook his head.

"It seems so odd, doesn't it . . . a flag half-mast on the roof and the balloons and smilax all up downstairs. But the flag comes down at sunset, doesn't it, and the band doesn't start up till ten." She shrugged lightly. "That's life, I suppose, isn't it. How long had you known Polly Randolph, Fish."

"Not long enough. Why?"

"I really want to know."

"No reason you shouldn't. Last night was the second time

98

I'd met her. An old classmate of mine from Ithaca brought her to dinner once, a long time ago." It seemed like a long time to him then. "She was a nice person."

Mrs. Emlyn shrugged again. "Unless she had her hooks in you. I'm afraid Dodo's going to regret her last night's girlish confidences. Or alcoholic confidences. Whichever they were."

"Am I supposed to know what you mean?"

"You'll know soon enough, I expect."

She regarded the remains of her sandwich with distaste and pushed it aside. He lighted the cigarette she took out of her bag, watching her, remembering the way she'd watched him the day before, seeing she was too involved now with something inside herself to be concerned with him. She leaned forward then as if she'd suddenly made up her mind.

"I want to talk to you, Fish."

"What about?" he asked pleasantly.

"About a lot of things. About Dodo and Nikki. About Jennifer."

Then as if aware she was being too intense, she relaxed, letting the smoke feather lightly from her lips, smiling at him, delicately ironical. "And about myself. And Peter."

He shook his head, smiling. "Too many . . . and none of them any business of mine."

"Not Dodo? Not Jennifer?" Her brows arched. "I thought they were intensely your business?"

"Their financial behavior only . . . within defined limits, and very narrow limits at that," Fish said. "And not a matter for me to talk about . . . as I'm sure you know."

"Very discreet, Mr. Finlay." A lazy smile curved her lips, but for a moment the pupils of her dark eyes had contracted. "Let's talk about something else. Jennifer's orchids, for instance. The ones she had in her hair last night. They were lovely, weren't they? Who sent them to her, I wonder?"

"Peter, I'd assumed."

"Peter? My God." She laughed, eyebrows up. "Are you being comic, Mr. Finlay, or aren't you an orchid buyer? Have you any idea how much a spray of fourteen white butterfly orchids costs?"

"Afraid not."

"Well, an awful lot more than Peter has, I assure you. Even if he'd thought of it, which he wouldn't, not before he'd seen her at least—if after." She shrugged again. "But that would be someone else's financial behavior, wouldn't it. I must say I didn't see her with anyone who looked that filthy rich last night."

"I guess we can all relax, then," Fish said. "It's not our problem, is it?" He rolled up his magazine and stuck it in his pocket. "And you're in a frantic hurry. Remember?"

"That was a lie, darling. I'm not in any hurry except to do

exactly what I'm doing. Please sit down. I must talk to you, it's terribly important."

"To whom?"

Her eyes narrowed. "I'm not joking, Fish," she said quietly. "You listen to me. I have no interest in either Dodo or Nikki. None whatsoever. But I have a great deal of interest in myself and Peter. In myself *for* Peter, to put it precisely. Peter belongs to me. Everything I've ever done—and I've done some pretty shocking things by your standards—I've done for Peter, and there's nothing I won't do for him. So you must listen to me. Time's getting short. Peter has *got* to have a rich wife."

He controlled the sudden anger flashing up in him. What was the use? The woman simply meant it. He smiled at her.

"If you're determined to make a first-class bum out of him, it's obvious we must act at once. What do you propose?"

Her cheeks flushed a little. "I propose that you answer one question I want to ask you," she said evenly.

"Fire away, lady. I'll certainly answer it if I can."

"How much money has Jennifer Linton got?"

She put her hand up quickly. "I know that's horribly bald, Fish." She smiled, her old mask slipping lazily back into place. "But you might just as well be realistic about it. If Peter wants her, he'll get her. He has a really astonishing gift, and Jennifer hasn't had enough attention in her life to resist his kind of excitement." She smiled again. "And if you try to warn her, she won't believe you, darling, you'll only make her more determined. She'll be like her mother. I was worried, last night, but as long as the donor of the orchids is *in absentia* I have complete confidence in Peter. The only question is whether he wants to go all out. If she's dependent on Dodo for an allowance when she marries, it would be stupid for him to bother. Dodo's not too generous unless she wants to be."

He looked at her across the table for a long instant.

"If she was as rich as all the seven seas, you don't think I'd tell you, do you?" he asked quietly.

The smile on her lips hardened. She nodded slowly. "But you have, haven't you," she said softly. "She isn't, is she. I was rather afraid of that when I saw her dress last night. It didn't cost $39.50, if that."

He felt the blood crawl up the back of his neck, leaving his spine clammy cold. *The viper,* he thought. *The female viper.*

"In fact, Peter gathered as much," she added calmly. "But there's still her grandfather, isn't there. Is he alive . . . or dead?"

"I expect you know as much about that as I do. More, if Nikki's told you about what he found in the newspaper

100

morgue the three days he spent in New York looking up the Maloney files . . . or if you've read the photostats Western Union sent you."

He moved out of the booth and got to his feet.

"I thought you two pooled your findings. If not, maybe you'd better find out what really happened to Polly Randolph, Alla. And to a little waiter whose name was Ferenc Blum. Or was that what gave you the touch of sun you had when you came in here? You'll excuse me . . . I've got a touch of something not the sun, myself, and I'd like to get to the curb before it's too late."

He went over to the counter and paid the girl. He put down an extra dollar bill. "Sorry I was sore. It was at myself, not you. Okay?"

"Oh, sure. I know how you feel." She blinked. "Gee . . . thanks!"

He grinned at her and went out, acutely conscious of Alla Emlyn still rigid in the frozen pool of silence behind him. He was halfway out Bellevue Avenue to Enniskerry before his mind cleared away enough for him to think. When it did, the two dimes and five pennies in the fountain girl's open palm slipped quietly onto the retina of his mind's eye.

She's broke. She's flat broke, he thought. *She's broke and she's scared.*

He slowed down. Maybe he'd better go back and let her talk to him. . . . But no. Let her sit there and think awhile. He looked at his watch. He still had time to meet Caxson Reeves for lunch at one, and time to stop by the stable and wash up.

As he turned in between the mortuary urns of Enniskerry, something else struck him about Mrs. Alla Emlyn. She wasn't thinking about Dodo being dead. That wasn't part of her scheme. She was thinking about Jenny's share of the estate and with Dodo still alive.

He came through the rim of purple beeches. Two men and two cars were in the drive. One car, with the Newport police tag on it, was in front of the stable. The other was over at the porte-cochere. The heavy-set man standing by it was talking to the lieutenant of detectives, Bestoso, whom Fish had talked to on the Randolphs' fishing platform as dawn was breaking. When they saw Fish the lieutenant headed his way, the large man got into his black sedan and drove on around toward the beeches. Fish saw the government tag on the back of his car.

"Who's that, Lieutenant?"

"Federal," Bestoso said. "Nothing to do with us."

Fish's attention sharpened. "F. B. I.? Who did he want to see?"

Bestoso shook his dark stubby head. Second or maybe third

generation Portuguese, short, stocky, weather-beaten, with bright black eyes, he looked more like a fisherman than a policeman.

"He didn't talk much. Says he'll be back at four. Mind if we talk a little? I hear you were down at the Azores this morning."

"Come on in." Fish opened the clock tower door and led the way up to the living-room.

"Nice place you've got," Bestoso remarked. "My grandfather was head groom when the hay burners lived downstairs. Used to tell us kids about it. Before the Maloneys' day. The old lady lived here was crazy about horses. Broke her back jumping one. The grass out there was a sand track, two boys did nothing but keep it raked. Built the house so they could wheel her out to watch the horses do their stuff. *Haute école,* the works. Big show, grampa said. It's the waiter named Beyle I came to talk to you about. You heard about finding him? Before you went to his place or after?"

"After," Fish said. He sat down and waited for Bestoso to make a tour of the room.

He came back grinning. "Sure gone to hell since grampa's day. Somebody went through Beyle's stuff, the landlady said."

"I wasn't the first. I looked around, when I saw somebody had."

"Why?"

"Curiosity, I guess. One of the drawers was in crooked, and the rest of the place was so neat."

"Why did you go there, is what I meant," Bestoso said. "If you'd gone after you heard about finding him, I'd have understood your curiosity, maybe. I guess you've connected him with what Mrs. Winton said about the little black man, same as I have?"

"Not till a few minutes ago. I thought she was seeing things."

"So did I, last night. Why did you go there?"

Fish Finlay lighted a cigarette to give himself a chance to think with the sharp black eyes resting steadily on him.

"Look, Lieutenant," he said. "If you'll give me a little time, there's a hell of a lot I think I can tell you. But I need time."

"Any particular place you want me to send your remains when we fish you out of the Atlantic?" Bestoso inquired coolly. He put his hand in his pocket and brought out a small book. "This mean anything to you?" He handed it to Fish.

It was a French passport. Fish opened it, and looked at the face of a man without a Gallic mustache. Clipped to the cover was a typed note from the Sûreté Générale, stating that the bearer was a private detective in good standing and that his efforts had the blessing of the Sûreté. His name was Ferenc Jean Baptiste Marie Blum.

"Blum brought that to me when he got to Newport," Bestoso said. "He wanted time to play it cagey too. Cocky little frog. I thought he was a laugh. But he had plenty on the ball if it was worth somebody's while to bump him off. If he'd played it straight, I could have helped him. Afraid I'd horn in on his fee, or his glory, I guess."

"You knew who he was this morning?"

"Sure. I was hoping for some kind of lead to somebody else. Like you, for instance."

He went on as Fish started to speak.

"The rest of the day I've been looking into a note he had in his pocket. Written with one of those ballpoint underwater pen deals. There's one of 'em on the stand by the Randolphs' telephone. It looks like Miss Randolph—"

He went on coolly as Fish made an abrupt movement. "I said 'looks like.' But it's funny she'd sign it 'Polly Randolph, Paris Edition, New York *Courier Graphic*'—if she wrote it and it was her he was after."

Fish Finlay took a deep breath. Miss Lanson had left that out.

"The handwriting doesn't look much like hers either," Bestoso said. "It's sort of a disguised backhand. You wouldn't think she'd do that and sign her name and life history. And she'd write 'make a deal,' not 'do a deal.' We found her body."

"Did she have a note too?" Fish asked quietly.

Bestoso looked at him for an instant. "Stuffed down in her bra. The paper was different. The salt water mushed it up, we can't read it. But you can see the picture. Her family didn't want an autopsy on account of Mrs. Winton. We did one. She was dead before she hit the water. Have you seen this before?"

He reached in his back trousers pocket and brought out the jeweled leather flask Fish had seen when the men picked up Mrs. Winton's unconscious form.

"It's full. Not liquor—lead shot. Colonel Randolph gave it to me. They keep it hanging on the porch, it's a souvenir, washed up from some place in the big blow of '38. Randolph used to show it to everybody. Blum was drowned. His skull was thicker than Miss Randolph's, I guess. Now I can't see Helen Winton doing that. Course, she was drunk as a skunk."

"You haven't got a carbon of Blum's typed report to his client in your other pants pocket, have you, Lieutenant?" Fish inquired. "Brother, you don't need any help from me."

"You need some from me," Bestoso said tersely. "We got a sensitive deal here in Newport. The Navy at one end, you millionaires' colony at the other, the town in the middle. We like to treat you people the way you like to be treated. But we don't go for murder. And we don't need a New York newspaper man editor to tell us when to do an autopsy."

He went to the door. "The Randolphs had five hundred guests from all over, drunk or sober or semi-each. I could waste months and get no place. You play square and I'll give you a little time. I won't trail you. I don't have the men. So watch yourself, brother." He went to the door. "I want somebody now who knows the fellow Blum to identify him. That could be a lead. Miss Lanson says you know somebody. Who is it?"

Not Caxson Reeves. Fish had already seen the error of that. Reeves would have been far too cagey ever to let Blum see him in the flesh.

"There's a man named Durban," he said. "A hunchback. At the Colony Hotel. He was talking to the bartender this morning. I got the impression he'd retained Blum once . . . a long time ago and in another country. I was just an anonymous guy buying him and myself a milk punch."

"Thanks," Bestoso said. "I'll drop in there and buy myself a shot of straight rye."

CHAPTER : 15

Fish followed him out to the stairs. They stopped, looking down at the taxi just pulled in, a man working his way out of the door, wrong end to.

"Who's that?" Bestoso asked.

"Looks like the hind end of a tall, lean, sandy-haired character totally unfamiliar to me," Finlay answered. "Name him and you can have him."

Bestoso grinned. "Okay. You'll find me in the phone book. Arturo Bestoso. And watch it, Finlay. They don't have banks where Blum's gone." He went on down, meeting the sandy-haired character coming in the clock tower door.

"Finlay?"

Bestoso hiked his thumb back toward Fish at the top of the stairs.

"Hi, Finlay. B. Meggs. Joe Henry sent me."

"Come on up," Fish said. He heard Bestoso speaking to the taxi driver. B. Meggs came shambling up the stairs. He was not only tall, lean and sandy-haired, he looked as if he'd heard the alarm but hadn't waked up enough to turn over and shut it off.

"Cops?"

Fish nodded. "Come in." He led the way into the living-room.

"Nice place you've got."

"All right. Don't tell me your grandfather—"

"He owned a grocery store in Pendleton, Oregon."

B. Meggs gave him a sleepy grin and put his hand inside his coat. "Joe said to give you this."

It was a folded piece of news copy paper, jagged where it had been ripped off the typewriter. It was a letter from Polly, the lines crooked, the punctuation mostly dashes, the sentences elliptic and the meaning plain.

"Joe," it said. "Important!!! Get picture, color if possible, Exhibit No. 43, Zirolli show Berdan Galleries Connecticut Avenue—La Dame aux Oeillets. I went to cover society angle —big deal for Zirolli—customers loaned portraits—all loaners named except the Dame with the Carnations best in show by long odds. Should be called La Dame aux Rubis and the rubies are what rang a bell. Talked with Zirolli— story off record but la dame is first Countess de G. Rubies terrific—I THINK I know where they came from—Blood all over them. Get your friend Fish Finlay for Lunch Friday—and picture—before I go to Newport. Will be in N Y Thurs. but Ive got a man to see—he wont talk over phone but 9 PM Thurs is a date. Get Picture before anything happens to No. 43."

"Polly R." was scrawled in pencil under it, and there was a postscript.

"Thanks for your efforts in re. Newport but I won't mind going up if I have the picture. I'll steer clear of dusty passages. Also grateful for Paris assignment I know you filched for me. Youre an angel. Love, P.R."

Fish read it a second time and looked at B. Meggs, propped against the paneled fireplace, squinting sleepily through his cigarette smoke.

"She was okay," B. Meggs said without moving. "Polly Regina, we called her, when her uncle dumped her on us. That 'R' after her name. I owe her twenty bucks she loaned me. I was going to buy flowers but I guess Scotch for the boys in the back room. She'd like it that way."

He rubbed his cigarette out on the brick lining of the fireplace.

"I've got the story, I guess, from the taxi driver and the AP man downtown. Any ideas? Joe'd like to help if he can. He loved her too."

"You'd better see Bestoso. He's probably waiting for you downstairs, anyway," Fish said. "The only thing I can think of would be to see this Mrs. Winton. But it can't be done. She's six deep at a place called Shepherd's Vale."

"Always try," said B. Meggs. "A week's rest, Joe's expense, sounds fine."

"If they let you out."

"Sure. We'll see. What's your phone listing?"

"Enniskerry, stable."

"Okay." He shambled over to the door. "You don't think the Winton dame shoved her over?"

"She shoved her all right," Fish said. "It's whether she killed her."

"She'll need a nice long rest, anyway."

"It could be longer. Much longer if they think she pushed the waiter in too. He was alive when he went in. He was a private detective named Blum."

"The AP man told me, off the record."

He ambled out onto the balcony and looked down. "I I guess Bestoso's through brainwashing my rickshaw boy. Gone, anyway. So long. I'll see you."

Fish thought of the empty beds in the two rooms next to his.

"I'd ask you to stay here, but I'm a guest myself."

"Thanks, all set," B. Meggs said. "Place called the Azores. Room seven. There's a strawberry blonde across the hall doesn't look too bad. Or too good. Whichever way one states a simple relative proposition. Joe wants Polly's letter back when you're through with it."

Fish nodded. B. Meggs, like A. Bestoso, seemed to get around a hell of a lot faster than F. Finlay, F. Finlay decided, deciding also to offer no advice to B. Meggs, gratuitous or otherwise. He looked back at Polly Randolph's letter, at the last typed line.

"Something did happen to Exhibit No. 43, I take it."

"What Joe says. Sent a man around next day. Couldn't get to first base. Called Joe, Joe called Zirolli, Zirolli clammed. Scared. Nobody's figured the deal yet."

"Polly knew Ferenc Blum in Paris," Fish said.

"No foolin'?" For a second B. Meggs looked alive and awake. "I better call Joe before I act on that one. What about Bestoso? He know about that angle?"

"I think not," Fish said. "But I wouldn't sell him short. He's a lot smarter than he looks."

"A shabby thing for the human race if most of us were not," B. Meggs commented, and departed without unseemly haste.

Caxson Reeves came out of the Chalet with Jennifer and Dodo.

"Finlay didn't get my message, I expect." He looked at his watch and raised his stick for his sister's chauffeur. "If you see him, Jennifer, will you tell him I'm conferring with the

106

'undisclosed principal'?" There was a bleak momentary gleam in his eye. "He'll know. Tell him I'll be around to see him at four. Or may I take you ladies home?"

"No, thanks, Mr. Reeves," Jenny said. "I have my car." She glanced at her mother stopping to talk to some friends behind them. "I'll tell him, sir. Mother wants to go by the Randolphs'. Just a minute, Mother."

She ran down the steps. She wanted to get her mother away from there before anybody else got hold of her to tell her how lovely her daughter's orchids were at the Randolphs' party. Just once more and she'd begin to wonder and then to ask, and it meant inventing a beau or telling her Mr. Vranek sent them, risking an explosion when everything was lovely. She hadn't even minded leaving Nikki playing backgammon in the cabaña. Nikki couldn't pay a sympathy call in shorts and a flowered shirt. And Peter had happily found himself another blonde. Now Jenny knew Fish Finlay wasn't coming, she wanted to get away herself. But getting her mother away from the butterfly orchids was the immediate problem. And it was already too late.

"Darling!" she said as she got in beside Jenny. "Those orchids. Shows what kind of a mother I am. They were so perfect with your hair I thought they were artificial. Not Peter?"

Jenny felt the laughing blue eyes examining the side view of her face, and knew she had to answer. She couldn't avoid it.

"Did *he* send them to you?"

"Who?" Jenny kept her eyes ahead as she turned the car away from Enniskerry, round to the Randolphs' on Ocean Drive.

"Your own lamppost lover, darling? Or have you forgotten about him in the whirl you. . . . Why, Jenny, baby! I didn't mean that. Pull over to the sea wall and stop, darling. I didn't mean to upset you. . . ."

It was the general strain, and the disappointment of not seeing him, that had upset her, and the sudden image of the flag at half-mast on the Chalet that was caught there in her side mirror, bringing Polly Randolph back and with Polly her own numb misery at the table after Polly left it. That's why Mr. Finlay hadn't come to the Chalet, of course, and why he hadn't wanted her around that morning in the stable. He really had been in love with Polly.

"Pull over, darling," her mother said gently. "Don't look so miserable, baby. What's the matter?"

Jenny stopped the car at the ledge. She fished out her handkerchief and blew her nose.

"It's nothing, really, Mother. It's . . . well, I just shouldn't have said anything, that's all. Because it's no use. He . . .

107

he wouldn't ever care anything about me, anyway. Not really, I mean."

Her mother hated the sun and the wind but she was sitting there being . . . being just like Anne Linton, Jenny thought, with a sudden surge of tenderness toward her that was new even in their new and warmer friendship. "You'll get all blown to pieces, Mummy."

"It doesn't matter, darling," Dodo said gently. "What's happened? Maybe I can help. Who is he, Jenny? Is it someone I know? I know how ghastly it is when you're young. I remember when I thought your father was in love with one of Polly Randolph's cousins. It was simply horrible."

Jenny closed her eyes a moment. That made it worse instead of better.

"I won't say you'll get over it, darling. Or some sleep would help. It's all true but you have to learn those things yourself. Where did you meet him?"

"On a road in Virginia," Jenny said. "It was when I was terribly upset about Anne getting married. I didn't want to come up here, because I didn't think we'd get along. I . . . I didn't know you could be so nice."

"I'm a stinker, Jenny."

"No you're not. You're wonderful, Mother." Jenny blinked quickly. "You've been marvelous. I'm . . . I'm so glad I came."

"Thank you, Jenny."

"But that's where I met him. He gave me a lift back to school. He . . . knew who I was but I didn't know him. And afterwards, he pretended we hadn't ever met. But I . . . just couldn't get him out of my mind. All spring I kept looking for him. I thought he liked me too. I thought he'd come back to the school, but he . . . but he didn't. It's Fish Finlay, Mother."

She put her head down, waiting, not wanting to look at her mother, waiting and almost holding her breath as the silence got longer and longer. She looked up then, not looking at her mother but seeing her, sitting perfectly still, her hands folded in her lap, her eyes fixed straight ahead of her out over the sea.

"You're . . . you're not going to be—"

"Oh no, Jenny. I was just thinking how . . . enormously wise we can be when we're very young. I think Fish is wonderful, Jenny. He's kind. He's self-contained. He's fun. I think a girl would be terribly happy with him, Jenny." She turned her shining gold head and smiled at her daughter. "But I don't think he'd marry a girl he *wasn't* in love with, and he'd never pretend to love one he didn't love."

"I know it."

108

"He's older than you," Dodo said gently. "But that wouldn't matter. You've had a miserably disjointed sort of life, so . . . dispossessed. You probably need somebody who's steady and . . . dependable. A boy your own age would have all your problems. I've thought about that, Jenny. It's funny, it was Fish who started me thinking about it, last April. I like to think maybe I'm not as much of a stinker as I know I am sometimes."

"Oh, Mother. . . ."

"No, sweetie." Dodo took her hand and squeezed it. "I've been a lousy mother. And if Fish. . . ." She shook her head. "I don't think there's anything I could do to help. It's something you'll have to work out yourself, Jenny dear. It's a little like birth and death, that way. Nobody can help you much." Then she smiled. "But I'd love it, Jenny. I'm very fond of him. I wouldn't feel I'd been as grim as I have been, if you had somebody like Fish to make up for all the things you . . . you haven't had."

She laughed suddenly. "There's one thing I *can* tell you, sweetie. Don't let him fall in Caxson Reeves's sister's hands. She'll marry him off to that walleyed grandchild of hers. Let's go home. That's probably why Caxey's coming around at four, to get him for her for the dance tonight. You keep your eye on him, baby. Nikki and I can go to the Randolphs' later. He ought to go, they're so devoted to him. Come along, let's go home. You're probably dying to see him anyway. And be terribly careful. Don't let Alla and Nikki know it. I've decided you and Fish were right . . . They both have their eye on you for that lout Peter. I wouldn't have you marry him for all the world, my pet."

As they turned in between the marble urns of marble flowers in the gate of the serpentine wall she said, "And I'm ever so glad you told me, Jenny. I'm ever so glad!"

The mauve shadows of the purple beeches on the shining blue of the car dyed it the color of the wine-dark sea until they came out into the sudden white and emerald of the courtyard as the chimes in the clock tower struck half-past three.

"His car's here, Mother," Jenny said quickly.

But her mother was looking at the black sedan standing in front of the porte-cochere, a United States government tag on the back of it, and at the heavy-set man with a briefcase just getting out. Jenny heard her catch her breath sharply, and turned to look at her.

"Mother . . . what's the matter?"

Her mother shook her head.

"Nothing."

But her face was thin and haggard, dead-white, almost

109

green from the reflected light of the emerald turf in the courtyard of Enniskerry. "Just let me out, Jenny. Then run and get
Fish. Tell him I need him. Ask him to come as quickly as he
can."

CHAPTER : 16

Jennifer Linton walked until she got inside the clock tower,
well out of sight of the man in the government sedan. Then
she ran up the stairs and knocked on the living-room door.
"Fish!" She waited a second before she opened it. He wasn't
there. Through the windows behind her she could see the
large heavy-set man taking off his gray felt hat and wiping
his forehead, waiting by the porte-cochere. She called again,
and ran through to the kitchen. The doors of the small foyer
were open, and she saw him on one of the bird's-eye maple
beds, his coat on the back of a chair, shades drawn, sound
asleep. She ran quickly through, catching her breath as she
stopped at the side of the bed, her whole young heart alive in
her face.

I hate to wake him, he must be worn out. She put her hand
on his shoulder. "Fish."

Fish Finlay opened his eyes.

Who can say how long a dream is, or how long it took the
phoenix to rise? How long the instant's iridescent brush of an
angel's wing as it passes to drop a single feather of its pure
incredible gold? It was to such an instant that Fish Finlay
awoke and saw the face of the dream he'd banished, and for
such an instant held it. Then he smiled.

"I thought I sent you home, Miss Linton."

Her cheeks flushed scarlet, bright. "Mother wants you,
quick. There's a man from the government. . . ."

"I'll be right there. You scoot along. He wasn't due till
four."

He reached out one hand to turn off the alarm he'd set for
ten minutes to, and the other for his coat.

"I'll go on over," Jenny said. She ran out, her knees trembling, her cheeks still fire hot.

*Now he knows I'm crazy about him . . . and he laughed
at me. He just thinks I'm a silly fool. And I shouldn't have
gone in his bedroom.* She rubbed her cheeks quickly. *I'll just
never dare face him again.*

She quickened her pace down the stairs, hearing him coming, and kept half a dozen steps ahead of him across the

courtyard. Dodo was on the porch with the man from the black sedan. He was putting his billfold back in his pocket.

"This is Mr. Finlay, and my daughter, Miss Linton," Dodo said. "Mr. Northrup." Her face was dead-white but her voice was steady. "It's all right . . . I'd like Mr. Finlay to be here." She turned to Fish. "Mr. Northrup is a United States Customs Agent from Boston."

Fish nodded to him, thinking intently. *The long distance call to the Collector of Customs, Port of Boston.* The operator hadn't been mistaken. . . ?

"Jenny, will you go upstairs and bring down my ruby necklace," Dodo said. "It's in a blue leather case on the second shelf of the safe in my dressing-room. Hurry, darling. I'd like to get this over with before the rest of them come home. It's a flat case with gold tooling around it."

Fish waited silently, his eyes on the large man with thinning gray hair and quiet manner.

"Will you sit down?" Dodo said. "And you, Fish." She sat down herself, took out her handkerchief and wiped the cold moisture from her upper lip. "It was very stupid, Mr. Northrup. I must have been out of my mind to do it."

She turned to Fish. "I didn't declare them," she said simply.

Fish Finlay took his own handkerchief out and wiped the cold sweat off the palms of his hands as two things Polly had said at the Randolphs' flashed into his mind. The first was about her cousin who'd called Dodo a moron. *She's bright bitter green about Dodo's new red necklace.* The other Polly had said when she was baiting de Gradoff about the ghost-woman who'd come in with the de Gradoffs to the party and whom she'd last seen looking at Dodo's rubies. Neither one of them had meant anything to him at the time, or meant anything now. He hadn't been close enough to Dodo to see the necklace, and he knew so little about jewels that it wouldn't have made any impression on him if he had been. Taken with the long-distance call and Polly's letter there in his pocket about the rubies covered with blood, it added up to a confusion that was nevertheless staggering. He wiped his forehead unobtrusively and put his handkerchief in his pocket.

Northrup opened his briefcase and consulted a notebook.

"We understand, Countess de Gradoff, that you brought a necklace and earrings of star rubies, set with diamonds, into this country through the Port of New York on June 10," he said. "You purchased them in Paris from a private owner?"

"That's correct," Dodo said. "May I ask who told you?"

He brought a receipt book out, laid it down on his briefcase and took out a pencil. "The source of our information is not given out."

111

There was a dull unhappy flush under the tight flesh over Dodo's cheekbones, her eyes were a cold hardening blue.

"I think I know what the source was," she said evenly.

"How much did you pay for the set of rubies, Countess de Gradoff?"

The flush deepened along Dodo's cheeks. For a moment she sat, her lips tight.

"Fifty thousand dollars."

Fish's hand on the way to his pocket for a cigarette stopped, and dropped quietly to his side. Jennifer Linton stopped in the doorway, the gold-tooled blue leather case in her hands, her face white-lipped, her gray eyes startled. She came across the porch and put the case in her mother's hands, moved back quickly and sat down on the end of the chaise, her face impassive as she watched her mother hand it over to the agent.

Northrup put the case by him on the table, calmly finished his writing, put his pencil down, picked up the case and opened it.

"They're very handsome."

Fish saw the stars caught in the sunlight gleaming out of the liquid pools of blood-red fire, the diamonds' blinding rays of molten sunlight around them.

"I've put down fifty thousand dollars, Countess," Northrup said. "I expect they'll have to be appraised." He counted the rubies. "Forty-eight. I'd say approximately eighty-five carats? Do you know the figure?"

"Eighty-seven," Dodo said impassively.

"And the diamonds?"

She shook her head.

"You got a bargain at fifty thousand, ma'am. It's a pity you didn't declare them."

"As a matter of fact, I never intended to wear them while I was here. I shouldn't have brought them in. I should have left them over there. It's not much of an excuse, but it's the only one I've got."

He tore the receipt out of his book, handed it to her, put the blue leather box in his briefcase, closed it and locked it.

"Paying the duty would have saved you a good deal. If it's any consolation, it's not a criminal offense. You've only to pay."

"How much will it—"

"The domestic value plus the penalty, if you wish to recover the jewels. It depends on the appraisal. If we take your figure of fifty thousand, that plus fifteen thousand duty you should have paid, or sixty-five thousand, is what we call the domestic value. The penalty is one hundred per cent. That makes one hundred thirty thousand, doesn't it."

He picked his hat up from the floor.

"We'll notify you about the hearing. It'll be at the Assistant Collector's office here in Newport. Either you or your attorney can attend."

As he got to his feet, Jennifer Linton said quietly, "How much will the person who gave you this . . . information get, Mr. Northrup? You call it . . . isn't there a name for it?"

Northrup hesitated. "Why, it's a matter of public knowledge, I expect. Yes, it's called moiety. A person furnishing original information may receive twenty-five per cent of the total net amount recovered by the Treasury, up to fifty thousand dollars. If there aren't any expenses in the present case, you can easily figure what twenty-five per cent of one hundred and thirty thousand dollars is."

Finlay had already figured it.

Northrup turned to Dodo. "Thank you, Countess de Gradoff." He included Jenny and Fish in his "Good day," went calmly down the front steps and got in his car.

On the porch was silence. It was broken by the sound of the black sedan starting, and leaving, by another car entering the drive between Enniskerry's purple beeches, and by Dodo.

"Oh my God," she said, and put her head in both her hands. "What will I do, here comes Caxson Reeves."

A Rolls Royce of the vintage of Reeves's yellow poplin suit came sedately into the driveway. Jenny got up quickly. "Oh, I forgot to tell you, Mr. Finlay—"

The chauffeur, old and almost clerical-looking, had seen them on the porch and came on, stopping where the Customs Agent's car had been.

Dodo sat with her head thrown back, gazing up at the ceiling, until she heard the door shut and Reeves's feet on the scallop shells. Then she brought her head back into normal position, remarkably composed, Fish thought, under the circumstances.

"Hello, Caxey," she said. "You've always been a bird of evil omen. Except that you come after the fact, not before." She stirred without getting up. "Sit down, will you, dear. Jenny, I think we could all do with a drink of some kind. Would you ring for Moulton. And you sit down, Fish. Don't just stand there looking like you'd swallowed a dead octopus."

"I'll get Moulton, and then I have to go, Mother." Jenny waited for her mother to get through with Fish before she started for the door. "Is that all right? I have to run downtown a minute."

"Rats deserting the sinking ship," Dodo remarked. "Do run along, darling. I'd like to go myself."

She turned back to Reeves. "You might as well have it straight, Caxey," she said calmly. "I bought a ruby necklace for fifty thousand dollars and I didn't declare it. The man you just saw is a Customs Agent from Boston. Somebody told them."

Caxson Reeves had pulled up his narrow trouser legs and sat down, putting his old panama hat on the floor. He looked as sere and yellow a leaf in Newport as he did in New York, lids hooded, as dry and detached as ever.

"I expected as much when you asked Fish the day you landed if you had any money floating loose and said you'd take a chance," he remarked. "The amount involved in all that surprises me."

"All right, Caxey." Dodo turned her head as Moulton came in wheeling the bar. "Just leave it, Mr. Finlay'll pour for us. I'd like a Martini, Fish. And before I forget it, I'm expecting you to dinner tonight." She smiled at Reeves, not at Fish. "He belongs to *us*, darling." There was a touch of malice in her voice, just over or under its matter-of-fact, slightly bitter quality, indicating that she and Caxson Reeves were on a level of discourse that each entirely understood, if Fish did not.

"I'll have a small bourbon, Finlay. Water. No ice."

"You don't need ice, darling."

Caxson Reeves gave her a wintry smile. "I haven't said a thing, Dodo. Everything I have to say I said a long time ago."

"And I haven't asked you for anything, have I? It was a gamble. I took it. I lost it. So that's that. The fifty thousand was my own money. I saved it between husbands . . . for the rainy day when my child's twenty-two. I bought the rubies as an investment, actually. I got them absurdly cheap. I don't particularly like them for myself, I'm not the ruby type. I was just going to put them in a vault and keep them. I don't know why in hell I ever decided to wear them last night. Maybe I *ought* to be under observation."

Her eyes were coals of molten sapphire.

"And how I got tight enough to shoot off my bloody mouth to Polly Randolph I'll never know. The little witch. But maybe, if all I had was seventy-five dollars a week, I'd sell my friends down the river too. Thirty-two thousand five hundred is a lot of seventy-five dollar weeks. But it's my own fault. I'm not asking anybody to weep with me or for me. If I'd tossed my fifty thousand away in the stock market you wouldn't just sit there saying I told you so, though, Caxey dear. You'd at least be sorry. Or say you were."

Reeves sipped his bourbon and put the glass on the table.

"Are you through now, Dodo?" he inquired. "I don't wonder you're angry. But frankly, I don't believe Polly Randolph informed on you."

"It wasn't Polly," Fish said quietly. "Someone here put in

114

a long-distance call over the phone in the stable, last night, to the Collector of Customs in Boston."

"That's nonsense, Fish, unless you did it yourself," Dodo said sharply. "Or unless it was that old devil Vranek, and the maid told him I was wearing them. He'd take a chance to get me in trouble if he could."

"That's ridiculous, Dodo, and you know it," Caxson Reeves said. "Vranek—"

"Well, some stinker did it, and you can't expect me to like it, can you?"

"I could have expected you to remember the other times it's happened. The bolt of lace we paid three thousand five hundred for. At which time—"

"At which time you said if it happened again I could go to hell, only in more becoming terms." She smiled at him without warmth, picked up the olive at the bottom of her glass and threw it at a robin perched inquisitively on the verandah rail. "So that's that, and the hell with it. I'm certainly not going to give you the satisfaction of hearing me implore you to bail me out, or the equal pleasure of refusing . . . or even capitulating, with another lecture on the evil of my ways. I've made mistakes that cost me less and made my heart ache a lot more. So that, Caxey darling, finishes the saga of the rubies. The hell with them. Jenny's promised not to let me starve. And so, much as I love both of you, the very sight of you gives me a terrific pain in a portion of my anatomy you don't know exists, Caxey darling. I'm getting off it now."

She got abruptly to her feet.

"And going upstairs." She moved a step toward the door and stopped, looking back toward the beeches. "Please stay if you like, but if you hurry you'll avoid my husband and his cousins, which I'm definitely doing for the moment. I'll break the news to Nikki later. He'll be livid. Goodbye, my dears . . . I'll see you at eight, Mr. Finlay."

She went rapidly into the house. They could hear her heels on the stairs as the sleek black car swerved dramatically in and alongside the ancient Rolls. Caxson Reeves picked up his hat without haste but without visible delay and rose.

"How do you do, Mrs. Emlyn . . . de Gradoff." He bowed slightly to each of them. De Gradoff's eyes were confidently clear, his casual arrogance untouched, a handsome man entirely at ease on his own verandah, being cordial even, in an offhand way. In his shorts and flowered shirt, sun-browned hairy bosom bare, he seemed as symbolic of something, there beside Reeves in his antiquated yellow poplin, as the black car was beside the Rolls and the clerical chauffeur. Symbolic of precisely what, Fish Finlay did not get to in the sudden interest provided him by Mrs. Emlyn's complete recovery of all her lazy lacquer . . . plus a diamond hard and diamond bright something he couldn't define and could feel rather than see, lurking deeply behind the dark velvet luster of her eyes as they met his and moved on.

Tiger! tiger! burning bright, in the forests of the night. . . . It flashed into his mind as she crossed the porch to the bar with the liquid grace of the tiger's sister, a panther with her young behind her, if that wasn't ridiculously farfetched for Peter following her with a panther-like ease of his own. He had scarcely more than nodded to Reeves, who had done still less toward him, and his "Hi, Finlay" suggested unsubtle olfactory nuances.

"We'll see you this evening, I'm afraid," Caxson Reeves said, pleasantly, so that it sounded as if he'd said "I expect," unless they bothered to think about it after he and Fish went down the steps. He stopped at the Rolls. "You needn't wait, Hanson. Tell my sister Mr. Finlay's taken for dinner, and that it's my fault, I didn't get her message to him in time."

"Very good, sir."

"We'll go over to your place, Finlay. I'll have a drink to get the taste of the other one out of my mouth. These people offend me. Not Mrs. Emlyn, she's quite lovely. The de Gradoffs. I find something intolerably blatant about the public display of too much human flesh, female or male. Except on the beach."

Jenny's blue convertible was gone. Fish had seen her come around, backing her car out so she would not have to pass in front of the porch. There was probably nothing in his belief that the sun was not so bright as it had been before. He waited for Reeves to pause a moment before starting up the clock tower stairs.

"What about the rubies?" he asked. "Someone did call the Customs from here."

"It could have been Vranek, if he knew about them. He dislikes her enough. As for the rubies, I'll need information she's in no mood to give rationally at the moment. The value of the stones is important. I like the way she's taking it. Reminded me of her father. Especially her saving up the fifty thousand," he added dryly.

In the loft room he put his hat on the table. Fish went to get glasses, water, ice and soda. When he came back Reeves was sitting on the sofa gazing absently into the empty fireplace. He looked up.

"Did Jennifer give you my message?"

"She forgot. The Customs Agent caught us all flatfooted."

"I told her to tell you I was having a conference with the 'undisclosed principal' who made the friendly inquiry into the progress of our plans for paying de Gradoff's debts. I must be very blind. I'm utterly incapable of seeing what it is de Gradoff has that softens the brain of hardheaded people. I understand old Randolph loaned him five thousand dollars last week."

Fish handed him his bourbon and water. "How much does he owe Durban?"

"You know him, do you?"

"Polly pointed him out to me last night. He was with Mrs. Emlyn at a table across the garden." He poured soda into his own glass and stirred it. "The police are looking for him," he added deliberately. "At my suggestion."

"What for?"

"I think he can identify your French detective Blum. I assumed you probably couldn't."

Caxson Reeves' hooded lids raised abruptly. His colorless eyes rested on Fish for several moments. "I've never seen the man in my life," he remarked quietly.

"If we could give Lieutenant Bestoso the report Blum made to his client," Fish said, "plus the information that last night Blum discovered the one thing he needed to finish his case, he could nail de Gradoff down. The bank wouldn't have to come into it at all. Bestoso's plenty good."

Reeves's foot switched back and forth like a cat's tail. "I'll see what can be done," he said abruptly. "Young Dr. McNair told me you'd been to see him. What's the matter with Dodo?"

"She could be taking Benzedrine, or something of the sort, without knowing it. She's afraid of cancer. She looks a lot better today. When I saw her yesterday. . . . She doesn't look good, but after the load she had on last night—"

"I saw her." Reeves shook his head. He was silent for a moment. "Durban's been told she may have cancer," he said then. "Mrs. Emlyn told him. That's one of the reasons he hasn't gone to her. The other is something else Mrs. Emlyn told him. If he insists on going, he may kill the golden goose. If Dodo's disillusioned, she might react so violently, in her present state, that she'd divorce Nikki and nobody would get anything."

"Did you tell him to go and see her by all means?" Fish inquired.

"A temptation I resisted. I don't want to force de Gradoff's hand, if you're correct. Durban believes he got the dirty end of the stick from the Argentine outfit. That's why he took over some sixty thousand dollars worth of de Gradoff's debts —at Mrs. Emlyn's request. She told him if Nikki could be tided over he could marry a rich American. He was paid twenty-five thousand six weeks ago. Where it came from, I don't know. He'd like the rest. I understand that. I don't understand Mrs. Emlyn's concern. Have you any information?"

"Only what she told me. Her nephew, period."

"The young man?"

"He must have a rich wife. Obligatory, for some reason."

"Jennifer Linton, I presume."

A knock at the door cut him off.

"Jennifer Linton, till this noon, anyway." Fish went over to the door and opened it.

"Why, Miss Linton," he said.

Her cheeks flushed, defensively hot, as he smiled at her.

CHAPTER : 17

"It's Mr. Reeves I came to see."

Caxson Reeves had started to rise, but hearing her and seeing her, and seeing Fish, he sat down, very abruptly for anyone so inured to the human race, including the Maloneys. *Well, bless my soul. I knew that he. . . . I'd never dreamed that she. . . . Bless me.* He picked up his glass, and put it down again. Then he got up, courteously, as she brushed past Fish Finlay, her cheeks still warm, avoiding his eyes.

"I'm sorry to interrupt, Mr. Reeves," she said. "But I thought you'd listen to me. Mr. Finlay won't. I came over last night to tell him, but he just sends me home. . . ."

"As indeed he should," said Caxson Reeves. "But sit down, young lady. I'm more than happy to listen. What—"

She sat down on the edge of the sofa, conscious of the hooded scrutiny leveled on her.

"It's ridiculous for Mr. Finlay to pretend I don't know anything that's going on," she said hotly. "I told him last night that I didn't believe poor Mrs. Winton hurt Polly. And I still don't believe it. Because I heard Polly talking to Nikki . . . about the woman with the carnations. I told Mr. Finlay she shouldn't have done it. I told him I knew where she got it all . . . from that portrait in Washington."

"Portrait?" Reeves was puzzled. "I'm afraid I don't follow."

She pushed her hair back impatiently. Fish Finlay reached in his pocket for a cigarette, watching her intently.

"I'm sorry," she said. "I told Mr. Finlay when he was in Virginia—I think I must have known without knowing it who he was, because I'd never told anybody before—about the Argentine girl at school. Nikki's first wife was a cousin of theirs. It's a big family and terribly important, and Nikki's wife was sort of a black sheep for marrying him. And this girl . . . she's a very good friend of mine, and her parents told

118

her a few more things so she could tell me. The portrait was one of them."

"What portrait, Jennifer?" Reeves asked patiently.

"It was a portrait the first wife was having painted for Nikki as a surprise, for his birthday. The first thing anybody knew about it was when the artist had a show in Washington, and there was a picture called 'La Dame aux Oeillets.' But a friend of theirs recognized it and told them, and they got hold of the artist right away, and he told them. He told them she was terribly pleased with it, and just had one more sitting the next day, so he couldn't believe it when he heard next morning she'd killed herself."

Reeves listened impassively.

"The portrait's gone now, Jenny," Fish said. "Did you know—"

"Of course," she said impatiently. "They bought it. They didn't want it just hanging there like that. And the reason it was was that the artist wrote Nikki and told him he was painting it and how much it would cost and Nikki said he'd better scrape the paint off and use the canvas for something else. So the artist finished it and just called it 'The Lady with the Carnations.' You see, Nikki didn't know—"

She broke off and looked at Fish. "The Argentine family weren't just being callous. They had her body exhumed, and there was nothing there. But they had a letter she'd written just before she went to bed that night, that her maid had posted, saying how happy she was and how divine Nikki was, and to prove it how he'd given her the de Gradoff rubies. When they came to look over her things, there weren't any rubies. But there was a canceled check for $60,000, in francs, and on the stub she'd written 'to redeem de Gradoff rubies.' Nikki brought the rubies out then, and they took one look at them and said he could have them. They knew right away there was something wrong with them. They didn't understand how he'd given them to her if she'd paid that much to 'redeem' them, though if they were in pawn you could say he'd given them to her, because they were worth an awful lot more. And they told Nikki he could have them and the letter she wrote the night she died if he'd give up any claim to the rest of her estate."

She stopped a moment, frowning, and looked back at Fish Finlay.

"That's what I thought Polly was talking about last night. When she was describing the woman with the carnations I knew she'd seen the portrait. She'd told me she'd been in Washington. And when she said she'd seen the woman looking at my mother's rubies, the way Nikki looked at Polly scared me. I was sure he thought she knew about the rubies
119

some way. And this morning, when mother said Polly was so excited about them, I could see him just waiting, standing there all tense, to see if Polly had told her anything about them. I think now he was scared Polly might have told her she'd bought the rubies that had belonged to his first wife. But I didn't know then what was wrong with them."

"Do you know now?" Caxson Reeves asked patiently.

She nodded. "That's what I just went downtown for. And what gave me the idea was the way the Customs Agent looked at my mother when she said she'd paid fifty thousand dollars for them. He didn't believe her. It was like the Argentines not believing it about the sixty thousand dollars."

"It seems like a lot of money to me," Reeves said.

"Especially when they didn't look like much, until you saw them lying out there in the sun. Then they were fabulous . . . and that's just the point. I went down Bellevue Avenue to see the man at Chenier Frères—mother's a customer of theirs in Paris. And he just laughed at me. He said there's no such thing as a necklace of star rubies. It would be a 'criminal waste,' because they're dull unless the light strikes down on them to show the star. And they're too valuable to waste, he said. One star ruby as big as I described would bring fifty thousand dollars. He thought I was being funny."

She managed a smile herself. "And there's another thing. This morning, when Nikki realized Polly hadn't told mother about the rubies, he caught himself and said it was surprising Polly'd be excited about jewels she wouldn't look well in. But she was almost the same coloring as the woman in the portrait. So I asked the man at Chenier's what type of woman would wear rubies, and he said, 'Why, Miss Linton, you have the perfect type at Enniskerry. Your mother's friend, the lovely Mrs. Emlyn.' "

Caxson Reeves was watching her intently. "What inference do you draw, Jennifer?" he asked quietly.

She flushed a little. "I don't mean to sound brash. But I think Mrs. Emlyn's just the one they do belong to, or did. If there's something wrong about them and you couldn't sell them openly, you'd sell them privately—to one woman who wants heirlooms and to another who doesn't but loves a bargain. If you just sell them to Nikki's wives, they'd still be in the family. And if mother smuggled them in and you reported her and got the moiety of thirty-two thousand five hundred dollars, you'd be sure she'd pay up and get them back . . . and that isn't bad business, is it?"

"It isn't," Caxson Reeves agreed dryly. His eyes met Finlay's. Jenny had left the verandah before Fish had told them about the telephone call to Boston.

"Polly may have known something about them," Fish said.

He took the letter B. Meggs had brought out of his pocket and handed it to Reeves, who took out his half-spectacles and read it. He handed it to Jennifer.

"She shouldn't have told him," Jenny said again, when she'd read it. "It was just a . . . an invitation to murder."

Fish started a little, and Reeves's saurian lids twitched just once, as if a grain of desert dust had blown too close.

"Have you told Jennifer about your visit to Dr. McNair?" he asked. "If not, you'd better."

She listened gravely. "I thought there must be something wrong with her. Last night. . . . I've seen people drunk. They go to sleep. My mother was wide-awake all night, and the maid told me it's the same every night. Anyway, she hasn't had anything today. I tipped over her martini and I traded my iced tea for her coffee at lunch." She got up. "I didn't drink it. But tonight. . . . One dose wouldn't hurt me, and we'll see."

"No." Fish and Caxson Reeves said it together. "You can't tell," Reeves added. "It might be more than Benzedrine."

"But you saw how she looked last night. It scares me. So maybe I'd better get back home. I just wanted to tell you. . . ."

Reeves got up. "I'll go down with you."

"Shall I run you home, sir?"

Fish went over to the door with them.

"I'll walk," Reeves said. "I'll take the short cut through the gardeners' lane. I'll see you at the dance."

"Is he going with you people?" Jenny asked as they went out the tower door into the drive.

Caxson Reeves looked at her with a dry smile.

"He's going with you people," he said. He saw the quickening glow he kindled. "Did you know he was engaged to a girl once? His sister told me. She threw him over when he lost his leg. If you want to marry him, Jennifer, you'll have to ask him. He'll never ask you."

He tipped his old yellow panama. "Goodbye, I'll see you this evening. Be careful, Jennifer. If you were married, I'd feel a great deal easier about both you and your mother."

He left her standing there and went through the cedar fence to take the short cut home. He had reached the gate and closed it behind him before Jenny Linton could untangle the curious skein of multicolored astonishment that held her there, and then sent her suddenly dancing feet across the emerald medallion and up the steps. She was hurrying around to her own back entrance when she heard her mother's voice in the hall.

"Darling . . . you're being positively hysterical!" Dodo

was saying. Her own voice was pitched not far from it. "I don't see what you're making such a ghastly row about it for. Nobody—"

Jenny swallowed quickly and went through into the hall. They were all on the second floor balcony, her mother and Alla Emlyn in dressing gowns, Peter with a bath towel wrapped around him, de Gradoff in his shorts, and the servants Moulton, Elsa, the other maid and the cook, all properly dressed, all of them shaken, de Gradoff standing alone outside his open bedroom door, his face transformed with impotent rage, turned on the servants, drawn together protectively behind Moulton at the corner of the spindled rail.

Jenny stopped cold, staring up at them. Alla Emlyn was holding on to the rail across the stair well, her face a different kind of white, her dark eyes grown so they were the only part of it Jenny really saw.

"I think you're crazy, Nikki." Peter de Gradoff was openly rude, almost contemptuous. "You're making a damned ass of yourself. You lay off the gin awhile, your brain's soft."

He turned and strode back into his room, slamming the door. But de Gradoff hadn't heard him. His eyes, blue and swift as dragonflies, had darted over to Jenny, fastening themselves, frigidly malignant, on her, as naked for an instant as his own rigid torso above the polished rail. He started to speak, but Dodo had seen her too and moved abruptly forward.

"Nikki." She put her hand on his arm, her voice taut but controlled. "You're being fantastic, Nikki! Moulton's told you what happened." She turned to him. "I'm sorry, Moulton. Mr. de Gradoff isn't himself. Go get them, and throw them out. Pitch them over the cliff, get thoroughly rid of them and see that it doesn't happen again. The rest of you go on with your work. I'll be down to talk to you. Alla, you'd better go dress. Jenny, go on to your room, darling."

De Gradoff jerked his arm from her hand, his anger still rigidly focused on his stepdaughter. Dodo turned and spoke quietly down to her.

"Jenny, did you bring Nikki a basket of flowers?"

Jenny stared blankly up at her. Still dazed by the suppressed violence of the scene above her, she took the question as literally as it was asked.

"What would I be doing, bringing Nikki flowers?" she asked incredulously, and with such complete conviction that there was instant silence on the balcony.

Moulton went to the bedroom door.

"I'm sorry, sir," he said stiffly. "Elsa went to hang up your evening clothes when the cleaner brought them at one o'clock. She saw the basket sitting on the floor beside your bed. She thought you'd brought them in. She put them in a

122

vase and put them on the table. None of us were aware you had a . . . an allergy, sir. However, I'm sure the staff understands, madame." He bowed to Dodo. "I'm sure no one will feel obliged to give immediate notice." He turned back to Elsa and the other two. "Carry on, please. Cocktails at a quarter to eight is correct, is it not, madame?"

"Thank you, Moulton."

He went into de Gradoff's room. Jenny was at the top of the stairway going to her room when he came out and passed her with a crystal bowl of pink and white carnations, their spicy fragrance filling the hall. She hurried on into her room, closed the door and stood there, startled at the chill running up and down her spine. After a moment she opened the door quietly. Nikki and her mother were gone, so was Mrs. Emlyn. Elsa was coming down the hall from her mother's room. Jenny beckoned her into her room and closed the door again.

"What happened?"

"They were just there on the floor, miss, like somebody had set them down and forgotten to pick them up, in a willow-plaited basket, by his bed. But he acted so strange, miss. He came rushing out. He wasn't angry at first, he was shaking all over. Then he got angry and called everybody out and started accusing us. I didn't think he was right in his mind for a few moments, miss. And I hope Mrs. Huggins stays to finish dinner. She thinks this house is . . . is very strange, anyway. Her sister's a medium in Boston and she feels vibrations. I don't know what she'll make of this. But your mother's gone down to speak to her. Shall I run your tub, miss?"

"I'll do it. But you can come back later and zip me up if you will."

She locked the door when the maid had closed it and stood there, the chill still along her spine as she glanced over at the spray of butterfly orchids on her desk. That would seem to be the immediate explanation . . . but the gardeners wouldn't know about the portrait, and there were no carnations in the greenhouses across the cedar fence. She knew, because she'd looked when she went to explain to Mr. Vranek about the rut in the turf edge. And Polly Randolph was dead, so Fish was the only other person who'd know.

The threshold between the natural and the supernatural was very ill-defined in her mind then, as she stood there, rejecting and not rejecting.

I wonder if the woman from the Argentine could have come . . . if the rubies and everything could someway have brought her back, to try to help my mother?

Two things were sure. Her mother had no idea why Nikki was so beside himself, and Alla Emlyn did know. . . . The way she was holding to the balcony rail with one hand, clutching her robe with the other, the look in her eyes, as if she'd seen the ghost walk right there in front of them. *But there are no such things as ghosts . . .* and the carnations were real.

She went quickly across the room to the alcove, pulled the telephone across the bed where she could watch the porch through the grille and asked the operator for the stable number.

"Fish . . . this is Jenny. Did you put a basket of carnations in Nikki's room?"

"Did I do what?"

The surprise in his voice gave his answer the same convincing quality her own had had. She repeated the question.

"No," he said.

"Somebody did."

"Maybe it was the lady herself. Maybe Enniskerry's really haunted."

CHAPTER : 18

Fish Finlay meant it to sound mildly amusing, but he knew it had no such content, for he had just seen the semblance of a ghost of sorts himself. He had stopped at the sink for a drink of water and looked down into the vegetable garden. A dusty blue gnome in a faded brown hat was in one of the cordoned squares, spraying the mauve-green plums, one of the two old gardeners. He sprayed and moved back, raising his head to avoid the wind drift, and Fish saw the face under the faded brown hat. It was a face he'd seen before, and as he stared down at it, puzzled, it came suddenly into his mind. He'd seen it that morning, passing him in the doorway of room No. 7 of the Azores in Thames Street . . . the sad-faced man in the blue work denims and blue denim hat.

It was just at that moment that the phone rang. When he'd answered Jenny, he put it down and went back to the kitchen window, puzzled by the carnations, but still more puzzled by what one of the Enniskerry gardeners had been doing in room No. 7 of the Azores. Until he looked over at the greenhouses. Caxson Reeves was in the doorway, just leaving, his short cut a matter of distance, not time. The other gardener was trotting along behind him. Old Right Hand Reeves checking with another of the hired left hands. . . . Because, of course, it had to be the gardeners who superintended the locks on Jenny's door and windows, and Caxson Reeves would be too conspicuous going to the Azores himself to check on M. Blum's personal belongings before the police arrived.

"Well, well," Fish Finlay said, with a sardonic salute to his own retarded development in the field of intrigue. With his known interest in tree planting (Finlay of the banished dreams), Reeves had no doubt counted on his visiting the gardeners himself. If anyone could guess what went on in Reeves's mind, that is. Finlay abandoned it, when he heard the clock strike seven and remembered abruptly that his only white dinner coat had been a mess when he took it off at six A.M. He went in to take a look at it before he called Dodo to regret, and found that Moulton was as far ahead of him in his department as Reeves was in his. It was there in the closet, clean and pressed. He had no excuse to avoid the dance, and no particular wish to, he realized, his only regret, in fact, that Moulton hadn't provided a red carnation for his buttonhole.

His heart was strangely quiet. It had been, since he opened his eyes to see Jenny Linton's face bending over him and knew the decision was his to. make. He'd make it, and could face himself in the mirror knowing the loneliness would come again, but come with a difference. For the moment a curious muted peace seemed to hang over him there in the loft. No premonitory shadow wavered, or light flickered, to suggest how frayed the rope or deep the abyss, or how near its edge they were.

At half-past seven he went down the clock tower steps and looked across the courtyard. No one was on the verandah except Moulton bringing ice and glasses and stopping to straighten the chairs. Fish paused inside the hexagonal hall. There was a door at the side of the staircase. He opened it. It led into a passage. On the right was a door opening into the part of the stable under his bedroom end, where the cars were kept. At the end of the passage an open door led into the gardeners' domain. He went through it and strolled out into the vegetable garden. A path along the cordoned fruit trees led toward a terraced garden under the spindled balustrade between the stable and the house. He looked back toward the greenhouses, and seeing neither of the little blue gnomes, went on along the path to the terraces, looking into the stable windows, at the elegant box stalls made of polished walnut, waxed and gleaming, the rails between them decorated with sheaves of ripe wheat and faded cornflowers. At the end of the cordoned path, he glanced back up at the porch again. Its only occupant was Nikki de Gradoff at the bar, a circumstance that he viewed with no interest. He turned down the center corridor of turf between the shallow-terraced rose gardens and went along until the roses ended and he came to the rocks, heather flowing like spilled wine over them, creeping out into the narrow trail along the cliff to the right, where the sound was coming from.

Sound was all he could call it, hearing it first halfway down the turf stairs. It was a roar, but quite distinct from the roar of the surf he could hear beating at the bottom of the cliff. As he went along the trail toward it, it changed abruptly. It sounded exactly as if some gargantuan unseen beast was suddenly and violently sucking air into his mouth just after he'd spewed out some scalding mess . . . unless the gargantuan beast was the Satan himself, as this must be the Devil's Chasm, he thought, that Caxson Reeves had said ought to have a rail around it and that Dodo had called the Rock and said not to go near when he'd had a drink, one of their friends had tried it. He had not had a drink for a couple of hours, but he approached it cautiously nevertheless, by ear alone, and found himself abruptly much closer to the edge than he'd imagined, even warned by the purple heather cringing back from the spume-poisoned rim. There it was, the deep jagged cleft in the rock, full of the tumultuous rage of the white sea horse, captive in his box stall of living rock, before the long withdrawing roar of the crested waves released him and the unseen monster sucked in the air to breathe, until the rearing sea charged in again.

He watched it, its violence fascinating. The cleft was perhaps not five feet in width, the rocks on the far side as flat and as barren, except for the poison ivy growing out of the shallow fissures. He could understand the impulse of the young man in the bathtub-gin days who'd tried to leap it. He felt it himself . . . and then, for a fraction of an instant, he thought the cold chill crawling up his spine was fear, a sharp reminder that it took two good legs to make a broad jump. But for a fraction of an instant only, and then he knew it was not that, and that someone was there close behind him . . . and knew also, with a sudden flash of knowledge, that what was happening to him was what had happened to Polly Randolph and to Ferenc Blum. The place and the time were different, the menace was the same, and his bad leg made him as unequal in the event as each of them had in different ways been unequal.

He braced himself and swung around. The instant held rigid . . . the sea roaring and the rising terraces hiding the verandah where help could have been, as the sea had roared and the rose-covered rock had hidden the garden full of people from the Randolphs' fishing platform. There there had been a rail. Here was nothing. He was caught in the apex of a triangle, one side the sucking chasm, one side the cliff down into the sea, and from the base of the triangle de Gradoff was moving deliberately toward him, his whole body alert as a tiger's is alert, except that a tiger wears no smiling mask to charm and deceive.

How narrow is the escape from death? Or is there a wide band of unseen shadow across which an unseen hand may reach and save? Was it chance alone that an angry order had been literally carried out, a crystal bowl of fresh-cut flowers pitched over the cliff into the sea, and by chance alone that one of them was caught, clear and lovely pink, on the mane of the white sea horse and carried back to toss on the vortex of swirling foam in the Devil's Chasm sucking the wave into its jagged mouth? And that de Gradoff saw it as he took his last forward step?

Fish Finlay knew only that something had happened as the smiling mask was ripped apart and the taut body went flaccid. He stepped around de Gradoff into the path between the heather-covered rocks to the turf stairs, and turned back then.

"Coming up?" he asked.

"Yes," de Gradoff said.

It took him a moment to say it, a curious pallor behind the vivid blue of his eyes.

"I . . . came down to speak to you about Dodo's necklace. She has the mad idea she isn't going to try to recover it. You must—"

"Sorry. You'll have to talk to Mr. Reeves."

There was a chill at the base of Fish Finlay's spine as he looked past de Gradoff at the Devil's Chasm. It would have been a natural . . . Nikki his own eyewitness. Poor Finlay with his bad leg got too near the edge. Treacherous spot, should have been railed off. Another murder no one could ever prove.

He reached in his pocket for a cigarette, aware that de Gradoff was watching him intently without seeming to watch him at all.

He's not sure if I know.

It was a curious sensation, walking casually up through a rose garden with his own murderer. More curious that Alla Emlyn should be coming swiftly to meet them. Her geranium-red evening dress was like a raw flame blowing in the wind. She stopped short when she saw them, between the urns on the balustrade, and stood stock-still an instant before the taut swift lines of her body were fluid again and she waited, half-turned to go back to the porch.

"I thought you'd both deserted us," she remarked, moving lazily up the steps. "Dodo has, and Peter's being perfectly horrid to Jenny. He says her driving's a menace to—"

"It's not either, Mr. Finlay," Jenny said hotly. Fish looked at her. There was a martini glass in her hand. Her eyes were bright and her cheeks flushed. "Peter thinks I'm afraid to drive over forty, but I was just waiting for my one-thousand mile check-up. I had it made while we were at the Casino playing tennis, and tomorrow I can drive seventy. I'll prove it to you if you don't believe me."

"It's a deal." Peter grinned at her and pulled himself up out of the wicker chaise. "Anybody want a drink? Jenny?"

"No, thanks. Mother and I have had our quota. I think mine's gone to my head." Fish looked at her again as she laughed. "But Mrs. Emlyn needs one. You look cold, Mrs. Emlyn."

"Cold. . . ."

Fish heard Alla Emlyn repeat the word slowly. Nikki had moved over to the bar and was pouring himself a drink. Alla was standing where she and Fish had stopped, Fish to look at Jenny Linton and Alla, because she seemed to need to steady herself a moment, her hand on the back of a chair.

When she spoke then her voice was so low, the quality of it so extraordinary, that Fish glanced around at her, not knowing if she meant him to hear her.

"Cold. . . ? My God, I'm horribly horribly cold. . . ."

He felt more than saw the shudder that went through her before she moved on and sat down, composed again. "Thanks, darling. I think Peter can get me a small spot of Scotch. On the rocks, no water."

Then, before Fish could unravel any of the odd confusion in his mind, Dodo came out onto the porch.

"Look, all of you," she said abruptly. Her cheeks were pale and her eyes bright, but with a glitter of anger, not the hectic glitter of yesterday. "My cook's walked out. She says she's psychic and the place is haunted. That's for you and your damned carnations, Nikki, dear. But never mind, angels. I've called Peel's and they've got a table. I've ordered you cocktails and a lovely meal, so put your glasses down and scoot."

"But, my darling—"

"Listen, Nikki." Dodo's voice was nearer the cutting edge than Fish, and certainly Nikki, had ever heard it. "You can't speak to servants in America the way you can abroad. They leave. The cook's left. Now I'd like to keep the rest of them. So you people kindly get the hell out, for my sake, as well as theirs. I'm at the end of my rope too, and if you don't get out I'll scream. And don't come back, any of you. I'm going to bed and I'm going to *sleep.* Now get out, *please!*"

Her voice was like a piece of wet silk ripped apart.

"Certainly, darling." Alla's voice was lazy, but she rose at once. "Come along, everybody. Fish, you go with Peter and Jenny, and see she doesn't drive any seventy, will you? Nikki and I'll come along after you. I know exactly how you feel, Dodo, dear."

128

Fish Finlay hesitated, the warning click of a switch in some cold dark room of his mind, until Jenny stopped close beside him.

"It's all right," she whispered quickly. "Elsa's staying with her in my room. She's going to lock it, and I've got the key. And tonight . . . I'm going to *tell* him."

Then it was a sharper fear dragging him along, not knowing what she was going to tell, until abruptly halfway through dinner he heard her across the table in the crowded room of the lobster palace on the pier.

"But Nikki, dear. . . ." Her voice sounded so like her mother's that Fish Finlay put his lobster fork down on the blue-and-white checked tablecloth. ". . . she can't *get* the rubies back. She doesn't have that much money. It would have to come out of capital . . . and surely she's told you that doesn't belong to her? The Maloney Trust belongs to me. She only has the income while she's alive, and not for too long at that. It's a couple of years or so. You can ask Mr. Finlay how many, I've forgotten whether it's one or two. It's just the way the Trust is written. Isn't it, Mr. Finlay?"

She was looking across at him, her eyes too bright, her cheeks flushed. He stared back at her, too stunned to speak. Beside him he could feel Alla Emlyn's cold taut body relaxing very slowly, and see her breast rise and fall as she drew in a long deep quiet breath and let it softly out, her eyes closed, opening then and going across to Peter de Gradoff, the faint shadow of a smile creeping into the corner of her scarlet mouth. And he saw Peter's head move, barely perceptible, in understanding and affirmation.

Jenny Linton was looking at Fish, Alla and Peter looking down at the lobsters on their plates. None of them looked at Nikki de Gradoff, frozen in complete silence, until they heard his chair move sharply back.

"You people stay. I must go."

For an instant Fish Finlay saw his face, gray and ghastly, and he was moving swiftly through the tables. Fish pushed his own chair back. He was in the telephone booth when he heard de Gradoff's car leap to the spark and roar out of the parking lot.

Dr. McNair's wife said, "He's at dinner."

"Get him, quick. Tell him it's Finlay. Tell him to get over to Enniskerry. It's life or death. For God's sake, tell him fast."

He put down the phone. Only then did he remember Dodo was in Jenny's room and the door was locked and Jenny had the key. He went back as swiftly as he could.

"Where's Jenny?"

"Oh, darling," Alla Emlyn said, "I've sent them to get me some aspirin. But I don't really expect them back, and Peter knows it. Do sit down, Fish." She smiled up at him. "You told me a story, didn't you. It's only the grace of heaven that saved me. Do relax. At least till you pay the bill. We can get a taxi then."

CHAPTER : 19

The headlights of Fish Finlay's taxi caught the blue-and-white insignia on the back of the car turning down Nantucket Avenue as the taxi turned into it at the other end of the serpentine wall. Dr. McNair had been to Enniskerry and was leaving it. The tension holding Fish forward on the seat broke with a relief so intense that he could taste the sudden gall-bitter irony of the fact that an equal tension had broken in the silent woman beside him. Alla Emlyn stirred in the seat. The movement of her body, the sound of her breath quieting, as she relaxed, had a quality of resignation so tangible and so extraordinary that it had a macabre humor. If she had not actually and overtly hoped for what he'd feared, she'd been waiting for it and could have borne it with fortitude, as an act of God or the devil clearing a way that wasn't clear.

De Gradoff was on the porch. The taxi lights picked him up for a moment, stretched comfortably out on one of the bamboo chaises, smoking a cigar, a glass beside him. With the taxi gone, the blur of his dinner coat and the round red tip of his cigar were still visible in the shadows made by the dim lights in the balcony hall. The rest of the house was dark.

Mrs. Emlyn was the first up the steps.

"We'd have been here sooner, darling," she said lightly, "but we had a perfectly foul time getting a taxi. Saturday night with the Navy on the town. Dodo's all right, I take it. Was that a doctor we saw leaving?"

"It was," de Gradoff said calmly. "Finlay called him. For what reason I've no idea, except I'm sure it was kindly meant. It was very awkward, as a matter of fact. He insisted on seeing her and she was sound asleep in Jennifer's room . . . much quieter of course than the front of the house. But he was pleased she was sleeping without any of his drugs. So, why don't you run powder your nose, Alla, darling, and let's you and I go along to the dance."

"I won't be a moment." She moved gracefully on into the hall.

"As I say, Finlay," de Gradoff went on evenly, "I've no idea what you had in mind. Under ordinary circumstances I certainly shouldn't bother to explain any conduct of mine to you. But I did leave the table rather abruptly, under circumstances that can hardly be called ordinary."

The dull end of his cigar glowed, the fragrant smoke came so directly to Fish that he realized de Gradoff must have blown it at him.

"Of course I'm astounded I hadn't been told. The impression is offensive to a degree. However. . . ."

Fish could hear the returning arrogance in his voice.

"The appalling thing that hit me there was that I knew, when Jennifer said that, what's been wrong with Dodo these last two months— the horrible anxiety she's been under. You know as well as I do that her relations with Jennifer haven't been too cordial, and money means a great deal to her. It means nothing to me. I've been used to great poverty and great wealth. I prefer wealth, but I can take poverty. You Americans find that hard to understand, but you've been very spoiled, of course."

Fish waited, with a controlled coolness that took some effort. De Gradoff sat up and put his feet on the floor. "My one thought, when I heard the truth, was to get home to my wife and tell her for God's sake to stop worrying herself to death. I found out, fortunately, that Jennifer has promised not to cut her off with that shilling the English talk about . . . which explains, along with a good many martinis, I'm afraid, why she was sleeping quietly at last. It's unfortunate she didn't have more confidence in me."

He turned to Alla coming back onto the porch.

"I've been having a needed chat with Finlay, darling, before we go. The whole atmosphere needed clearing. Tomorrow, I'd like a quiet day alone with my wife. Why don't you and Peter and Jennifer take the day and go somewhere, the Cape or some place amusing. I'm sure Finlay can occupy himself."

"Oh, that's a divine idea."

"Because I think we'll all go back to France next week and take Jennifer with us. It's a lot less expensive . . . now that I understand our financial situation." He put his cigar down in the ash tray. "Do stay and have a drink, Finlay." He passed Fish and went down the steps. "Coming, darling?"

Alla Emlyn moved gracefully across the porch and held her hand out to Fish. "Good night," she said. When she took her hand away from his there was a piece of paper in it.

"Good night," Fish said. He waited until the sleek black car had roared away from the porch, took out his cigarette lighter and held it to read the hasty ink-blurred scrawl.

"Don't worry about J.," it said. "Believe me, dear, she couldn't be safer. Both Peter and I will see to that."

"I'll bet," Fish Finlay thought.

He held the paper for the flame to eat, dropped it into an

ash tray and crumbled it to carbon dust. He went over to the bar, poured himself a Scotch and soda and sat down to give McNair a chance to get home before calling him to find out what else had gone on at Enniskerry, knowing already that nothing had and that de Gradoff had won another round. A romantic tomorrow alone with Dodo would only consolidate his gain. And if he took her and Jennifer abroad. . . .

He sat there in the dark listening to the roar of the sea, the swirling maelstrom of the Chasm imprinted on his inward eye, and beside it on the same stuffless negative, the fishing platform and the rock and the sandal caught in the black shag of mussels. Getting out of the country was the shrewd move of a superb opportunist turning every checkmate into victory with the ease of a magician at a birthday party for the blind. He put his head back against the cushions, closed his eyes, trying to think, and raised his head abruptly, hearing a new sound out in the drive.

He bent forward, listening more intently. It was somebody walking, feet softly scrunching over the scallop-shell surface. He turned his head and looked out. It was too dark to see beyond the hazy rim of the verandah. The steps were coming closer, pausing, coming on again, curiously stealthy and, at the same time, direct. Fish put his glass carefully down on the table, gooseflesh creeping out along his spine as the steps reached the turf and were silent, moving closer or not moving, he couldn't tell. Then he heard them again, very close, just at the corner of the porte-cochere, scrunching very softly on the shell again. His eyes peering into the dark created forms that had no substance, his listening ears created sound that was not sound, until he heard the soft pad of a foot on the wooden steps. He turned his head toward it, and saw a dark shadow emerge to take form deeper than the shadows around it, and saw then, picked out in the frail sifted tendril of light from the hallway, a moon-pale patch that riveted his eyes, as his nostrils quivered with the sharp spicy fragrance of carnations and the goose-flesh was colder than lumps of ice on his spine. He dragged his eyes up, holding his breath, as a shadowy figure moved onto the porch and across toward the door and he saw the small sad-eyed gardener with the faded brown hat move quietly into the hall and disappear, the odor of the carnations lingering in the salt-damp air behind him on the porch.

Fish let his breath out quietly and waited, motionless, hardly breathing again, until he heard the soft padding steps return and the little man cross the porch, empty-handed. He went down the steps, his feet scrunching across the drive to the turf, and the only sound was imagined sound.

Fish Finlay picked up his Scotch and soda and took a

drink he badly needed. He started to take another, and stopped short as a light flashed on in the three high windows of the clock tower. He put the glass down, watching. In a moment he saw the dusty blue figure reach the tower balcony and disappear, and a faint light show in the windows of the loft living-room, dissolving the sea of darkness over the courtyard.

He sat up, his first impulse to go over and see what the little gardener was doing in his rooms, his second to stay where he was and watch. He stayed, his eyes fixed on the windows. Once he saw the brown hat or the shadow of it move across in front of the lighted lamp. He looked over at the hall door behind him. If he could get upstairs, he could look directly into his room. He hesitated, and was glad he had. He could hear a phone ringing distantly. A moment later he heard a stirring around inside the house. The lights in the stable were still as they had been. He waited, bewildered in some curiously expectant sense that he felt without knowing how or why. A door opened upstairs in the house and a light came on in the hall, making the porch brighter too. Then he heard the movement of feet on the stairs, not sharp or distinct but more like feet that were feeling their way uncertainly down an unaccustomed path.

He stood up. It was too light for concealment, too dark for him not to be frightening, seen unexpectedly there.

The steps were steadier now, clear on the polished floor, dulled again as they reached the Aubusson carpet, and the light threw the shadow of a woman out onto the porch before she stepped out herself. He saw Dodo. For a moment he thought she was walking in her sleep, until he saw her eyes open, staring out of a face that was whiter than the robe she wore, her hands clutching jerkily to tie the belt around her waist. She saw him and stopped, again almost like a sleepwalker disturbed for a moment on her way. He saw her lips move without hearing any sound, until she moistened her dust-dry lips and stepped closer to him on her way to the steps, her eyes fixed, wide open, not a sleepwalker but a walker in some frightening kind of hypnotic trance.

"My father. . . ." Her voice was like sandpaper on polished wood. "He's . . . sent for me. I must go. He's waiting . . . out there."

She raised one hand as though brushing something off into the night, and Fish stared at her, a sharp chill along his spine again as he saw her hand go out toward the rose garden and the cliff above the sea and the Rock, and felt a sudden doubt of his own sanity as well as hers.

"I must go alone," she whispered "Don't come."

She went down the steps. He moved after her quietly and stood there, tense, until she passed by the opening in the balustrade, going on like a white ghost in the light filtered down from the stable windows, and he saw her open and close the clock tower door. He saw her reach the balcony and stop, her hand on the rail, for several moments, before she moved on toward the living-room door and out of his sight. He stood there staring up at the windows, for how long he could not have told, before he made up his mind, went down the steps, across the courtyard to the tower door and up the stairs, making no attempt to deaden his footsteps.

He opened the living-room door and went in. The gardener was gone. Dodo was there alone, on the sofa, a sheaf of thin blue papers in her lap, staring at a photograph in her hand, her lips parted. If her face had been white in the frail light on the porch, it was dead-white now, blank, too dazed to hear him enter, her eyes dazed, resting on the photograph. She looked up as Fish shut the door.

"I . . . don't believe it," she whispered. "It's a lie."

She moistened her lips and turned the page of the sheaf of papers, her hand trembling, her eyes darting over the lines. "It's all a lie."

"What's a lie, Dodo?" he asked quietly.

She sat staring down for a moment. "That was . . . my father," she said then. Her voice was suddenly sharp. "He's been here, every winter. Right here at Enniskerry. Right here with Vranek. I knew it, the other day—I saw him in the greenhouse, from your kitchen window. But I didn't believe it, I thought I was mad. But now . . . I've seen him, I know it's him. He stayed this summer . . . to watch me. *He* hired the detective in Paris. This is his—"

She broke off, holding up the sheaf of papers. "This is . . . oh, it's just lies! And he gives it to me!"

The pitch of her voice rose. "*I'm* to do what I like with it. *I'm* to accuse my husband of murder! My own father . . . he's had my husband watched, like a common criminal! It's horrible, Fish . . . and it's all a lie!"

He went over to her. "Will you let me see it, Dodo?"

She flashed to her feet, her eyes blazing.

"No! They haven't proved anything. They admit they haven't proved anything. There was a maid but the maid is dead. There was a letter that woman wrote the night she died but they haven't got the letter. They say the family gave him the letter in return for his interest in the estate. That's a lie. The whole thing's a lie. They exhumed the body to prove he poisoned her but there was nothing. And they call their suspicions *facts!* And this—"

She snatched the photograph up savagely, her eyes blazing at it for an instant before they went suddenly gray and sick as she dropped it on the floor. "It's his wife, a photo of a portrait . . . and she's wearing my rubies. Oh, Nikki couldn't have done that! He wouldn't have let me *buy* his own family jewels. . . ."

She flung the papers down. ". . . Unless it's true, he was in debt to that man and . . . afraid to tell me!"

Her lips were dry again. "Get me some water, Fish. Water with ice. I'm burning up! Oh, I hate my father! I've always hated him! I know now! He was the one who called up the Customs people!"

He went out to the kitchen, got a tray of ice and a glass from the cupboard, raised his head sharply then and went quickly back into the living-room. She was standing in front of the fireplace, her eyes as hot as the flames licking the sheaf of papers on the hearth behind her.

"There!" she cried. "My father said they were mine to do as I liked with. I've done it. And don't you try to—"

"I wouldn't think of it, Dodo. Here's your water. Or don't you want it now?"

"No." She took the poker and stirred the charred papers savagely.

He put it on the table. "Just one thing. Your father wouldn't have given you that, Dodo, if he'd known what happened tonight. He wouldn't have put Jenny's life in your hands. You're perfectly safe, for the moment—thanks to her. But when you burned that report—"

"I don't know what you mean, thanks to her," she said sharply. "She promised me she'd not tell about the Trust and she gets one martini. . . . But she did me an enormous favor even if she didn't mean to. Nikki was divine about it. If I trusted him as he trusted me—"

"All right, Dodo. I've heard all that. Here."

Under the charred mass there was still a part of the picture. He pulled it out and knocked off the ash. The head was gone, but the necklace was there and the hand holding the basket of carnations. He handed it to her.

"The original of this has been hanging in Washington. She was having herself painted in the rubies as a surprise birthday present for him . . . she'd just got them from him two weeks before she died. You can see they're the ones you bought. When she died the portrait wasn't finished and Nikki refused the commission. He never saw it and didn't know she was being painted with the rubies. The painter finished it and called it 'The Lady with the Carnations.' "

"Carnations?" She looked at him white-faced. "Nikki hates carnations. . . ."

"Since when?" Fish Finlay asked quietly. "But I'm not arguing with you, Dodo. Take that home and think it over. He's planning on a quiet day at home with you tomorrow. Ask him."

135

He went to the door and opened it. "Would you like me to walk you home?"

"No." Her voice was curt. "But I would like you to find another place to stay. Nikki doesn't like you any better than you like him and I'm wondering why I ever thought I did. And I've changed my mind about your marrying my daughter."

"I didn't know the point had ever come up, and I'll move the first thing in the morning. Good night."

She still had the fragment of the portrait print in her hand as she went out . . . whether because she wanted it or had been too angry to throw it away he didn't know. When she got it home, if she did, to look at in the silence of the empty night. . . . He shook his head, went over to the telephone and called Dr. McNair.

"I've been waiting," McNair said. "De Gradoff and I got there together. He was badly shaken for a few minutes. There was a small bottle on the table by her bed in the front room, but she wasn't there. I was afraid something had already happened when he insisted she was all right. But she was okay. When I came back to the front bedroom, the bottle on the table was gone. I'd heard the toilet flush. That's all I can tell you. But I hear the Maloney Trust goes to Jennifer. Somebody called my wife half an hour ago. News travels fast, doesn't it."

"It seems to," Fish said. "Thanks a lot."

He put the phone down, turned off the lights and saw that Dodo was back in her own room across the courtyard, not Jenny's. Half an hour earlier he would have drawn some confident conclusion from that. Sitting there now gazing into the fireplace where lay the fine ash of his most persistent assumption, he hesitated to draw any at all. How wrong could you be? If Caxson Reeves hadn't known it was James V. Maloney who had hired the French detective, he must have guessed it from the first. And no doubt he'd known for the last seven years that Maloney was quietly and happily there in the gardens of Enniskerry. He remembered Dodo coming out of the kitchen looking as if she'd seen a ghost, as indeed she had. He'd at least been right in assuming that was the only place from which she'd ever see the greenhouses, and see a figure that would have a kind of inner familiarity before the external appearance put her off and she took it for granted that she was overwrought . . . as indeed she had also been. Was her father only carrying on his educational theory that Dodo should be allowed to cut her own throat in her own way if she wanted to, and Jennifer, if she survived, would be the better for it?

His room was abruptly dark then, Dodo had turned off her light. He got up and looked out of the window. There was still light in Jenny's room. He could see it at the end of the porch. Whether Dodo had gone back there or merely left the light on when she came out of it he had no way of knowing. He reached for a cigarette, lighted it and held the flame to his watch. It wasn't twelve. The dance wasn't over til two, and what time Peter—and, no doubt, Alla Emlyn—would bring her home was something else again. At least she was safe. Until she got home? He didn't know. There seemed no reason for him not to go to bed. One thing was sure . . . she wouldn't come to the loft again.

Nevertheless he turned on the reading lamp behind the sofa and settled down, his feet up, his head on his arm, and closed his eyes for a minute.

CHAPTER : 20

When he opened them the clock was striking three and the rain was beating on the shingles. It was neither sound that had waked him, but the door opening.

He took one startled glance. "Miss Linton, I thought I——" He broke off and got quickly to his feet, seeing her face, her dripping raincoat and the sodden tennis shoes on her feet. "Jenny!"

She ran to him, buried her head against him, clinging to him, her body trembling as he'd felt it trembling beside him in the cab of the battered truck, her heart pounding. He could feel it through the clammy wet raincoat as he bent his head down to hers in a moment of exquisite warmth before he shook himself out of its intoxicating loveliness and tried to release the grip of her arms around him.

"Jenny, what is it?"

"Oh, don't . . . don't let me go, Fish! Hold me tight! Please, don't ever let me go! I'm afraid, Fish! He's . . . out there. . . ."

He held her tighter a moment longer.

"Stop it, Jenny. Stop it and tell me what's happened. Let's get this thing off."

She was shivering under the raincoat. When he unbuttoned it, he saw that all she had on was her evening dress.

"Hold on a minute." He started to his bedroom, but she tagged along like a frightened puppy while he got his wool bathrobe and put it on her. She came back with him into the living-room and sat huddled in a corner of the sofa, watching him while he closed the windows and drew the blinds and turned up the thermostat to warm the place a little for her.

When he came back and sat down by her, she was quieter but still pale, her eyes wide open and bright.

"What's happened?"

"I don't know really." She·shook her head. "They were home when Peter and I got here—Nikki and Mrs. Emlyn. I don't know when they left the dance. Peter and I went for something to eat and they were gone when we got back.

"And my mother was in my room, waiting for me. Nikki was with her. I thought she was going to be terribly angry, because I'd promised not to tell about the Trust, and I . . . I hated to do it, she's been so nice to me. But I *had* to. I changed cocktails with her and I didn't drink all of hers but there was something in it. I'm just like she was last night, and I'm not sleepy at all. And I didn't just run out with Peter, from the restaurant. I called up from the drugstore, and Elsa said my mother was fast asleep. But tonight, with the Benzedrine I got instead, I thought she wasn't supposed to sleep?"

"Or to sleep forever. The Benzedrine would make her so desperate she'd take whatever anyone suggested. Dr. McNair saw a small bottle on her table. It was gone when he looked for it again."

She was silent for a moment, her face paler. "Nikki never took his eyes off me at the dance, or when I got home. And over there, he was telling my mother she mustn't scold me, and she said it wasn't my fault, it was yours, you were the one leading me on. And . . . that you're leaving here tomorrow, and I wasn't to see you any more."

She pulled the bathrobe tighter around her. "And he said they . . . they'd take me abroad with them next week and tomorrow I was to go with Mrs. Emlyn and Peter somewhere. I just felt . . . trapped. He thinks you put the carnations in his room, but he wasn't scared this time, the way he was before. So, my mother said I should go to bed and Nikki said I wasn't to make any . . . visits over here, because he'd be watching me. He said it as a joke but it wasn't one. Then Mrs. Emlyn came in, after Nikki took mother into his room."

She stopped for an instant.

"Mrs. Emlyn said . . . I'd better sleep in her room with her. She made it sound like a joke too, but it wasn't. So . . . she's afraid something's going to happen to me. And she said, why didn't I marry Peter and . . . and get out of the way."

She put her head down in her hands for an instant. "I'm just so dead tired I don't know what to do. So . . . I lay down till everything got quiet, because I *had* to see you, and then I sneaked out. I was just at the end of the porch when I heard him coming. I ducked down into the rose gardens. That's how I got so wet. I couldn't see him but I could hear him. He was coming over here, looking for me. I hid in the

138

garden. It seemed just ages. He had a flashlight, I could see it in the garage sort of off and on, and once he came out the gardeners' door and I was afraid he'd see me then, but he went back and I heard him in front again. And that's when I came in, and if he comes back he'll see my wet prints on the stairs."

She looked over at the door. "Lock it, Fish. Please."

He went across the room and opened it. The hall was empty and there was no sound but the beating rain, sharp on the windows, hollow on the shingled tower. He closed it again and turned the key in the lock. Then he went into the bedrooms and looked at the smooth dry surface of the floors before he locked the door there and came back to the living-room.

"Fish." She raised her eyes to his for an instant, the color seeping into her cheeks as she looked down then at her hands pleating the fold of his bathrobe around her knees. "It's . . . it's a horrible thing for me to . . . to ask you, but . . . would you marry me . . . and take me with you when you go tomorrow? Because I really love you, Fish. I don't want to marry anybody else but you. That's what I came over for . . . to ask you if you would."

The wind tore in sharp gusts, whipping the white sea horses bounding up the cliff. The rain beat on the windows and on the shingled roof. Fish Finlay sat quietly, his hands folded between his knees, hearing none of it in the maelstrom of his own heart.

"You . . . do like me, a little bit, don't you?" Jenny asked.

"I like you very much, Jenny."

He could hear his voice, not believing it was his own.

"I love you very much, Jenny. But I couldn't marry you. It . . . it wouldn't be fair, Jenny. You're too young, you've got a lot of time—"

"I won't have any time, unless I get away from here," she said quietly. "And that's not the real reason, is it? It's because of your leg, isn't it. And what some other girl did. Mr. Reeves told me. But that doesn't make any difference—except to you. You're just afraid, that's all. The other night at the Randolphs', you were limping when you came in with Polly . . . but you weren't limping when you ran down the steps to the fishing platform. You could do all sorts of things if you'd just forget yourself a minute. And I know very well the way I feel. I don't want anybody else, Fish. I want somebody just like you. And there isn't any use of my having to hunt him when I've already found him, is there? We both know all that. There's no use arguing about it."

"My dear child," Finlay said. "You—"

He broke off, listening. They both turned their heads

139

sharply. It was a sound scarcely audible in the beating rain.

"It's the garage door," Jenny whispered. "Peter and I closed it."

They heard a motor starting. Fish got to his feet, but she put her hand out.

"That's Peter." She reached and turned off the light, and ran to the window. A faint streak of blue showed under the parking lights that cast a gray rain-slanted film bright enough to point up the white shell drive as Jenny's car crept quietly out toward the purple beaches.

She turned back. "That's Peter," she said again. "He took it last night. It's some girl. She's got reddish hair, because there were bronze bobby pins between the seats. But it's all right, I've decided I don't care. Let him use it."

The tail lights crept into the purple blackness, a misty glow filtered through as the head lights came on, out of sight of the house.

Jenny came back to the sofa, turned the reading lamp back on and looked at Fish. "I feel sort of sorry for him," she said. "He'd have been all right if it hadn't been for his Aunt Alla. She's babied him so. He asked me to marry him tonight. He was very nice about it. He didn't pretend he was in love with me. Just that we could have a lot of fun together, tennis and dancing and all that stuff. He swims like a dolphin. But that isn't what I want to marry for. I want a family and a home . . . and somebody who doesn't go chasing redheads."

Our kind of fun. The words repeated themselves in Fish Finlay's mind, their false spell gone, like the ritual of a god whose clay feet had crumbled to meaningless dust, a form remaining in the mind long after the substance of belief was gone. The bitter shrine was empty. He looked at the place where it had been, and that was gone too. The scar was healed. He moved abruptly, dizzy with the knowledge of release.

"Fish," Jenny said. "I'm not going back there tonight."

He looked at her, still dazed.

"If you wouldn't let me stay here in one of your rooms, I was going to Mr. Reeves's sister's house, except it would be all over Newport by morning. But I can't go there now, because I haven't got my car. Or I can go to Mr. Vranek's." She reached for her sodden shoes. "Except that my grandfather—"

"Your—" He stared at her.

"You didn't know?" she said simply. "I'm sure Mr. Reeves does. And I remember Mr. Vranek and Mr. MacTaggert. Mr. MacTaggert was tall and quite stooped. And Mr. Vranek would never have thought to send me the orchids. That was my grandfather. And if you'll look at him, you'll see how much my mother looks like him around the eyes when he smiles, and he smiled at me when I went over and told Mr. Vranek I was sorry my car had chewed the turf. He didn't know I saw him. And if he doesn't want us to disturb him, I don't think we should, but it's just nice to know he's here, doing the sort of thing he loves to do. And he's not crazy. It's my mother who's crazy . . . and I'd be crazy if I went back home tonight. So, if you'll lend me a pair of pajamas, I've got a toothbrush in my raincoat pocket, and if I could have some warm milk, maybe I could go to sleep. If we can turn this light off so nobody'll see me through the windows, I'll go make me a bed. You can call Mr. Reeves and tell him I'm here, if you want to."

She reached for the light and turned it off herself.

"And maybe you'd just kiss me good night. . . ."

"I would not," Fish Finlay said firmly. "Look—"

"You're afraid to, that's all. You can lock the door on your side. I promise I'll never stir till morning."

She picked up her raincoat and padded into the kitchen. He heard her get out the milk and a pan to heat it in. She smiled at him as he came through the passage to go to his room and get her the pajamas.

"I'm just terribly sorry to be such a problem. But the Maloneys have a strong sense of personal survival. I've heard my father say Mr. Reeves said so. And I know this isn't fair, because if it gets out you'll have to marry me, won't you."

"Miss Linton," Fish began, and stopped again as he saw the tears spring into her eyes and her chin tighten to keep from trembling.

"It's okay, baby," he said. He smiled at the youngest Maloney, with a saucepan in her hand and an outsize bathrobe hitched up around her middle, runs in her nylon stockings, no lipstick left and the rain curling her hair in tight ringlets. "As an officer of the Maloney Trust, I'm honored to have you sleep in your own stable."

"Thank you," she said. "I . . . I just don't want to be dead tomorrow morning."

She poured the milk into a glass and padded on into the room next to his. "I'll stay put till you call me."

He remembered that with sharp relief at a quarter to nine the next morning, when he heard a car stop in front of the clock tower and feet on the clock tower stairs. He was up and dressed, the alarm clock under his pillow waking him after he'd finally given up listening for Peter's return, and moving around quietly, making coffee. He heard the knock on the living-room door. The door into the bedroom passage was closed, but he looked to make sure before he went out, carefully closing the kitchen door behind him. As he opened the living-room door, his heart took a downward jolt at the sight of the first man standing there and hit solid rock bottom at

141

the second. He stood staring into the sleepy eyes of the lean sandy-haired reporter B. Meggs and the tired black eyes of Lieutenant Arturo Bestoso.

"We come in?"

Fish jolted himself back to life. *I'll stay put till you call me.* Thank God, he thought.

"Sure." He moved back, glancing hastily at the sofa. She'd taken her raincoat and tennis shoes with her. "Sit down."

The two of them had been up a long time. Neither was shaved. Bestoso's black beard and B. Meggs's sandy one gave the first a disreputable and the second a raffish character that the streaks of smut across their faces and on their clothes did not help.

"What's up?"

Bestoso sat down, dead-beat. B. Meggs propped himself against the fireplace as before and got out a cigarette, very quiet, not looking anywhere except at the cigarette.

"This is B.'s idea," Bestoso said. "He thought you could brief us before we barge in on 'em over at the house. It's about a blue convertible, Virginia license."

There is a point below which the human heart cannot sink, and Fish Finlay had thought his was already there. He sat down on the arm of the sofa and reached in his pocket for a cigarette. His lighter was on his bedside table, so he reached for a match, lighted the cigarette and flicked the match into the fireplace, his eyes resting for an instant on the black ashes of the papers there, less than a yard from B. Meggs's mud-stained feet.

"What about the blue convertible?"

"It's a wreck," Bestoso said shortly.

Fish had already heard the movement in the kitchen. B. Meggs had heard it too. There was nothing to do. Fish was beyond the point of doing anything, when Jenny Linton pushed the door open and flashed into the room.

"What's a wreck? Not my . . . Peter didn't wreck my new car?"

CHAPTER : 21

Fish Finlay put his cigarette in the ash tray. She was bare-footed, his rumpled striped pajamas rolled around her ankles, his bathrobe hitched up around her waist, one corner dragging, one sleeve rolled up and the other hanging, her head tousled, face pale, eyes wide with alarm. Bestoso's black-bearded jaw had dropped, so even had the sandy stubbled jaw of B. Meggs, for whatever hollow satisfaction Fish Finlay could get from that as he pulled himself together once more and got to his feet.

"This is Miss Jennifer Linton, gentlemen," he said calmly. "Miss Linton, Lieutenant Bestoso of the Newport Police, and Mr. B. Meggs of the New York *Courier Graphic*."

Her eyes widened and she swallowed. Then for a fragment of an instant, Fish could have leaped across the intervening space and kissed her. He was proud of her. She straightened her shoulders just a little and moved her tousled head, looking from one to the other of them with simple dignity.

"How do you do, Lieutenant Bestoso . . . Mr. Meggs." She looked down at her bare feet and over at Fish. "I'm sorry I haven't any shoes on. They're too wet." She looked quickly back at Bestoso. "What about the blue convertible? And Peter? He . . . he wasn't hurt, was he?"

She came over to the sofa and sat down, putting her feet up under her, her face paler. Fish sat down. It took Bestoso a moment. He rubbed his hand over his eyes. B. Meggs relaxed his spine back against the fireplace, looked intently at the ash that had lengthened on his cigarette, moved his hand down and knocked it off into the fireplace.

"It's your car, Miss Linton?" He took a slip of paper from his pocket. "Virginia tags." He read the license number.

She nodded. "What's happened to it?" Her voice was taut. Fish saw her hands gripped tightly in his bathrobe sleeves.

"We traced it through the people serviced it for you yesterday morning," Bestoso said gravely. "This Peter you mentioned. Who is he?"

Jenny looked at Fish, her lips dry.

"Peter de Gradoff," Fish said. "We assumed it was he who took Miss Linton's car out this morning, round three-thirty or so. He's a cousin of Miss Linton's stepfather, staying here at Enniskerry."

"Tall? Dark-haired?" B. Meggs asked. Fish nodded.

"He's dead, isn't he . . . ?" Jenny whispered. She looked from one to the other of them.

Bestoso nodded. He seemed reluctant to go on.

"Tell her, Art," B. Meggs said quietly. "She can take it."

"You tell her then. You saw it."

B. Meggs nodded. "He had a date with a girl roomed across the hall from me, lodginghouse on Thames Street. Picked her up round three-thirty. Went out the West Road. Going fast. Raining. Road's wet. Made a sharp right turn. Next thing I saw, burst of flame. I got there, minute later, thing was a mess. Couldn't get near it. Hit a stone fence. Jar must've released top, it was back, girl thrown out, over in the field. He was caught, didn't have a prayer."

143

Jenny's lips were ash-white. "Poor Mrs. Emlyn," she whispered.

Bestoso looked at Fish.

"His aunt. She's visiting at Enniskerry too. She's the one you'll have to tell."

He looked from one to the other of them himself. There was more than this. They weren't saying it because Jenny was there. There was an uneasy gap between things. Why B. Meggs had been on the road behind them, for example. He glanced at Jenny, uneasy about her too, she was sitting there so white and silent.

"You knew he had your car, Miss Linton?" Bestoso asked.

She shook her head. "I just assumed he did, because I thought he'd taken it the night before. There were some bobby pins between the seats and thirty-five miles extra on the speedometer. I knew, because I was—well, it was my first car, and I was watching for the one thousand miles, for the checkup. That's how I noticed somebody had used it after the Randolphs' party. And I didn't mind him using it, so much, except he made fun of my driving . . . not fast enough for him."

"He's not making fun of it now." Bestoso hesitated, rubbing his hand over his beard. "If it's okay with you, Finlay," he said abruptly, "B. and I'll wash up before we go over to the house'."

B. Meggs unwound himself from his espaliered position against the mantelpiece and followed them through the kitchen into Fish's room.

"There's the bath," Fish said. He nodded toward it and closed Jenny's door.

"Come on in," Bestoso said. He went into the bathroom, B. Meggs and Fish filing in after him, closed the door, went over to the washbowl mirror and looked at himself. B. Meggs sat on the edge of the tub, Fish straddled the bathroom chair, waiting.

"I didn't want to say too much in front of the kid in there. There's damn near nothing left of the car."

He pulled off his coat and tie and turned his shirt collar under.

"Or Peter. The girl's in the hospital. May pull through, may not. They're going over what's left of the car now. It's B. here that—"

"I admit you've got a beef, Art," B. Meggs said. "If it'd worked, been swell."

"No beef." Bestoso turned on the hot water and changed the blade in Fish's razor. "You bastards just make it harder, that's all. It's my job. I don't expect you to do it for me."

"Told you about the strawberry blonde across the hall." B. Meggs turned to Fish. "Seems the Frenchman gives her an envelope, sealed and stamped, mail if anything happens to him. Had some reason think he could trust her. Anyway, she was willing to sell. Landlady told her I was a reporter. From way she described it, got the idea was addressed to Sûreté. She wanted cash on barrelhead, I said no dice."

"I use a straightedge at home," Bestoso said, swearing quietly from the washbowl.

"She said okay, if I didn't want it, society fella did," B. Meggs went on. "I'd have called Art but phone's down front hall, didn't want society fella to show up while I'm gone, figured if I tagged him Art could pick him up with the goods. He came in the blue convertible, she was waiting in the hall, popped out with envelope, popped in car, I tagged along in mine, rest you know. Hadn't been for car burning, I'd been Art's white-haired boy."

"No trace of any envelope left," Bestoso said through the towel. "If B.'s telling the truth."

"It's the truth, Art. If I'd found it, I'd put in anonymous call for ambulance and left. Wouldn't hung around."

"Okay, it's burned up then." Bestoso swore again. He moved away from the bowl. "Your turn, B." He put on his tie and coat and took B. Meggs's place on the side of the bathtub. "What I'm getting at is something else." He looked intently at Fish. "Say the society fella is this de Gradoff. It's the first tie-in I've had with anybody interested in the frog dick. That's a help. So I come here and find Miss Linton's spent the night here when her own house is just across the yard. She doesn't look to me like she's been here for fun, Finlay. So who's she scared of? Or did she have a row with her family? What's this de Gradoff's interest?"

He got up, looking over at B. Meggs. "You look better. Make it snappy if you're coming with me. I'm not asking you for an answer yet, Finlay. What I want you to do is keep Miss Linton here till I get back. That's a police order. I want her here till I check on a couple of things. And I could hold the two of you as material witnesses. I'll let it ride if you'll give me your word. . . ."

"Sure." Fish opened the door in the bedroom passage to let them out into the clock tower hall.

"Wouldn't like to hold everything till I get a camera man, would you, Finlay?" B. Meggs asked.

"You go to hell," Fish said. He said to Bestoso, "I don't think her mother knows she's here, yet."

"She's had plenty time to get here since breakfast," Bestoso said calmly. "I don't have to mention the rig she's wearing. If you're smart, you'll get her out of it. I'll have to say I've seen her."

He went down the stairs, B. Meggs trailing. Fish turned and went back into the kitchen. Jenny was at the counter

145

heating up the coffee. She stopped, her back to him, her head down a little.

"I'm sorry," she said. "Just terribly sorry. I didn't want to go to the Reeves's because it would be all over Newport, and now . . . now it'll be all over everywhere. Another Maloney gone to the dogs, all over the front page. I'm . . . I'm awfully sorry. But I'm sorrier for Peter, and that girl. That's a horrible thing to happen."

Fish nodded. His impulse to give her unshirted hell for not staying in her room had died quietly as she spoke. He went over to put his arms around her and caught himself just in time. He cleared his throat.

"The present point is to get you some clothes."

She stiffened a little. "It's perfectly simple. Just call Enniskerry and ask Elsa to bring me some. There's no use trying to lie about it now. What's done is done. If you don't want to do it, I will."

He went in to the telephone and gave a number. She came to the kitchen door. "That isn't Enniskerry."

"Mr. Reeves, please," Fish said, and saw her eyes widen. She went to the sofa and put her coffee cup down, watching him miserably.

"Fish Finlay, sir. I've got a problem here. Could you come right over? To the stable, not the house."

"Five minutes," Reeves said without a pause, and Fish heard the foggy buzz of the line in his ear. He waited a moment and gave the operator the Enniskerry number. It was Moulton who answered, for what temporary relief that was.

"Mr. Finlay, Moulton." He tried to make his voice sound as matter-of-fact as Reeves's "Five minutes" had been. "Miss Linton would like Elsa to bring over some clothes. From scratch."

There was a pause. He was about to repeat it when he heard Moulton's voice.

"I'm sorry, sir," he said. "Miss Linton is not in. She left half an hour ago. She's having breakfast with Mr. Finlay at the stable. But the maid is going over in a few minutes to straighten the apartment, if you'd care to leave a message, sir."

"Heaven bless you, Moulton," Fish said.

"Thank you, sir. I'll ask the maid to tell Miss Linton you called."

He put the phone down. "Moulton says you left half an hour ago to have breakfast here, and Elsa's coming. So what about an egg, Miss Linton?"

He expected her to smile back at him, at least, but her face, blank at first, went slowly paler, her eyes wider.

"Jenny . . . what is it? He's just trying to help. Nobody knows you weren't at home."

146

"I know." She had to moisten her lips before she spoke. "That . . . that's the trouble."

"I don't understand, Jenny."

She got up, hitching his robe to keep from falling over it, went quickly to the phone and asked for a number. He waited blankly.

"Oh, Mr. Vranek . . . this is Jennifer. How are you people this morning? Oh . . . good. I just . . . wanted to know. There was an accident last night. Peter de Gradoff had my car out. It skidded on the wet road. Yes, it's terrible. The police are here now. I'm at the stable. With Mr. Finlay. Thanks . . . goodbye."

She put the phone down, swallowed hard, and pushed her hair back from her forehead. "I was afraid something could have happened to my grandfather. Because Nikki *was* out, Fish. I didn't make that up. He . . . he mustn't have seen me, after all. He'd tell my mother if he had, just to make trouble for you. But I *know* he was out . . . and he must have been doing something."

He looked at her, troubled. "Did you *see* him, Jenny?"

She shook her head. "I didn't see him. But I *knew* it was him. It was so dark, and it was raining. But I heard him, Fish. I knew it was—"

She broke off and looked at the hall door, then turned and looked back through the kitchen. "Thank you, Elsa," she said steadily. "Just leave them in the second bedroom. Thanks ever so much. You can do Mr. Finlay's room. I'll do mine if you're in a hurry."

"You'd better go and put them on."

She shook her head. "No. I'll wait till Mr. Reeves comes. He might as well know the worst before he sees it in the papers."

"I don't think B. Meggs is a swine."

"No. He's a reporter and the Maloneys are news. My mother always has been and I'm her daughter. I don't expect him not to do his job because of me."

A car stopped in front. Jenny waited with her eyes on the door. Caxson Reeves knocked and came in. He was dressed for church, and shockproof as Fish had always known him to be, he was not impossibly so. He stopped dead in the doorway.

"Well, bless my soul."

Jenny's pale cheeks flushed. She sat down and pulled Fish's robe around her. "I've got clothes," she said. "But this is the way the newspaper reporter saw me. I thought you'd better know."

Reeves looked at Fish. His hooded lids that had opened wide for a moment drooped back. He came on into the room.

147

"I can see what your problem is." He cleared his throat. "Hippolytus," he added dryly.

Fish Finlay flushed.

"Hippolytus? That's Nikki's middle name," Jenny said.

"The wrong man has it then." Reeves sat down in the wing chair where Bestoso had sat.

Jenny looked blankly at Fish.

"It's the name of a Greek play," he said curtly.

"I've never had any Greek plays."

"He was a young man whose exalted opinion of his own virtue offended the gods," said Caxson Reeves. "And got everybody in a great deal of trouble, including himself."

"But . . . it's me that's got Fish in trouble," said Jenny calmly. "It's my fault. My mother's making him leave the stable, and I wanted him to take me with him, because I'm afraid to stay over there."

"And he refused," Reeves said quietly. "That's what I meant by 'Hippolytus.'" He ignored Fish Finlay, uncomfortably hot under the collar. "It would have been a very simple matter for him to tell the reporter you were going to be married, and make a romantic story instead of an unpleasant one." His voice was even crustier than usual.

"I asked him to marry me," Jenny said, also as if Finlay were anywhere else. "But it was a mistake. He doesn't want to."

"He wants to," Reeves said. "It's his pride. Because he's lost part of a leg. Because you're very young. Chiefly, because you're very rich."

"Rich?" Jenny's eyes opened wider. "I've never had money enough to do anything any of the other girls at school did. Yesterday I didn't have money enough to buy gas for my car. I had to ask the man to let me pay him when I get my allowance next month. And I won't get it unless I go abroad with my mother and Nikki. She didn't say so right out, but that's what she meant. I know that tone of voice. And now everybody knows I won't have anything for a long time. At the Randolphs' dance they thought I was rich. Last night at the Chalet what I told Nikki at the restaurant had got around and I didn't have more than two or three beaux left. Except Peter. I don't know whether he and Mrs. Emlyn knew mother was supposed to be killed. Maybe it was because I'd said I'd have the whole Trust in a year or two and they figured the wait would be worth it. But I've . . . I've got to get a job next week, because I won't go abroad with mother and Nikki. Maybe I could stay with you people, Mr. Reeves, till Anne comes home or I get some place to live."

"You're welcome to, Jennifer."

Caxson Reeves looked at Fish, aridly inscrutable.

"And as for being young," Jenny said soberly, "even my

148

mother said she thought I'd marry somebody older, because I've been . . . dispossessed, is what she said."

She got up, hitched the robe higher and went to the kitchen door. "I'll go get my clothes on. And I don't want him to marry me if he doesn't like the idea." Her face was a pale heart-shaped blank. "I didn't mean to try to . . . to force him. I didn't think about the money, because it's never meant anything but trouble to me, and I didn't think about my age. I just thought it was because of his leg he wouldn't ask me, and I had to ask him. Because Rusty Red, he's a horse at Dawn Hill, he tore his leg on the barbed wire and we thought we'd have to shoot him, but we didn't. He can't run but his foals are the only one's we've ever sold for anything like a decent price."

Fish saw Caxson Reeves start, and he himself started practically off the arm of the sofa before he managed to steady himself enough to speak.

"They don't sell human foals at any price, Miss Linton," he said.

"I know they don't," she answered soberly. "You want good ones if you can get them, though. But it doesn't matter. I shouldn't have asked you, and I'm sorry. I'll go get dressed now. I'd like to go home with you, Mr. Reeves, if you don't mind."

She padded off through the kitchen. Neither Fish nor Caxson Reeves moved for a moment. Then Reeves uncrossed one leg and crossed the other. He cleared his throat again.

"I regard that as a very flattering estimate of your potentials, Mr. Finlay," he remarked gravely. Then, as Fish looked at him, he saw that the Vice-President and Trust Officer of the Merchants and Mechanics Bank was shaking with silent laughter.

He flushed again. "Very funny," he said. But as Caxson Reeves went on laughing, he gave in at last to a grudging smile of his own. "To hell with both of you," he said.

Reeves sobered gradually, his face returning to its desert dust. He took a deep breath—he must have used muscles he had no idea were there, Fish thought—stretched his diaphragm, breathed deeply again, and sobered up in real fact.

"What's this about young de Gradoff? I hear he skidded and smashed up on the West Road last night? Is that what the police are over at the house for?"

Fish nodded. "And you can't take Jenny home with you. Bestoso wants her here till he gets back."

The phone rang. It was Bestoso speaking from Enniskerry. Fish felt his spine stiffen and the gooseflesh crawl again. He turned to see Jenny come in from the kitchen, still in his bathrobe, and stand there watching him.

"Say that again, Lieutenant," he said quietly. He listened

149

as Bestoso repeated, and put the phone down. Jenny had come silently on into the living-room. Reeves waited impassively.

"It was Bestoso," Fish said. "He's got the report on Jenny's car. I don't know the technical language, but the drag link at the base of the steering column was filed and the feed line tampered with. At high speed or on a sharp right turn the car was bound to leave the road and almost certain to burst into flames. Skidding on the wet road had nothing to do with it. It . . . wasn't meant for Peter."

He couldn't look at Jenny, but he knew she was moving over to sit down and steady her own shaking knees. Then he heard her voice.

"It wasn't meant for Peter alone," she said, very quietly. "But it was meant for Peter and me . . . and Mrs. Emlyn too. It was meant for all of us. Because we were all supposed to be in the car, on this trip we were to take today. Nikki'd arranged it. All three of us were supposed to . . . to burn up on the road. On Sunday morning, nobody would have given it a second thought. A new car and a girl driving. And Peter and Mrs. Emlyn and me, all of us, dead. All of us burned."

She said it with perfect calm, her voice steady, and quietly folded up and started to topple over. Fish caught her before she hit the floor.

CHAPTER : 22

Fish Finlay came back into the living-room. "She's just worn out, the poor little devil. The maid's with her." He went over to the sofa and sat down, his head in his hands. "If Peter hadn't taken that car out last night . . . Dear God."

Reeves looked silently at the polished toe of his black boot.

"Finlay," he said at last, "may I ask you a question that I grant seems to be none of my business?"

"Shoot."

"Are you in love with Jennifer Linton, or are you not?"

Fish steadied himself. "I am, sir," he said evenly. "Very much. But I'm not going to marry her. For the reasons you both stated, and one other. She thinks it's me she's in love with. But it isn't. It's the romantic beauty of self-sacrifice that she's got herself all mixed up in. First it was for Anne Linton. I met her on the road then and gave her a lift and some azaleas. She saw I was lame, and unhappy too, so she included me in the deal. Up here she's sacrificing herself for her mother, and I'm still on the scene. A couple of months of normal life and she'll come out of it. I don't want her coming out of it and finding herself tied to me, no way out but the divorce court. I don't want it to happen to her . . . or to me."

Reeves shook his head. "That other girl. I should think you'd have thanked your stars you escaped her. Curiously, in my opinion, Jennifer is the only person here who's not in the least mixed up. It's Jim Maloney's theory . . . the flower against the weed. However. . . ."

He was silent a moment. Fish glancing up at him saw that he looked tired and very old.

"Why, may I ask? I mean, why do you ask?"

"I'd hoped you were in love with her and would marry her, and produce one of those . . . foals, as soon as possible."

He was not being funny. He was deeply in earnest.

"I'm thinking about the Maloney Trust," he said, "and my own responsibility to it . . . to be honest and accurate. It is very important to me for Jennifer to marry and have children. Her safety would be assured as it is not assured now. As she certainly is in love with you—for whatever reasons—I had some idea you'd be enough concerned about her safety to marry her at once, so there'd be no question of her going back to her mother. I have a number of reasons for not wanting her at my sister's house. There is, in fact, no place for her to go."

"Her grandfather?" Fish Finlay asked quietly.

"You've got on to that, have you?"

Fish nodded at the scattered black ashes in the fireplace. "There's the report he got from Ferenc Blum. I owe you an apology, I guess. How long have you known it was Mr. Maloney who hired him?"

"I assumed it must have been he when you kept bringing the fellow up. You took Dodo's word that no one else cared who she married. There was one other person. But I told you I've never seen Jim Maloney since the morning he walked out of my office, and that's still the truth."

"You knew where he was?"

Reeves nodded. "From the February after he came. When he got pneumonia, Vranek was alarmed and called me. I'd have known it at the end of that year, however." A gleam half-flickered under his lids. "The greenhouses paid for themselves. The next year they showed a profit, and the gardens the same. Jim Maloney can't help making money. He always left in June, for the season. This year he stayed on because of a letter he got from an old Frenchman who'd lost touch during and after the war and didn't know Maloney had disappeared. He addressed his letter to Enniskerry. Maloney got it, and instructed him to keep on the job and keep his employer's name out of it. I did write to Vranek explaining why

151

you were here. When you said yesterday a report Blum had made his client would enable the police to lay de Gradoff by the heels, I went by the greenhouses and told Vranek to tell him. Vranek told me that Blum had phoned from the Randolphs' that everything was set. You and Blum and Maloney were to meet here and decide how you and Blum would present the whole thing to Dodo and Jennifer, with de Gradoff present. Blum's death wrecked that. I assumed Maloney decided to present what he had left to Dodo when he knew she was alone. You see what happened to it. I can hardly ask him to take Dodo's daughter, in addition to what he's done."

The sound of heavy feet scrunching the scallop-shell drive broke the silence in the shadowy loft. It came from the clock tower stairs a moment later. Fish opened the door. Lieutenant Bestoso came in. He nodded to Fish and went to Caxson Reeves.

"Glad to see you, sir." They shook hands. "Where's Miss Linton?"

"In the other room," Fish said. "She keeled over when she heard about the drag link. I suppose they told you over there she and Peter and Mrs. Emlyn were scheduled for a long drive today."

"They did." Bestoso sat down. "De Gradoff told me. He was knocked cold. He's a nice fellow."

"That's what everybody thinks. That's just the trouble."

Lieutenant Bestoso's jaw dropped for the second time as Jenny came in, unconcealed admiration and pleasure sparkling in his black Latin eyes. She had on shoes, for one thing, simple and very Newport, her curls tight, still damp from the shower, lipstick on, a young lady, not a barefoot kid in an outsize bathrobe and somebody else's pajamas drooping around her ankles. Fish felt the sudden spark of pride ignite in him again, and something more than pride, or less, a sharpening of his own sense of acute unworthiness.

She's lovely. It was the moment of seeing her on the porch again.

She came over to the sofa without looking at him. "Everybody thinks he's charming . . . so he can just go on murdering everybody he wants to and nobody can stop him. You needn't look surprised." Her eyes rested gravely on Bestoso's. "It's the truth. If it hadn't been for Mr. Meggs knowing that girl, and following her and Peter, and connecting them up with the Frenchman and Polly, you wouldn't have had the car gone over, would you. You'd just have had it towed to the junk yard, wouldn't you."

Bestoso nodded uneasily. "That's so. But your stepfather—"

"Don't call him my stepfather." Her eyes blazed. "He's—"

"That's one of the troubles here, Miss Linton. You're accusing him of murder. He doesn't accuse you of anything, he just says you don't like him. Animus against him, was the way he put it. He said you'd probably say—"

"Wait a moment, Art." Reeves interrupted him. "I'd like to get straight what happened to Miss Linton's car. Then I think Finlay and Miss Linton ought to tell you, without acrimony if possible, just what their reasons are for feeling the way they both do. I think it's time one responsible person was told the whole story. I've known you, and your father and grandfather before you. You're all good men, in the summertime anyway. I've never had the opportunity to observe you in the winter."

Bestoso grinned. "And you wouldn't want to get yourself out on a limb."

"I'm talking for Finlay and Jennifer's benefit, not yours."

"Okay. The car was tampered with. The drag links down at the base of the steering column. They connect the steering arms to control the wheel. A link was filed. I'm no mechanic, it's what the boys told me that worked the car over as soon as it got cool enough. It could go along at low speed and make a left turn without anything happening. High speed and a sharp right turn and it'd go out of control; the gas line that was tampered with would catch fire and you'd be off to hell in nothing flat. The driver wouldn't have a chance, the other passengers might get thrown loose. In this kind of a country they'd probably land on a rock and be killed, or paralyzed like the girl was. Whoever doctored that car was a mechanic. It'd take him about eight minutes, they tell me."

Jenny Linton nodded. "It didn't take him much longer."

Bestoso looked at her, startled.

"I was out in the garden in the rain when he was in the garage. Around three o'clock this morning."

"You saw him in the garage?"

She shook her head. "I heard him. I knew it was him."

Bestoso drew a long breath and sat back in his chair. "Okay. Go on. Tell me what else you know but don't know."

"Fish," Reeves said quietly, "you'd better start. At the beginning. Jenny can add anything she knows that you don't. Jenny, will you be quiet until Fish is through."

She put her head back on the sofa and closed her eyes, her long lashes fringing her cheekbones, her hands folded in her lap, and sat motionless.

"As far as I'm concerned, it began when I found de Gradoff listening at the keyhole when I was having a conference with Mrs. de Gradoff in early April," Fish said. "Then I met Miss Linton on a road in Virginia a week later, and she told me about the Argentine girl."

Bestoso listened. At the end he stared silently down at the mass of charred paper in front of him.

153

"This hunchback fellow identified the little detective," he said. "That's all. He must have known it was de Gradoff the little guy was after."

He got up and took four or five turns around the room, came back and sat down. He rubbed his scalp vigorously, his weather-toughened hands like coarse sandpaper on the curly stubble of his black hair.

"Sure. I can arrest him." He was abruptly answering the question no one had asked. "How long would I hold him? Long enough for Dodo Maloney to get to the telephone. There'd be a lawyer down there to spring him before I got the cell door shut."

He glared angrily from Fish to Caxson Reeves and around to Jenny.

"Okay, you people," he said bitterly. "Maybe somebody knows he murdered his first wife, but nobody can prove it. They got a crazy drunk locked up in a fancy sanitorium says she's the one knocked off Miss Randolph. Miss Linton says it was him in the garage but she didn't see him. His wife tells me it's funny she and he didn't hear Peter take the car out because they stayed awake talking until the clock in this tower struck four. Miss Linton says he was out in the soggy wet rain and over here in the garage fixing up a death trap at three or shortly after. I don't think Miss Linton's lying about what she thinks is the truth and I damn well don't think Dodo Maloney is either. The burden of proof's on Miss Linton. How would she hold up on the witness stand?

" 'You love your stepfather, don't you, Miss Linton?' says the prosecutor. 'Yes,' says Miss Linton, eyes blazing hell-fire and black brimstone like just now, and the jury knows she damn well hates his guts. 'Animus!' shouts the defense, only they don't shout, they say it nice and gentle. 'Isn't it too g.d. bad the girl hates her poor stepfather just because he married her mother and she's a jealous brat.' "

Jenny Linton didn't open her eyes. "That's what they'd say. They've been saying it for years."

"Okay," said Bestoso. "I'm just telling you what I'm up against. People think the cops are dumb. Hell, they read stories. The big-brain private eye gets everybody together over at Enniskerry. At the psychological moment he points to de Gradoff. 'You,' he says. 'You were all fixed to poison your wife last night. But your stepdaughter tells you you won't inherit, because the dough belongs to her. So you've heard her say tomorrow she'll drive at seventy because she's got her thousand-mile checkup. So you say "Peter and Mrs. What's-her-name and my stepdaughter must drive to the Cape" and you run out and file the drag link so the minute they hit seventy or make a sharp right turn they're off to king-

154

dom come and no trace left. But I've got you, de Gradoff!'
And de Gradoff turns pale and reaches in his pocket and takes
out a pellet of cyanide and he's dead and the case is solved.

"And the lame-brain cop, that's me, is sitting in the corner, surprised as hell. Sure he's surprised . . . he knows if
de Gradoff had sense enough to file a drag link he'd hav
sense enough to know all he had to do was look at Big-Brain
and say 'Nuts, where's my lawyer?' "

He stopped for breath, still glaring at them.

"Motive? Sure you've got motive, and it points the finger
all right. But that's all you have got and it isn't enough. What
does de Gradoff say after he's said that to Big-Brain? Exactly
what he did say half an hour ago. 'I understand the Maloney
Trust officers feel I'm pathologically interested in my wife's
money. They're so wrong that I rather wonder if they aren't
. . . let's say, the interested ones. Has anyone examined
into what motives *they* might have? It's particularly diabolical
because they know—or Finlay knows—that my one and only
job was in an automotive works and I'm perfectly competent
to perform the clumsy operation you describe—if I was stupid enough to do it.' That's what de Gradoff said to me and
B. Meggs half an hour ago."

Fish looked at Caxson Reeves. "He couldn't have heard
that the Maloney Trust, or some document thereto apper-
taining, has been laughingly referred to as 'Invitation to Murder,' could he?" He asked it with admirable coolness, or so he
thought. "In the privacy of the office only, of course."

He saw Reeves draw in his breath and expel it, slowly.

"Which is precisely what I've been talking about ever since
I came here, Finlay," he said evenly. "If de Gradoff has heard
that, it must have come through Dodo from Jim Maloney
himself, last night; and I doubt that Maloney would put in
her hands the weapon he personally designed against just
such adventurers as de Gradoff, to protect both his daughter
and Jennifer. Especially as Vranek told me yesterday the only
time he'd seen the old man moved—he put it differently—
was when Jenny came and took time to go through the greenhouses, obviously loving them. That's why he sent her his
prize orchids."

Jenny still sat motionless, but Fish saw her lashes move, a
glint of moisture on them.

Reeves turned to Bestoso. "You weren't surprised when
Finlay mentioned Maloney. You've known he was here?"

Bestoso moved uncomfortably. "Well, there was some talk
I didn't put much stock in," he said gruffly. He colored a little. "A few people talked about it, among themselves. I guess
they had a lot of sympathy for the old man. It was sort of like
one fellow said. Quotation, I guess. The world forgetting,

155

by the world forgot. So if I knew it, it wasn't any of my business. He wasn't breaking any law. You were talking about some weapon."

"The reversion of the Maloney Trust." Reeves looked at Fish. "The reason I suggested you and Jenny get married at once and have a family." He turned back to Bestoso. "It's a document Jim Maloney signed in my office that morning he walked out, going on seven years ago. He brought a rough draft of it for me to draw up. It was witnessed by the president of the bank and one of the legal officers. They were the ones who originated what Finlay calls 'the gag' about Invitation to Murder. And it is that. It puts a . . . a terrible responsibility—" He broke off for an instant. "It was an act of faith. Of a faith I myself would not have in any human being without a soul-searching that only a higher power would be capable of performing."

He moved in the wing chair and drew his breath in again. "In the event of the death of Dodo Maloney and of her daughter, if Jennifer died without issue before she reached the age of twenty-two, the entire corpus of the James V. Maloney Trust was to pass, without restraint of any kind, to a third individual, named in the document Jim Maloney drew up."

Bestoso leaned forward. "And who does it go to?"

"To myself," Caxson Reeves said.

His voice was expressionless. "He assumed I would lean over backward to see that nothing preventable happened to Dodo and Jennifer. My colleagues at the bank called it 'Invitation to Murder' . . . as indeed it was if I had coveted the Maloney money. In that sense de Gradoff is unwittingly correct. If possible motive points the finger, then I'm your man, Art. It's me you arrest . . . and I shall say, 'Nuts, where's my lawyer.' "

The gleam in his eyes died instantly. "But we've wandered. The point is Jennifer's safety. We can't afford to gamble on what de Gradoff knows or doesn't know. The reasonable assumption on his part is that in the event of Jennifer's death the Trust will go to Maloney's one remaining heir, namely de Gradoff's wife."

His voice was like a brittle stick scratching out letters in the desert sand.

"Jennifer is obviously not to go back to Enniskerry. I'd prefer, for a reason that is now obvious to you, that she doesn't come home with me. She can't spend another night here with Fish, if only because he's being put out himself. That leaves two courses."

He stopped as the clock in the tower struck, and waited until the last resonant murmur had died.

"Art can put her in jail and keep her there, while he gets to work to scrape up evidence. Her mother, of course, may force her release at once." He nodded down at the hearth. "And it may be that's the fate of all the evidence once available. We should remember also that a wife cannot be made to testify against her husband. There is an alternative."

A faint undertone of irony came into the grit-dry level of his voice.

"Fish here can nobly sacrifice himself, and marry the girl. He can then keep her with him, in a suite in a hotel, her guardian if not her husband, for so long as it takes Art to find what he needs. Then we can have the marriage annulled. That seems to me the sensible course. I don't feel it's too much to ask of my Assistant Trust Officer, in line of duty, in this emergency."

CHAPTER : 23

"No," Jenny Linton said. She opened her eyes quickly and sat up. *"No,"* she repeated.

"You serious?" Lieutenant Bestoso demanded.

"I'm very serious, indeed," Caxson Reeves said.

Then Lieutenant Bestoso, a plain man, spoke plainly.

"Look, sister. You spent the night with the guy here last night. What's poison about him now? It's just a couple of weeks of the same thing. Nobody's asking you to marry him for keeps. It's just a . . . a ruse to protect your reputation at the same time we're taking care you don't get killed that's all. Unless you've got some other place that's safe you'd rather go."

"I . . . I don't have any other place," Jenny said unsteadily, the tears suddenly coming out along her lashes. "My stepmother's in Europe. The house is closed."

Bestoso and Reeves looked at Fish Finlay. He was the color of firebrick.

"All right," he said curtly. "I'll marry her. For protective custody only. I don't like any part of it."

"And I don't like it any better," Jenny said hotly. "I don't want . . . I just want to stay alive, is all."

Reeves looked at both of them, his eyebrows moving upward an impatient fraction of an inch. "Can you arrange it, Art? Or shall I."

"I'll do it." Bestoso looked at his watch. "I'll have to get the medical examination waived. It'll take a little time, Sunday, but I'll get hold of the Clerk and get a special license. I'll have it and a preacher over here." He took out his notebook. "Name, age, and place of residence, please."

"James Fisher Finlay, unmarried," Caxson Reeves said imperturbably, when there was complete silence. "Twenty-eight, Cransville, New Jersey. Jennifer Louise Linton, spinster. Eighteen, Dawn Hill Farm—"

"Better make it Enniskerry, Newport. So the Clerk won't think she's a runaway on account of her age."

Jenny Linton's eyes smouldered, but she was silent. Bestoso put his notebook in his pocket and got up, glancing sardonically from one to the other of them. "Anybody'd think it was the electric chair." He grinned at Reeves, and picked up his hat. He looked at the ash in the fireplace. "I guess that's too far gone for any use, but I'll scoop it up and send it to the FBI along with the note we got off Blum and a sample of de Gradoff's handwriting. But I don't put much stock in that for evidence."

At the door he stopped. "B. Meggs and I went down to the Randolphs' fishing platform last night. My guess is, what happened there is exactly what Mrs. Winton said. A 'Voice' told her Miss Randolph was down there and to shove her over and she'd get the job. Everybody says she was hunting Miss Randolph all night. The lanterns are still up down there. The way those roses cover the rock at the bottom of the steps, B. stood and bopped me over the head coming down, and I didn't see it even when I knew it was coming. Blum was first. He was dumped overboard. Miss Randolph was left hanging over the rail for Mrs. Winton to shove. I yelled my head off down there and B. up in the garden couldn't hear me even without the band and all the other racket. We found the white rope under the roses in the poison ivy. Neat setup. The few sober people were inside playing bridge. Mrs. Winton doesn't remember even wanting Miss Randolph's job. What on earth would she want Polly's job for? It doesn't make sense to her this morning, her doctors tell B. They won't talk to the cops but they'll talk plenty to the press."

He started out and stopped again at the sound of a car coming into the courtyard. "Who's that?"

Fish went over. A huge black limousine was slowly coming to a stop under the porte-cochere. The driver got out, opened an umbrella and the door, and a familiar grotesque figure emerged, was assisted down to the ground and escorted under the canopied carriage drive.

Fish turned back to Reeves. "It's Durban. What do you think he—"

"He's a friend of Mrs. Emlyn's. He may have come on account of Peter. Or," Caxson Reeves added, very calmly, "it's barely possible he's taking the advice I gave him at the dance

158

last night. To see Dodo and collect if possible. As Jennifer's indiscretion about the Trust was running like wildfire, I saw no use in being other than frank about the whole thing."

"Frank," Bestoso said. He grinned at Reeves again. "Ha. I'll give you one thing, though. You sure know the last ditch when you see it, sir. Most people figure there's always one more they can duck down in. I'm sealing the garage, nobody takes a car out till I've had the place gone over for filing traces."

Fish Finlay watched Durban go up the porch steps and disappear inside, and turned back, his eyes drawn unhappily over to Jenny Linton, the hinges of his heart dissolved in painful inarticulate yearning, the gates down, as he stood there wishing Reeves was somewhere else, wanting to go over, touch her, tell her. . . .

"Jenny. . . ." It sounded like the croak of an old frog buried in the mud at the bottom of the marsh, scarcely audible with the rain scudding in again, pelting the roof and the shingled sides of the stable. She heard it, or at least she moved. She stood up, steadying herself, not looking at him, just at Caxson Reeves.

"If you'll excuse me," she said, "I'm going to get a glass of milk and go to my room awhile. Till he . . . gets back. I'm sort of . . . well, I guess my knees are still a little weak."

"Lie down and see if you can't rest," Reeves said. "It's all this—"

"No, it's just me. I've always been a horrible nuisance to everybody. Maybe I'll feel better if I get something to eat."

She turned halfway to the kitchen door. "I really want to thank you, both. It's . . . it's terribly sweet of you to . . . to take so much trouble. Thanks, ever so much. I'll be all right if I just lie down awhile."

She managed a grave smile at Caxson Reeves and one not so steady somewhere in the direction of Fish Finlay, lowering her lashes to keep her eyes from meeting his. Then she went out. Fish heard the icebox door open and the scrape of a milk bottle and the door close again, heard it with a misery that numbed as it ate his vitals.

"I guess I'll go in and—"

He started forward, and stopped, hearing her heels click across the kitchen tiles and the door into the foyer swing shut. He heard them then till she reached the rug in his bedroom, and he imagined them then until he knew she must have reached the bed in her own room and thrown herself down on it.

"I guess I'd better let her rest awhile," he said.

If Caxson Reeves would just get the hell out of there. . . .

He stopped himself sharply. His conduct ever since he'd opened the door at nine o'clock and seen B. Meggs and

159

Bestoso standing there had been, in general and in particular, the conduct of a clumsy, self-righteous, wholly stupid, eternally to be damned so-and-so of a first-rate low-grade swine. He took a deep breath, got out a cigarette and lighted it. Reeves's foot at the end of his crossed leg was twitching. His hands on the arms of the wing chair were very still, his face the face of the patriarch of all Gila monsters, watching long and long, frozen in absolute immobility on the sun-baked rock, only his lids, half-opening, half-closing, and the turgid pulse in his throat, to indicate he was still alive. His face, expressionless by any ordinary standard, still managed, paradoxically, to convey a malevolent disgust that Fish had seen on it before but never in so concentrated a form as he saw it now.

"All right, sir," he said. "I've been acting like a bloody fool. Say it if you want to."

Reeves' foot stopped twitching. A kind of smoky film seemed to cover his eyeballs as he raised his lids and looked at Finlay. His jaw tightened, while he took a deep breath of his own, no doubt, because the fire and brimstone stinking up the air in the loft room dissolved slowly, like a miasma of some especially offensive nature, and when he spoke his voice was surprisingly its quite restrained and dessicated self.

"It's perhaps because I'm not in love with the girl that I can see your abysmal folly with such extraordinary clarity," he said mildly. But the effort made him pause and draw his breath full into his bony chest and let it out slowly before he could go on as mildly, succeeding in tone, if failing in content.

"Anybody, Mr. Finlay, anybody not totally blind, preternaturally deaf and dumb, feeble-minded to the point of Mongoloid idiocy and beyond, would have known that when Miss Linton walked out of this room she was giving you, instinctively, what I regard as an almost heartbreaking opportunity to retrieve your . . . your. . . . But it's Sunday, and we're in New England. In any case, I haven't the words in my normal vocabulary to tell you what I think of your ineptitude as a lover."

His eyeballs clouded smoky-gray again, his foot twitched dangerously.

"But if you don't quit standing, staring at me like a . . . like a paralyzed ox, and go in there to that girl, I swear, I swear to God, I'll . . . I'll. . . ."

He relaxed abruptly. "I swear I'll break a blood vessel," he said, to himself and to the empty space where Fish Finlay had been.

"Bless me. . . ." He pulled out his handkerchief and patted his forehead, listening to the doors opening and banging shut behind his assistant trust officer. He took a long

160

breath and settled himself back in his chair. Then the continued silence, suddenly ominous in its intensity, made him draw his brows together. In front of him across the end of the sofa was the window. He looked out, through the slanting rain, across the emerald courtyard, and dropped his hands to his sides. He turned them as Fish came back through the kitchen.

"I know," he said. "She's gone."

He took the sheet of paper out of Fish's hands. "I'm sorry. It's my fault, I shouldn't have waited for you to see it for yourself."

He took out his spectacles.

"Dear Mr. Reeves," the note said. "I was being a coward. It's like Mr. Bestoso's last ditch and I don't want Fish to be that for me. I don't want him to marry me because you tell him to or just so I'll be safe. Until he told Mr. Bestoso and us just now, I didn't know Nikki tried to push him over the Rock, and nobody can pretend that's a sacrifice he's supposed to make in line of duty, can they. Anyway, I can't go on forever being a nuisance to other people. I'll be perfectly safe, I really will. And thanks for trying, but it wouldn't work and I wouldn't want it that way if it did. I'd just rather take my own chances and not have anything happen to Fish or you, or anybody trying to help me. Love, Jenny."

It wasn't any tear-blotted scrawl. The pen had flown over the paper without hesitation, direct and to the point, from a hand with a mind made up. The only place the pen seemed to have wavered was in the postscript she'd added, a sort of last will and testament of Jennifer Louise Linton, spinster.

"Just in case," it said. "I'd really like the mortgage on Dawn Hill Farm paid. Anne won't want to take it, now, but she did it for me and it's what my father called a debt of honor and I wish you'd pay it—if you possibly could, I mean. Love, J."

"We who are about to die salute you," Caxson Reeves murmured. There was a faint smile on his face that vanished at once as he looked sharply at Fish Finlay coming back in from the bedroom, pulling his raincoat on, his jaw set.

"Where do you think you're going?" he inquired dryly. "Not to Enniskerry. You've been ordered out of here. You'd be kicked out of there."

He folded Jenny's note and handed it to him. "Here. It's the first love letter she's written you. Let's see it's not the last. Have the postscript copied when you get back to the office, pay off the mortgage and I'll okay it. And now, if you'll take that coat off, we'll begin to use our heads. There's no use your trying to see Jennifer. She won't see you, you'll make a bad matter worse. . . ."

His voice hung in an arid void for an instant.

". . . Hippolytus," Fish finished for him. "Go ahead, say it."

"No," said Reeves. "The parallel's gone far enough. I don't expect Jenny to hang herself for you, as the lady did for love of him. And de Gradoff is not going to do it for her. I've never killed a man, but I. . . ."

He broke off, shocked at himself. "That was a fool thing to say," he remarked evenly. "No doubt it's what's in your mind too. You'll get it out at once. We wouldn't be as clever as de Gradoff, we'd land in the electric chair. And there's no use saying that's agreeable to you," he added. "There's no sense being a damn fool twice in the same day. Get the phone book and get Bestoso's number. Let's approach this thing as intelligently as possible."

Fish took his raincoat off and picked up the telephone book to look for the number of Arturo Bestoso.

"You won't get him at home, but start there. He may have called his wife. We'll keep on till we find him."

It was while Fish was waiting for a busy line to clear on his fourth call, that his own phone rang.

"Perhaps that's him now," Reeves said.

It was not Bestoso. It was a woman's voice, a strange taut voice that Fish thought he had never heard before.

"Mr. Finlay, please," it said.

"Speaking."

"Sorry. You don't sound like yourself," the woman said, and he still did not recognize her. "Alla Emlyn, Mr. Finlay. I want to talk to you. It's stopped raining. Will you come down in the rose garden? By the back way . . . the way you came last night. I'll be there in a very few moments now. I want to talk to you . . . about my son."

"About your. . . ."

"Yes," the quiet voice said. "Peter was my son, Mr. Finlay. I'll see you in the garden in a few moments. I have a . . . a debt of honor that must be paid."

He stood there holding the phone, the line empty, eerily empty, until he heard the operator's voice. He put the phone down and turned to Reeves.

"Alla Emlyn," he said slowly. "Peter wasn't her nephew. He was her son. She wants me to meet her in the garden. *She's* got a debt of honor that must be paid."

"What debt of honor does she owe you?"

"None that I know of."

Reeves's brow contracted. "She doesn't think some way that it's you who killed her son? De Gradoff couldn't have convinced her of that kind of lethal nonsense?"

"I don't know. Unless she's off her rocker. I see now why she was so intense about Peter at the drugstore yesterday.

Maybe she thinks it's my fault Jenny didn't fall head over heels in love with him."

He picked up his raincoat again. "I'll go and see." He shook himself a little. "I'll also keep damned well away from the Rock when I do. Her voice came straight from hell. It didn't sound quite sane. Will you keep after Bestoso?"

He looked out of the window by the telephone. The rain had stopped, but long gray arms of fog still hung from the angry clouds. The sea was angry too. He could hear it churning, beating against the cliff, and see the white crest of the waves tossed over the heather-dark ledge. The tide must be high, he thought . . . the Devil's Chasm gorging and disgorging itself with the unleashed ferocity of hell itself.

He went to the door. "Well, so long," he said. "Take care of yourself, sir."

Reeves stopped on his way to the telephone.

"A man who contracts a debt of honor with a woman," he remarked evenly, "is hardly competent to proffer advice. And don't forget it was Neptune who rose and finished off the other Hippolytus. I'd watch him, if I were you. I shall be at Enniskerry when you return. If you will pack your bag, I'd like you and Jennifer to come to my sister's house with me tonight. Separate rooms will be arranged. I could insist Dodo let you stay on here, but curiously enough, I'm as interested in the preservation of your health as I am of Jennifer's. I got you into this thing, it's my duty to get you out of it, I'm afraid."

Fish grinned at him. "If it's one you find too painful to bear with your customary equanimity, sir," he said graciously, "I'll be glad for you to cease and desist from any further—"

"The lady's waiting, Mr. Finlay," Reeves said. "Go, and keep away from that infernal Rock. Both men and horses have died there. It's a grave fit only for a monster. Go, and come back. And shut that door . . . I don't like the sound the wind's making. There's a storm rising. My only prayer is we'll get through this thing without the devil taking another toll. The force of evil is strong at Enniskerry. Jim Maloney's trying to exorcise it has only strengthened it. God go with you, Fish, and for the love of heaven try to use your head."

Fish closed the door, shutting out of the loft room the wail of the wind funneling up from the door under the stairs, left or blown open. So was the door at the end of the passage. The salt tang of the sea was rich with the fragrance of ripening fruit ransomed from the captive branches, their leaves shivering, bound to the iron frame of the cordon. He buttoned his raincoat and stepped into the path and left toward the terraced garden. In the green turf corridor he stopped

163

and looked up at the stable. Caxson Reeves was in the hay-loft window at the gable end, watching him. He grinned and turned, looking for Alla Emlyn, the fragrance of wet roses in his nostrils, the pounding roar of the waves, the sucking vacuum of the Chasm and the lost moaning of the wind in his ears.

CHAPTER : 24

Jenny Linton came up the steps without looking back at the stable, crossed the verandah and came into the hall at Ennis-kerry, the raindrops glistening like diamonds in the short tendrils of her curly dark hair. In front of her, coming to the door, was Mrs. Emlyn, carved ivory with the gift to move, a shining black broadtail cape around her shoulders, her bag in her black-gloved hand. Beside her, shorter than she, heav-ily moving, was the thick misshapen figure of the hunchback whose limousine was waiting outside. Jenny went forward. In the door, half open, half closed, of the small reception room at the left she could see Nikki, hovering, restlessly, just inside it, his eyes darting like blue dragonflies. Behind him her mother was sitting, watching him impatiently, not aware of Jenny in the hall.

She put her hand out to Alla Emlyn.

"I'm very sorry. I wish there was something I could do. I liked Peter. I'm sorrier than I can ever say."

Alla Emlyn had stopped. She stood rigidly, not seeing the outstretched hand. Purposely, Jenny knew as she turned to the man beside her, his body stunted like a blast-whipped pine or a tree pruned hideously by a hook in a devil's hand, his head like the egg of some great prehistoric bird set deep into his twisted spine.

"I'm Jennifer Linton, Mr. Durban," she said. Her eyes looking into his lighted softly as he put his hand out and took hers. She smiled. "I saw you last night but I didn't have a chance to meet you."

"It's a pleasure, Miss Linton." His voice was deep and kind. "Alla tells me you were going to marry Peter."

Jenny's eyes were grave again. "No. That isn't true," she said. "I liked Peter. I didn't love him, and we wanted such different things from life. And I'm already in love with some-one else." She turned to Alla. "It's Fish Finlay, Mrs. Emlyn."

Alla Emlyn stood, carved ivory, the gift of motion taken away. Durban took Jenny's hand again, smiling at her.

164

"Whatever life you want, I know it's good. Goodbye for the present. Come, Alla, we must go."

"No. I'm staying."

She peeled off her glove with a gesture so abrupt that her white hand appeared like a magic hand shining out of a black drawn curtain.

"You go, Durban. I'll call you later."

He looked at her, his eyes clouding, shaking his enormous head. "Don't be impulsive, Alla. And don't stay too long, my dear." He bowed to Jenny and went out.

Behind her, Jenny heard her mother's voice. "Nikki, for heaven's sake can't you sit down and be still for half a minute?"

Jennifer Linton, can't you stop squirming for half a second? Go to your nurse, you'll drive me mad! Familiar words, sound the same. Nikki was beginning to irritate her mother too.

"I'm just waiting, my darling." De Gradoff opened the door full wide. "Seeing Durban doesn't come back and bother you. He's such a repulsive beast."

"He's not!" Jenny flashed around hotly. "He's not repulsive. He's beautiful. Look at his face. He's wise and wonderfully kind. Just look at his eyes!"

"Oh good Lord." Nikki's blue eyes were bright with relief. "Alla darling . . . I thought you were going with your Quasimodo. . . ." ·

Alla Emlyn's lips tightened. "Later. I'm going upstairs a moment first." She came over to the door and looked at Dodo. "Darling," she said calmly, "are you *quite* sure you heard the clock strike four? Are you quite sure it wasn't three instead of four?"

"That's strange, you know." Dodo was suddenly interested. "I've been bothered about it all morning. It seems to me it *was* three. I—"

"Nonsense." De Gradoff cut her off so rudely that angry sparks shot out of her violet-blue eyes fixed on him, seeing his own eyes fixed on Alla Emlyn with an instant's malevolence so intense that it was as if she'd reached out and touched a high-tension wire naked on the ground. Jenny saw her body contract then, her eyes suddenly pale ash-gray, motionless for a fraction of an instant. She seemed to draw herself slowly inward, the shrinking fabric of her whole being changing texture, color and pattern.

Nikki smiled at her. "My darling, it was four. Alla's trying to confuse you. She's really a witch, you know."

He looked around. Mrs. Emlyn was no longer there.

"It was four o'clock. You were so sleepy, my dearest girl, after your Scotch, you didn't know I'd kissed you good night. Tomorrow we'll be away from all this, thank God."

165

"Of course, darling." Dodo smiled quickly. "We're going abroad. Jenny, you'll adore flying. Icebergs, they're fantastic from the air." She looked at her watch. "Why don't you tell Moulton to bring us a cocktail, Nikki? The hall bell, darling, this one's out of order. Jennifer Linton!" Her voice sharpened petulantly. "Look at the hem of that skirt! Come here, you sloppy Joe."

Jenny moved, obedient . . . familiar tone, words the same, her cheeks warming at de Gradoff's lifted brows as he went smiling from the room.

"Quick, Jenny!" Dodo whispered the words desperately. "Get out of here. Go to Fish. Tell Alla. It was three o'clock, Jenny . . . not four. Hurry, for God's sake hurry!"

Nikki was coming back into the room. Dodo dropped Jenny's skirt.

"That's the trouble with cheap clothes, darling," she was saying. "Nikki, you're so right. A year in Paris is certainly what this child needs, to teach her how to dress. Go change to something else, please, Jennifer. Elsa will fix it in the morning. And *move,* child, for heaven's sake! You're slow as well as sloppy, my baby precious rat."

"Yes, Mother." She passed Nikki in the doorway, his smile tinged with mockery before he pushed the door to behind her. She crossed halfway over the thick carpet to the stairs and stopped, her throat tight. Nikki needed her mother now: he was depending on her to prove he was in the house with her until four o'clock. But if he found out she knew . . . Jenny turned back. She couldn't leave her mother alone with him now. She had her hand out to push the door open when she heard Dodo calmly placing the dagger square in Nikki's hand.

"—*was* three o'clock, Nikki. I set my watch by your bed-side clock when you were in your dressing-room putting on those horrible black pajamas. You put it ahead so when you counted the tower bell to four I wouldn't see it was three by your own clock there beside me. My watch is still an hour fast."

"My dearest—"

"No, Nikki." Jenny heard her mother's voice, dispassionate and cool. "Up to now I've refused to believe—even last night when I had the whole story in my hands. I wouldn't read past the letter the Argentine woman wrote telling her family you'd called from Dijon to tell her how unbearable a night away from her was and you were taking a sleeping pill, and there was one for her in the silver box beside your bed. Even about the rubies I wouldn't believe. I thought the person who showed me all that was just trying to destroy my happiness. And the Argentine woman's maid, Nikki . . . she was killed

166

in a motor accident—like Peter, last night. And Polly Randolph . . . and the detective. I see all of it, now. This one lie shows up all the rest. Even our meeting in the rain. Everything's a lie, Nikki. It makes me sick . . . really sick."

"Dodo, my—"

"No, Nikki! It's no use!" Her mother's voice was sharper. "But I'm like the Argentine family, I don't want a scandal either. I just want you out of here . . . away from where my child is, at once. Go call the airport. Tell them we want a plane, to run us up to Quebec. I'll go with you so Art Bestoso doesn't think you're running away. We'll switch and fly to Gander and you can get the first plane to Ireland. I've got money in my safe upstairs. I'll give you ten thousand a year for four years . . . as long as the Trust is mine. Use the library phone. And hurry, Moulton's coming. . . ."

Jenny caught her breath, hearing Nikki cross the room and Moulton coming from the pantry. She flashed back to the stairway, slipped off her pumps and ran up the stairs, opening the door of her room carefully so her mother wouldn't hear it and know she hadn't left the house. She closed it softly behind her, started breathlessly across the room and stopped.

"—Peter was my son, Mr. Finlay. I'll see you in the garden in a few moments. I have a debt of honor that must be paid."

Mrs. Emlyn was talking on the outside phone between the beds in the alcove. To Fish Finlay. Her voice was low and terrible. Jenny's throat went dry, her hands clammy cold. She shrank back against the door, blocking it, as Alla Emlyn came out of the alcove, her face, always white, so white it was marble made of snow, as hard and freezing cold, her eyes, filling it, obsidian black, blacker than pitch running before the flames. She had on sneakers and a misty blue film of a raincoat over her black suit. Her hand was thrust into the pocket and through the plastic transparency Jenny could see the dark outline of the revolver. Mrs. Emlyn stopped and stood there, her hand on the gun, her eyes burning into Jenny's.

"What are you doing here?" she demanded, her voice the same deadly monotone.

"It's my room." A sudden flash of anger released the paralyzing fear constricting Jenny's throat. "Nikki's leaving. My mother's helping him get away. She's paying him ten thousand a year to live on. He's down there now phoning for a plane. I'm going to call Lieutenant Bestoso."

She took a step forward. Alla Emlyn stiffened, her hand tightening on the revolver.

"No you're not. Stay where you are."

167

"I'm going to call Mr. Bestoso," Jenny said evenly. "If Peter was *my* son—" She broke off, flashing around toward the door. Nikki was coming up the stairs.

"They can be ready for us as soon as we get there, darling," he was saying, in the confident familiar voice. And down in the hall Jenny could hear her mother, directing Moulton, hear the casual quality of her voice, not the words.

Jenny steadied herself. "I'm calling Bestoso, Mrs. Emlyn," she said again, and started forward. But as she moved, Alla Emlyn moved too, brushing past her with the concentrated swiftness of a stab of lightning burning into the tree it strikes. She was past her to the door, brushing it open with one motion.

"Ah there, darling." Jenny heard Nikki's easy voice. "Dodo and I are just running out for a bite of lunch—"

"Or just running out? No, you're not, Nikki. Not this time, love."

The crash of the gunshot reverberated. The air was sharp and acrid. Without knowing she had moved, Jenny was gripping the door frame. De Gradoff's body on the floor twitched horribly once and was motionless. She heard Alla Emlyn's voice then, the words like writing, tangible, ivory-carved.

"Now you can call your Mr. Bestoso, Jennifer. And call Mr. Durban at the Colony Hotel too, please."

There was a long rigid silence, and out of its total unreality Jenny heard the dreadful dispassionate calm of her mother's voice, as she'd heard it when her mother was speaking to Nikki, telling him what she knew.

"I'll call them, Alla. Jenny, you and Alla come downstairs. Moulton—go to the stable, ask Mr. Finlay to come at once."

Fish Finlay waited on the turf stairs well up from the heather shivering purple over the rocks. Alla Emlyn's few moments seemed to have stretched. He moved back up the terrace out of the wind to light a cigarette and stopped abruptly, his mind refusing to register, his feet to respond to the absurdity, like an old swan walking, of Caxson Reeves hurrying, wind-blown, motioning urgently for him to come. He ran then, hollow-cold inside. Bestoso's car slowing down at the clock tower picked up speed, passing him halfway to the porte-cochere. He ran across the porch behind Bestoso. Dodo and Caxson Reeves were in the hall. He heard Reeves, aridly composed.

"Mrs. Emlyn has just shot and killed de Gradoff, Art. He's on the balcony. She's here, in this room."

Two of the other men in Bestoso's car passed Fish. One was a uniformed officer, one was B. Meggs.

"Upstairs, Miller. Call Headquarters, and take over." Bestoso started into the reception room.

"I've called them, Art," Dodo said. She stood erect. "I was flying him to Canada. It's my fault."

"Okay, take it easy," Bestoso said.

"It is not her fault, Bestoso. I killed him." Alla Emlyn's voice came through the reception room door. "The gun is on the table there. I'd like to speak to Finlay before I go."

Bestoso picked up the revolver and slipped it into his pocket. He motioned Finlay inside.   ·

"You'd better clear out of here, Dodo. My people are going to—"

"I'm staying." Dodo moved in front of Fish to the door. "Don't say anything, Alla, till we get a lawyer here. Caxey, will you—"

"Durban will have done that, Dodo," Alla Emlyn said.

Fish stopped in the door. She was standing in front of the hearth, her bag and gloves in her hand, white, rigid as her voice, and cold, so cold he caught his breath as he'd catch it coming around a protected corner into a slashing gale out of an arctic sea. Jenny was beside her, pale with shock, suddenly very far away, her eyes meeting Fish's and passing over him as if he were someone she'd met long ago in the forgotten country of the blind. Bestoso gave him a shove on into the room and waited for B. Meggs before he closed the door on the men suddenly filling the hall.

"For God's sake, why did you do it?" he asked.

Alla Emlyn's eyes flickered over him, tiger-bright.

"Because he killed my son."

Dodo, moving to the sofa there beside Jenny, caught her breath sharply. ". . . . Your son . . . not . . . Nikki?"

"No. His father was a Red Army colonel quartered in my aunt's house when I was fifteen. I told you, Finlay, everything I've done I've done for Peter. I've even been blind to Nikki, letting him fool me . . . me, who knew him as well as I know myself, and as long. I believed him that night in Dijon when he came from the telephone weeping because the Argentine girl was taking the divorce so hard. Until Polly Randolph and Blum died. Then a horrible fear crawled into my mind. Dodo wasn't sleeping. The Argentine girl was sleepless too."

Dodo's hand went slowly to her throat. Her peachblow makeup and scarlet lipstick were suddenly a plastic mask with no relation to the flesh behind it.

"You couldn't have made her believe it either." Alla Emlyn spoke to Dodo then without glancing at her. "And your daughter saved you, last night. By chance alone. I thought you were dead when Nikki staggered up from the restaurant table. He thought so too."

Her eyes were holding Fish's, but he could see Jenny beside her, luminously pale, a clear clean loveliness in the periphery of the pool of black intensity Alla Emlyn created.

"I wanted a rich American girl for Peter. That's why I arranged Dodo for Nikki."

"*You*—"

"From lampost to altar, darling. Because you had a daughter right for Peter. But you, Finlay, you said I was making a bum out of him. I decided then he could marry Jennifer, take your job and eventually Reeves's and be a man. We were going on a trip today. We'd show Jennifer it wasn't safe here. She could marry Peter and not have to come back. I was confident. I didn't see that Nikki had already planned it. None of us coming back, Peter, Jennifer, myself. We were all to end in the blazing hell that Peter—"

She closed her eyes a bare instant.

"I thought he was drunk—Nikki. Coming from the dance last night. I thought I was making him talk. 'Is it all true, how clever you've been?' I asked. He laughed. It was true. He and I would be rich forever. He told me, all of it. The Argentine girl. Polly Randolph and Blum, one blow for each from the Randolphs' lead-filled flask, at the foot of the stone stairs, and the drunk woman to take the blame . . . because Polly and Blum were in contact with Finlay. Finlay escaping the Rock, Dodo escaping because she was in Jenny's room, away from the little bottle there by the bed. He was drunk, but not with liquor, with his own brilliance, and he told me because today I would be dead, with Peter and Jennifer, and he'd be abroad with Dodo, and another chance at the Maloney money. We came home. I waited for Peter. I gave him the three hundred dollars he wanted. I sent him to hell . . . alone."

"You sent him to the girl at the Azores?" Fish Finlay asked.

"She was going to give Peter the envelope Ferenc Blum left, till people started searching his room—a tall man with a limp, Finlay, and a workman, and the police. She wanted money then. Blum told her it was his insurance policy, and it was addressed to the Sûreté Générale. I didn't have much money. But when Nikki told me what he'd done, I knew we'd need an insurance policy of our own. If we had Blum's story, Nikki would get money for us. I waited for Finlay's light to go out for him to get Jennifer's car and go to the girl. But it didn't, and we took the chance and I went to bed."

She turned to Bestoso. "I didn't know my son was dead till you came this morning. Nor did Nikki. He was sick, waiting for Dodo to remember the clock striking four. Finlay's light was on at three. He'd remember a noise in the garage when he was reminded later. And Dodo came through. You believed her, Bestoso. You are old fishing friends, she told us. Nikki had won again. That's when I decided to kill

170

him. But Durban came. He said no, there were other ways. I was going away with him then . . . until Jennifer came.

"—The girl Peter was to marry. Alive when Peter was dead . . . in the door, rain on her hair, cool lovely rain, with Peter burned . . . no lovely rain to cool the hair my hands—"

Her voice broke for an instant.

"She spoke to Durban, the hunchback. It was Finlay she loved . . . lame, ugly Finlay, not Peter, my beautiful Peter. She never saw Durban's terrible body. Only his kindness and his wisdom. And there handsome Nikki was, sweating in the door, afraid to open it, afraid to close it, because he was afraid Durban was there to tell Dodo that Nikki owed him money. And I was leaving Jennifer, knowing there was nothing would stop him from killing her. So I stayed. I went upstairs and called Finlay. I told him I had a debt of honor. Last night I promised him Peter and I would see that nothing happened to Jennifer. Peter had done his part without knowing it. I still had mine to do. If Nikki heard I was down at the Rock, he'd come. He had to kill me. Both he and I knew that. He'd tried to kill Finlay there, before dinner last night. That would have been an accident. Poor lame Finlay lost his footing. Today it would have been poor disconsolate Alla, bereft of her only son, a suicide. Nikki would never resist so easy a way out for me. I got my gun and called Finlay. I wanted him as an eyewitness, to see I killed Nikki in self-defence, close to the Rock. I was just going down the back stairs to ask Moulton to tell Nikki I'd gone there. . . . But Jennifer came. Dodo had made a deal, ten thousand a year and safety. Jennifer was calling you, Bestoso. Nikki came up the stairs. I shot him. I'm ready to go now."

She turned to take her cape from Jenny and stopped, her eyes fixed past her. In Dodo's hands was the half-burned fragment of the portrait print Fish Finlay had taken from the fireplace at the stable.

"What's that?"

"I thought you'd tell me," Dodo said. "I put it in my pocket to show Nikki on the plane."

Alla Emlyn looked down at it for an instant. She shrugged. "This is from a painting of her? Her hands, and the carnations . . . she drove Nikki mad always filling everything in the house with them, even his bedroom." Her eyes rested on it again. "So this is how Blum and Polly Randolph knew about the rubies. Nikki thought they saw them first on Dodo at the Randolphs'."

She spoke slowly, as if trying to absorb something she hadn't known before. "I see, now. This explains a lot we didn't know. How they were traced to us in the first place."

"They were stolen, Alla?"

"Stolen? Not if the Axis had won the war. There was an old man in Vienna who collected star rubies. He and his wife were in a concentration camp. He offered a friend of mine, a power in the land, three star rubies he'd hidden to get him and his wife out of the Nazi hell to New York where his son lived. They didn't reach the border and my friend got all the rubies, not three. He didn't know that star rubies aren't meant for a necklace. They were red, my neck is white. And I had to hide them after the war. The stones are known. I couldn't sell them except under the counter. The son has a claim in for them with the Occupation authorities. We heard last month they had been traced to us, we didn't know how. We had to get them out of France. Dodo kindly smuggled them in for us."

"At Nikki's suggestion," Dodo said, with sudden bitterness. "I can hear him now. And the other night he persuaded me it was all right for me to wear them to the Randolphs' . . . so he could go to the stable phone, to call the Customs. Very neatly done, Alla."

"Well, it was a gambler's chance for fifty thousand dollars, darling," Alla Emlyn said coolly. "The local Customs wouldn't know about the Austrian claim, you'd rush down and redeem them to save your own face if nothing else. That was another reason Nikki had to kill Blum and Polly, so they couldn't tell. Until Durban insisted on seeing Dodo, and Nikki knew he couldn't afford to wait to see if the gamble worked."

She put her cape around her shoulders. "A nest of vipers your lamppost brought you. But I was only cheating you. I never planned to kill you, dear. Shall we go, Bestoso?"

She walked to the door, waited for him to open it, and went out across the hall without turning her head again.

Dodo sat staring in front of her for an instant, and put her hands to her face.

"Don't, Mother . . . please," Jenny said.

Dodo shook her head. "It's nothing. Just what a ghastly fool I've been. Go away, Caxey. I can't bear to look at you. Go away, Fish."

Fish Finlay had not even heard Alla Emlyn, except in a dazed fog, since she'd said 'lame, ugly Finlay. . . .'

"Let's us go, Mother," Jenny said. "You and I. We'll go away some—"

She broke off as Bestoso came back into the room. "Well, she's gone," he said grimly. "Did I leave my hat?" He started out, and stopped. "There's this thing," he said. He put his hand in his pocket and brought out a paper. "I had a tough time getting it. It's going to be a hell of a lot tougher, explaining why—"

"Let me see it, Art." Caxson Reeves took it, took his half-

172

spectacles out of his breast pocket, polished them, put them on and read the paper, carefully and for a long time. Jenny's cheeks went pale at first and colored, miserably, hotly red.

"Let's go, Mother," she said quickly.

"Wait, darling. What is it, Caxey, for heaven's sake?"

Reeves looked over the straight bar of his spectacles gravely, at Fish Finlay first, and at Jenny Linton, the color seeping still more unhappily up into her face.

"It is a document," he said cautiously. "A document that purports to be a special license, valid for one marriage between James Fisher Finlay and Jennifer Louise—"

"Jenny!"

"No, Mother . . . *please!*" Jenny said desperately. "It's nothing . . . it was just a crazy idea—"

"No, Jenny." Fish Finlay moved then. "It's a beautiful idea, Jenny."

He went over to her. She shook her head, her lashes down, her cheeks burning. "Please, Fish. You don't have to—"

"Jenny." He turned to Caxson Reeves, Bestoso and B. Meggs. "Look, you carrion crows. Give a guy a break, will you? How can I tell a girl I love her with you three standing on the sidelines? How can I tell her I fell in love with her before I knew she was Jennifer Linton, on a back road in Virginia, when her face was dirty and her shirt torn, and I gave her my azaleas because they were all I had left . . . she'd already taken my heart. I can't tell her I love her with you people here. Or can I, Jenny? I love you, Jenny. Will you marry me?"

"I got a preacher out in the car too," Lieutenant Bestoso said. "I just got a Protestant, though. I didn't want to pull a fast one in the Church."

"The Maloneys of Enniskerry are all Protestants, Art," Dodo said tartly.

"Well, you find good people in all faiths," Lieutenant Bestoso said. "—I guess."

"Stinkers too," said B. Meggs.

"I love you, Jenny. Will you marry me?"

"Polly's beat, not mine," said B. Meggs. "Do my best, though. On Sunday, at Enniskerry in Newport, a motley crew assembled. . . ."

"Will you marry me, Jenny? Here? Now?"

Jenny Linton raised her face then, glowing, silver-bright as the new young moon.

"For protective custody only?"

"For protective custody," Fish Finlay said, "but . . . to take the intolerable burden of the Maloney Trust from Mr. Reeves's unwilling shoulders, it's our duty to produce a foal. Or two."

"Or more, Rusty Red," said Caxson Reeves. "None of

them for sale at any price." He looked at Dodo. "Just the influence of Finlay's living quarters here at Enniskerry," he said blandly. "Symbolic. But effective, I trust."

He took off 'is spectacles, folded them and put them back in his pocket. 'Ask our Protestant friend to come in, please, Art," he said.

www.ingramcontent.com/pod-product-compliance
Lightning Source LLC
Chambersburg PA
CBHW020642180626
46816CB00003B/1085